G F

"*The Kiss of the Shaman* is ⎵⎵⎵⎵⎵⎵⎵⎵⎵
to come into balance with ⎵⎵⎵⎵⎵⎵⎵⎵⎵
one foot in Spirit. This book will keep you
center and be more in touch with Spirit than they have ever
been."

–Lynn V. Andrews, www.LynnAndrews.com,
teacher and author of the Medicine Woman series

"Carol Simone has written a beautifully mystical meditation on transcendence, awakening, passion, facing your fears and following your bliss along the journey to finding love and your true self. I love it!!!"

–Patti Cathcart Andress, vocalist, Tuck and Patti

"What begins as a Hawaiian vacation turns into a journey into the core of the psyche. Part *Sex in the City*, part a woman's Carlos Castaneda, *The Kiss of a Shaman* is an awakening, a mirror realized...reflecting humor, insight, and the promise of love among the ruins of a wrecked marriage. It's a love story, yet the love that heals is the love and recognition of self. A terrific read."

–Jaan Uhelzski, editor-at-large, *Relix* magazine,
2013 recipient of the 45th ASCAP
Deems Taylor Award

"Carol Simone has created a heroine for our times in Kate, a woman with a delicious wit, huge heart, and enough gumption and sass to carry her through some massive changes in her life. This marvelous novel overflows with sensual charm, sneaky humor and profound wisdom about the inner workings of the human heart. Highly recommended."

–Jane Ganahl, author of *Naked on the Page:
The Misadventures of My Unmarried Midlife*

A spellbinding story of passion and spiritual unfoldment on the shores of Maui, *The Kiss of the Shaman* will grip your soul from the very first page. With humor, joy, and infinite wisdom, relax into this enjoyable read that deftly delves into shamanism, healing, and ancient Lemuria through the journey of a well-heeled, middle-aged female gynecologist who discovers just how powerful she truly can be when she opens her heart to the spirit of true love."

–Skye Stephenson, Ph.D., author of *The Spirits of Jade*

"The Kiss of the Shaman is a beautiful, sensual, spiritual journey rising out of the magic and mystery of Hawaii."

–Andrea Smith, international artist for peace

"Carol Simone's lively, questing *The Kiss of the Shaman* explores the mysteries of love, healing, and traditional Hawaiian culture with great frankness, reverence, and free-flowing humor."

–Cyrus Cassells, author of *The Crossed-Out Swastika*

"Listen to Dr. Kate, a jazz-loving gynecologist whose full-hearted communion with Hawaii and its Ancient Ones opens onto a spiritual entertainment grounded in the here-and-now."

–Al Young, California's poet laureate emeritus

"Against the edenic backdrop of Hawaii a successful gynecologist comes to reassess her life and career. A spectacular journey of self-discovery ensues, during which the reader is swept away on a thrillingly funny and deeply spiritual wave of self-transformation. A must-read homerun! Carol Simone touches all the bases."

–Scott Richardson, author of
King of the Shadows and *Hearts of Fire*

"There are stories that take us on a journey so deep into the imagination that we can disappear. Carol Simone creates this experience by asking us to let go of our excuses and live unafraid. *The Kiss of the Shaman* lures us to be free."

–Tish Lampert, photojournalist,
author of *America Speaks*

ALSO BY CAROL SIMONE...

The Goddess of 5th Avenue (*a novel*)

Networks: An Anthology of San Francisco Bay Area
    Women Poets

Why Women Wear Hats (*a play*)

Being Quan Yin: Becoming the Energy of Love and
    Compassion (*a CD*)

The Art of Introducing Yourself without Saying a
    Word (*a CD*)

THE
KISS
OF THE
SHAMAN

For Nicki —
with the
beautiful eyes.
Enjoy!
10,000 Blessings
to you — Simone

THE
KISS
OF THE
SHAMAN

BY

CAROL SIMONE

Turquoise Light Productions

Interior design and typeset by Jan Allegretti
www.ListenToTheSilence.com.

Published by
Turquoise Light Productions
Palo Alto, California

ISBN-13: 978-1490443768
ISBN-10: 1490443762

For Bob Longhi,
wisdom keeper, rascal,
ally, magician

And for the beloved Quan Yin
in each of us

PART ONE

"PEOPLE SAY THAT WHAT WE'RE ALL SEEKING IS
A MEANING FOR LIFE.
I DON'T THINK THAT'S WHAT WE'RE REALLY SEEKING.
I THINK THAT WHAT WE'RE SEEKING IS
AN EXPERIENCE OF BEING ALIVE."

—JOSEPH CAMPBELL

1

SEAL COVE, MAUI

IN WHICH MAX THE ROACH MEETS LADY VAL

I know I'm in trouble the first time I make my way up the sandy path and find a set of stepping stones arranged in some sort of helter-skelter design in front of the cottage. Presumably someone placed them there in a more or less misguided attempt to welcome me. Or to guide me. It was a good idea, unlike the words etched on the stone closest to the door. *How far will you fall down the rabbit hole?* This cryptic little message sends my coyote mind and stressed-out physicality in a whole other crazy direction. All of a sudden I feel out of balance and trip, and when I try to catch myself my pointy-toed stilettos stick into the wet Maui earth and send me sailing toward the peaceful Pacific. Not my best moment. But there, sprawled on the moist red soil in my white linen dress, I'm directly if involuntarily reconnected to the earth through the palms of my hands and my soggy butt.

I stop all the commotion and just sit a moment in the gentle rain and incoming mist, gazing out at the little bay called Seal Cove. No seal faces rise from the azure water, but a small wind comes up to welcome me. It's so soft, so tender, there's nothing for me to do but breathe and realize that I have finally arrived at a safe harbor. I pick myself up, gather my flute case, shoes, suitcase, handbag, and sandy sunglasses and make it to the front door.

I have worked hard for many weeks, making sure I'd taken care of all my responsibilities at home so I could feel I deserved to take a whole month off...a whole month away from my endless stream of patients and my futile efforts to resuscitate a dying marriage. I almost backed out of this self-prescribed timeout. But then Barb, my college roommate and bipolar pal, enticed me so artfully that I totally surrendered. She had me seeing her beach house as a contemporary cottage, painted a delicate pink, with white plumeria flowers framing the outside gate, wonderful works from Hawaiian artists gracing the inside walls, lots of Maui light coming in through huge windows facing the ocean, and little moments of serenity everywhere.

Oh, the many shades of mania—Barb's and mine! From my first glimpse of the tiny living area she's painted hot tangerine, to the even tinier bedroom painted turquoise with lime trim, I am in alien territory. It's not the color that bothers me so much as the application. I love turquoise...when it is set in silver and hanging around my wrist. On these walls it threatens to keep me up at night. What's even stranger is that there are no curtains or blinds. I'd have thought Barb's depression would have made her want to close out the world, but then with the highs and lows she cycles through you never know. By day she might be a hermit, at night a downright ho. I try to drop my judgmental thoughts while I go through closets and drawers to find extra sheets and thumb tacks.

Time to check out the bathroom. I open the door and gasp—clearly Barb hasn't wasted much energy scrubbing the place. Even so, I put my cosmetic bag on the floor because every shelf is jammed with oils and creams, waxes and hennas, salves, pills, gels, and remedies. I open the bottle of Kama Sutra Oil and take a whiff. Barb's been busy...there's not much left.

Ah-ha! Here in the medicine cabinet is her western stash: tranquilizers, including my favorites, Lady Val, Zan Man—and eureka, I have laid eyes on my personal favorite for sweet dreams, Little Amby. Don't get me wrong, I am not a druggie. But I do enjoy an occasional full-on sleep, especially after being at the hospital all night for a delivery. Or sometimes when David is racing and gone longer than a week, I get edgy and pace the living room at 3 a.m. thinking the anxiety will stop, but inevitably I give up and turn to Val. Looking at the filth around the sink, I consider taking one now.

Never mind. I head back to the bedroom to unpack.

My new suitcase got torn coming down the conveyor in baggage claim at the Kahului airport. Someone definitely went through my stuff, but I understand that it has to be done. My heart warms as I unpack and find a picture of my Jess in an inside pocket. I miss her so, but just looking at my daughter's smile gives me an infusion of her innate joy.

As I pull out my clothes I notice for the first time that almost everything I have brought with me is white. White shorts, white tees, white straw hat, white panties, white nightie—even the super white pearls I never wear at home. Maybe I unconsciously thought that since Maui is so colorful I should go white? Let's see: white rental car, white skin, forty-nine-year-old teeth newly whitened. It seems likely I am the standout white tourist of the season. I pray that I am deeper than that. Maybe underneath my fashion statement I secretly wanted this adventure to be a ceremony where I would be cleaned up, purified, and spun from white to some exotic tone...like this fuscia silk sarong that I mercifully find wadded up inside my white bathing suit next to my...uh...white bathing cap.

I open a little pine wood drawer to layer my silk undergarments and discover a pile of Barb's barely-there panties, probably relics of her younger days. When I move

them aside I am introduced to the first of my neighbors—
a cockroach the size of the palm of my hand. I scream, and
pile Barb's panties back on top of it.

C'mon, Katherine, it's a cockroach not a cobra...I lift
the thongs and take a second look. This thing is way too
big to smoosh! Besides, it only has three legs, so it
struggles to make itself mobile while it watches me freak.

I relax a little and try to ease into its presence. I
mean, the poor guy—or gal—is moving very slowly with a
kind of limp, trying to get out of my way. He definitely
needs cockroach crutches. I consider catching him and
depositing him outside, and look around for some kind of
container. But to tell the truth, the thought of handling
one of these filthy bottom feeders totally freaks me out.
For now I'll just let him be. When I go out later I'll leave
the drawer open so he can make his exodus. But then
where will I find him next?

On to the next drawer. I burst out laughing, because I
cannot believe that Barb has left behind every size dildo
imaginable. At last I have found a drawer I can relate to.

I open the minute closet and find super slinky dresses
designed for a seventeen-year-old, mixed in with what
seems like a thousand camisoles. Barb's older than me,
has lost one hundred pounds over the years, and when
she takes her meds is very self-accepting. I carefully fold
up a few of these handmade beauties to make room for
my whites, and that gorgeous fuscia sarong that I've been
fantasizing about wearing on the beach without a bra.

Granted, it will take a major shift in my self-image before I'll expose the downward slant. My girls are sweet enough, but are well on their way south toward the equator. Even so, I take comfort in knowing I still have a lovely body. Maybe that's because of all the years I've been around sick women who don't take care of themselves, and healthy women who do. I've pretty much seen every size and shape. And attitude. Attitude has everything to do with health. My husband was nice enough to let me know he noticed that my body is aging, that my arms are sagging a bit more. Brilliant, motherfucker. And your penis resembles a russet potato.

I laugh at my hostility—but hey, I am here to relax, to get rejuvenated and positive about my life again. As I warm up to the idea, the sun comes blazing into the little bedroom window for the first time. I pull out my one-piece suit, wrap a towel around my waist, open the cockroach drawer to enable his exit, and saunter down to the ocean. Every gentle wave seems to reflect a different interpretation of blue: royal, electric, cerulean, cyan....

I can't help but feel good.

2

WALKING INTO MY INNOCENCE

This ocean is bathwater warm! I sit myself down and splash around like a toddler. A rare sweet childhood memory rolls in...my mother and I are standing in the surf in Miami. She is in her thirties, I am four. As usual the sweetness quickly sours, as we go out a little further into the water where I can't touch the bottom, and I'm not happy. Mother has a hold of my arms and is twirling me to the right, then back to the left. I put my head back and force out a nervous giggle, then she tells me to dive down and swim through her legs. I am terrified of the water but more terrified of letting my mother down, so I hold my nose, poke my head down, and go right through her open gams. I come up searching her face for approval, and she rewards me with a wink. That was the only wink I ever got. Oh, here we go...and blah, blah, blah....

Be present, Kate! Come back into your body. Better. And why not—I can't remember when I have been totally alone on a beautiful beach before, and I am overwhelmed with feelings of gratitude.

I realize now why I have chosen to come to this little bay. The waves are soft and gentle here, just like the waves that frightened me so much that day in Miami with my mother—but now I can see that it wasn't the ocean I was afraid of. It was losing touch with solid ground that terrified me. Much as I hate to admit it, it still does. I've been floating on fear my whole life, been a wader and a sitter for more than four decades now, terrified of venturing out beyond whatever is most familiar, convinced I would be pulled under and rendered out of control. I'm ashamed of my fear. And anyway, in spite of my substantial efforts to be impervious and impenetrable, the high waves and deep ocean keep lapping at the edges of my life, threatening to wash away the shifting sand I'm trying so hard to stand on. I fight like hell to avoid revisiting that vulnerability I felt as a kid. But lately I've been wondering if I might be better off just letting myself get washed out to sea.

The sky is changing from swirling gold and tangerine to dark shadowy clouds. So dramatic and sultry! It must be close to dinnertime, so I get up and slosh back to the shore. My feet refuse to head back to the cottage. They take me further up the beach, and soon I encounter a massive rock formation with a much more commanding surf rushing toward me. Is it fog, or has a passing cloud swooped down to surround me in a shroud of mist? Whatever it is, I can barely see more than ten feet in front of me. It has me feeling kind of uneasy, so I decide to leave my exploration for another day and turn back toward Barb's. But suddenly a strange high-pitched moan comes floating through the mist. I follow the sound, and make out the outline of a small seal pup. Slowly I approach him, bend down, reach out my hand—and hear a deep voice behind me, coming through the mist.

"Do not touch," it says.

I look around, trying to figure out where the strange accent is coming from.

And there it is again, "Do not touch," more emphatically this time. He's directly behind me now, much closer.

"Why?" I ask. "What's the matter?"

"Some things must never be touched. They lose their innocence."

The accent seems to be some variation of British. I still can't see him, but somehow I feel him moving past me.

The cloud begins to lift, and the baby seal barks excitedly.

I can now make out the silhouette of the voice...a man who is large in stature with long dark hair. Crouched on the other side of the pup he looks powerful—light eyes in a dark face, and a blue feather hanging alongside his left temple. Maybe he's Hawaiian? Peruvian? Native American? Whatever, in this light he appears unapproachable.

"This monk seal is not doing well," he tells me. "He has been left here by his mother. If you touch him she may not take him back."

"Really?" I say, scared to move.

"This is not our business." He stands and turns to walk back down the beach.

I want to pick this baby up in my arms and hold him close to me. I want to reassure his little body that his mother will come. "It *is* my business," I whisper to me and the seal. "We're your caretakers! And I'll be back later to check on you. I promise."

I turn and begin the long walk back to Barb's. Mr. Friendly is not far in front of me. He walks as if he owns the land, with long strides, bending over several times to pick things up off the beach and pocket them...something I have been warned again and again not to do. If he senses I am close by, you would never know it. There's an inordinate amount of energy coming from his body, like a trail of red smoke. When I walk where he has walked, it feels like I am walking into a vacuum. I wonder what it would be like to place my feet in his footprints. He turns toward the water and steps nimbly across the rocks onto an outcropping above the waves. I opt for solid ground, and head up the path into my newfound sanctuary.

I finish unpacking and organize my stuff, but the vulnerable face of that baby seal doesn't leave me. Nor does the energy of that guy. In an effort to zero it out, I turn on the radio and tune it to a native Hawaiian station. I pretend to hula and embarrass myself.

I flip the light switch in the mint-colored kitchen where there must be twenty-five thousand black dots scurrying in search of a meal, their nano-ant-feet climbing over my mine in their oblivious scramble. Holy crap! I grab a faded dish towel and brush them off, then take a bottle of window cleaner and spray them silly. I don't feel good about this. I have nothing against ants, per se, but this is an onslaught.

Okay, enough! Where's the bucket and the cleanser, the broom and the disinfectant, the fucking toilet bowl cleaner, and all of the other accoutrements I can obsess with? I am going to spend the next few hours turning this place into a sparkling little refuge, a sweet spot in paradise. I turn off the radio and pull out my iPod, tune in to John Coltrane, discover some pink rubber gloves and get down with my sponge and Barb's barely broken-in Hoover. I have no words to describe what I find. I simply whisper, "*Ewwwwww!*"

I finish in the bathroom and place my lip liners and mascara around the sink. I rinse off my face with a puce washcloth and an old piece of soap that smells faintly like coconut. Below Barb's now shiny mirror is a little poem by Rumi, the Persian mystic. It says:

"Out beyond ideas of wrongdoing and rightdoing

there is a field. I'll meet you there.

When the soul lies down in that grass

the world is too full to think about."

For some reason this takes my breath away and I am momentarily ashamed of my attitude, my entitlement. After all, this place was a gift made from the heart—a reckless heart, sure, but still....

Over mojitos at the Pumphouse, Barb has confided, sometimes ad nauseum, about her many affairs and how she inherited her S.T.D.s. "T.M.I.," I told her. "Too much information for me on one lovely Saturday evening."

Apparently this upcountry area here on Maui is a hotbed of vaginal and anal polyps from a crazed human papilloma virus. And herpes, well, it's rampant in these parts, due to crack and ecstasy and sultry nights on the beach. I imagine that's hard to pass up when you're seventeen and in from Nebraska. Or approaching fifty, from San Francisco. And have just discovered the papaya coconut daiquiri mix in the TV cabinet. By the way, it's a Motorola TV from the fifties. I can almost see Howdy Doody and Buffalo Bob peering out of that screen.

After a feast of blue cheese, sliced papaya, and some peanut M&Ms I retire into the bedroom where I fear my new neighbor—whom I have named Max Roach after the legendary drummer—perhaps waits with his family. I pull back the red sheets and look for signs. I find no critters, but a lumpy sand trap, so I strip the bed and shake the sand outside. When the sheets are duly shaken and re-tucked, I climb in, turn on my iPod, and block my weirdo thoughts with some Brazilian jazz. Miraculously, within minutes I am out. I awake again at 2 and 4 and 5 a.m. to the lovely sounds of bells in the distance. While the faces of my patients float like ghosts before me I wonder if there is a church nearby. Finally the bells deliver me back into sleep.

3

BUT HE'S MY DICK

I open my eyes to my new bedroom cave and immediately fantasize about calling the Four Seasons. Then again, it feels so lonely staying in a place like that on my own—every room, every meal is filled with couples and families. Now that I think of it, I hardly ever see single women who look happy. Except in Manhattan, where it's chic to be on your own. Maybe.

I unhook the moldy shower curtain and come eye to eye with that nutty, gimpy cockroach. The poor thing tries to get out of my way by hobbling up the side of the tub, but he slips back down. He keeps trying, over and over again. I feel strangely empathetic and leave him alone. Neither of us needs the stress, and I hear that cockroaches actually have two brains. What a challenge if you're a worrier like me! Over last evening's daiquiri I googled that they have eighteen knees. Now that would be a real nightmare if you were a candidate for knee replacements. Let's see, so with a three-legged roach, how many knees would he have? Nine, right? I wonder how Max lost his other legs. Maybe his super stupid, faithful wife got sick of him cheating and shot them off with her teeny tiny handgun?

Well, now. I guess after ten endless years I'm really not finished with therapy. Behold! These are the erudite ramblings of a peri-menopausal Maui Mama.

I guess I might as well put "Suffer a Migraine" on today's activity roster. I've been migrainized ever since my early forties when I started approaching menopause. Twice a week at home I get light shows that put Monaco's fireworks to shame. But then, who am I kidding...even with the pain, sometimes it's a relief when one arrives on the scene. Illness is the ultimate excuse to take care of one's self and slow down. I apply the principle every now and then with my husband. I remember the time we were getting ready to attend another hideously boring fundraising event for one of his companies.

"Darling," I told him, "I'm not sure I can go. I have a miserable migraine."

The dude is stoned on adrenalin almost all the time, but he stood still long enough to give me a quizzical look.

"If you'd ever had a migraine you'd understand," I grumble, wishing for a little support.

"Sweetheart, I don't get migraines. I give them," he said nonchalantly, leaving the room. So much for compassion. I climbed between the silky covers of our big bed and escaped into guilt-free, bliss-filled nothingness.

Another time I mentioned my headache and he brilliantly proclaimed that getting laid would knock it out of me. He was probably right—but then he would've had to shower off that vague Eau de Younger Woman fragrance that hangs around his neck. It's hard to open my legs to that.

It's so easy to cast David as a one-dimensional jerk, but I know that's not fair. He's really funny sometimes, and a true adventurer if you like that sort of thing, which I do. I'd like to be more like him in that way, take more risks, care less what people think. It's cool that he's into opera as well as salsa and GaGa and the Bhagavad Gita....always aspiring and learning. The tough part—well, one of them—is that with him everything must be the best. He's authentic paella in Spain and sweetbreads in Paris. I'm all into home-cooked whatever's-in-the-fridge in my own dining room. But for David, if he doesn't get the best the shit hits the fan, and because I don't pretend to be perfect I am suspect. Maybe that's why he married me. Maybe looking into me as his mirror makes him remember it's okay to have foibles and bunions. That's it—I keep him real.

My head is still pounding, but there's no way I'm going to spend my first day in Maui in bed. I start to head out to the beach, but a twinge of guilt stops me, so I call my service. I've been gone less than thirty-six hours and already there are more than twenty messages. Most are just requests for appointments, which will be handled by Lisa, my darling receptionist. There is news of two clients who have discovered lumps, one in the left breast, one in the armpit. Marsha, an ovarian cancer patient, has decided she will go no further with chemo, she is done with her specialists and wants my feedback. I will listen and then pretend to know something about what else actually works to cure this mystifying disease.

I toss my cell phone on the bed. As if in protest it rings, and for a moment I am excited that it might be David calling to talk about us, ready to try and heal the mess our marriage has become. Or ready to get a lawyer and finish. Whatever, just some movement, please.

But it is Jess, my beautiful twenty-four-year-old truth teller, big-time-adventurer only child, who took off for the Congo a year ago to nurse women who have been traumatized and raped, who are having their genitals re-constructed so they can feel whole again. It's all happening in a place called Village of Peace. Jess says she gets healed when she holds these women in her arms, broken-hearted souls who have been cast out of their tribes. She says she likes to hold them deep into her chest until they cannot cry anymore, until there isn't one inch of separation. "Soul to soul," she says.

The sound of her voice brings up my own longing for a soul-to-soul connection to...something. "Come home," I plead. It's hard to believe that even though I am surrounded by all this beauty I am still selfishly trying to bring her back to me. Maybe that's the real reason she doesn't want to come home.

"Why?" she counters. "You're all right, aren't you, Mom? Is something wrong? What's the matter, you're there in paradise!"

"Nothing's wrong, darling. I want to share my practice with you again. I like having the Jamison girls running the show. There are plenty of women who need your nurse's heart in San Francisco, you know. Okay, the truth is I just want you to hold me in your arms the way you hold those other women. I want to be that close to you now. I crave your sweetness."

Jess will not be coming home because she's a dedicated being who is on a mission that both of us are proud of. Before we hang up she asks about her Dad and I give her a status report.

"What a dick," she sighs.

"Yeah," I tell her. "But he's my dick." We both laugh, knowing too well that it's not true. And then we are cut off by Maui trade winds.

It's not loneliness I feel...it's longing for newness. To reach out and connect to warm arms and an open heart. Maybe that's the panacea for these headaches. I swallow three Excedrins followed by my faithful migraine prescription. Nothing works. I am headed down that hideous path toward nauseous pain so bad that I feel like I am being stabbed in the eye. During the worst episodes I've been known to turn to Lady Val, just to knock myself out into a softer place. But it seems antithetical for me to take a tranquilizer in the land of mood-altering sunsets and the Seven Sacred Pools.

What the heck. In the spirit of this ridiculously holy place, Lady Val gets the day off. I do some yoga with the windows open to the symphonic surf and the trade winds moving through those terribly sexy palm trees.

At noon I decide to surprise myself with a guava margarita. Even yoginis have to celebrate now and then.

And then I'm not surprised at 4 when the sledgehammer hits my right temple and I am forced into bed, closing the curtains to block out the sun. Max has started to follow me from room to room, and now he sits next to the bed on the windowsill. I know this is crazy, but I feel his presence in a big way, like he is trying to communicate with me. I am losing it!

A slow wave of warm energy surges through my body, and I need to move. I raise my legs to my chest and rock back and forth very slowly. I get into the movement and before I know it the edge of the pain has softened. A little. I listen to some Miles, and at sunset I open the curtains to watch the waves of color drift across the sky in the fading light. The distant rhythm of the waves rocks me to sleep.

4

PERSONAL BOUNDARIES AND THE LACK THEREOF

So it wasn't a great sleep, and there is some kind of bird outside my window serenading me S&M-reggae style. He is definitely more crow than nightingale. I brush my teeth, slip on my flip flops, and by 7 a.m. I'm driving into town, straight into the morning sun. The narrow road winds past tree after tree of blushing pink plumeria, and fiery red hibiscus blossoms the size of human baby heads. The sight and scent of it all is sweet medicine for my throbbing skull.

I head to the little bakery known for its papaya coffee cake and turbo caffeine. It dawns on me that I have not seen one Hawaiian since I've been here. I mean, look around...the cook, servers, diners, and everyone walking by this café are white people. Seriously, there's no one in sight who looks the least bit Hawaiian. Where are the natives? Where do they work? Where do they live? Maybe they can't afford to live here anymore and they have fled Maui altogether? Or maybe they keep the Hawaiians hidden because if we knew how poor most of them are it would give the place a bad rap. Like in Jamaica...I remember when our family went there when I was nine. Everything was fine around the resort, but if we traveled too far in one direction or another we were met with such terrible poverty it was almost unbearable. Is that what's going on here? When the blonde Australian waitress comes to take my order, I ask her where everybody is. She doesn't know, either.

I sit next to a beautiful young woman who reminds me of my Jess, so I relax and we talk a bit about our lives. When she arrived here from Minnesota she was Penny, but the island has inspired her to re-name herself Maile like the maile flower. With her new name and Maui residency she has gotten certified as a massage therapist who specializes in calming, yet deep Thai massage. She says she can help me release my migraines, and follows me back to my newfound home. I am absolutely launched after three cups of Kona coffee and I'm talking a mile a minute.

Maile has brought a mat from her car and has me lie down on it.

"Oh my gosh!" Maile exclaims. "There's a *huge* cockroach on the sofa! Have you got something we can kill it with?"

"He's the house mascot," I tell her.

"But they breed filth," she continues, riddled with repulsion. "You'd better call Morris, the exterminator. Everybody uses him to get rid of these disgusting things. "

"Not to worry. He's the only one I've seen, and he's totally innocuous." And with that Max limps over the side of the couch and down the hallway.

Mysterious flute music wafts through the sheeted windows.

"That's so healing," Maile says. "Where's it coming from?"

"I have no idea," I answer.

And then begins one of the most painful experiences of my life.

"I know you can do this," she tells me in a soft voice as she bends my right leg over my head all the way in back of me so that my foot touches the floor.

I cannot breathe, and the pain in my thigh is excruciating. "Are you sure?" I keep asking. I can already tell I will be traveling on my hands and knees for weeks after this.

"Let's try this side," she says, lifting the left leg even further back.

Okay, this is where I really screw up in life. At this point I should be telling the little Maile flower, "Stop!!!!!! Are you fucking nuts?" But I don't want to hurt her feelings, so I say nothing. This is a problem with me, always has been. It's a Piscean thing. We're very bad at establishing and holding our boundaries in our personal relationships. I ask myself, "What are you afraid of?" Myself doesn't seem to know. Secretly I know it has to do with losing people—I'm even afraid of losing Maile, who I have known about sixty minutes and who will have caused me to file for disability. So here I am, an M.D., exposing a major schism in my psyche while Maile continues twisting, mangling, and wrenching. Finally after twenty minutes of torture I tell her it's enough, that my headache is getting worse, which it is. She is so sweet, I crawl to my wallet and hold out the sixty dollars but she will not take it. I can tell she feels like she failed, so I tell her, "It's me, not you."

She shakes her head "no," and does not believe me one bit. Here we have a standoff case of "I'm not worthy" meets "I'm unlovable." I push through my pain, hold on to the arms of a chair, and force myself up to take a stand.

"Here," I tell her, my legs wobbling. "Maybe next time you could ease into it a little slower?"

"You're very nice, Dr. Jamison," she mutters, finally taking the cash.

"I'll let you let yourself out."

The minute she leaves I crumble to the floor, crawl to the refrigerator, and pass Max on the way. It's hard to determine which of us is more disabled. Finally I pull myself up and throw some ice cubes into a towel. Hallelujah! I make it to the bed and center the ice on my throbbing forehead. Soon I am drifting into dreamland. Loneliness takes over after my noontime gin and tonic. I vow to stop drinking, but I know that isn't going to happen.

"What are you looking at?" I yell over to Max who sits on the faded round braided rug. What the hell does he want from me?

5

THE ADVENT OF
THE MEDICINE MAN

I force myself out of bed because I know I have to get moving before the stiffness sets in. It's not easy, though. The only way to get my walking shoes on is to lie on the bed with my legs in the air so I don't have to bend over.

It's late afternoon, and I head toward the spot where the seal pup was waiting the other day.

I think I see the little creature huddled in the sand, not far from where he was last time. But shit, a tall figure is moving toward him, and crouches over the seal just like before. Maybe I should just turn back and avoid the whole thing. All I want to do is make contact with the little guy, send some love into his ailing body. I grit my teeth and move on in.

The seal is gasping for breath—oh my God, I think he's dying! The strange, dark man is hovered over him making a muffled sound. When I get closer I can see that his mouth is on the seal's chest, his lips pressed against the furry coat, and he's blowing into the pup's body. I don't know what to do. I bend down and bow my head. Don't die, little one. Please don't go.

After a short while, the blowing quiets down and the seal's body is very still. All of a sudden he takes a deep breath and begins to move. The man moves back and the furry creature makes swimming motions with his arms. Is this a last movement before death? Is he swimming toward God?

I can't help myself. "Is he going to be okay?" I ask. "Or is he dying?"

"Shh! Do not bring your fears around him. It drains him of his energy."

"Okay," I whisper, closing my eyes, praying in my own way.

After a few moments the pup begins to breathe evenly. The man and I gently scoop water over his body with our hands, and soon the seal lifts his head and looks right at the man, unwaveringly, for the longest time. Everything goes silent. And then the baby does the damnedest thing...he puts his head down right beside the man's hand as if to say thank you. I look over at the man's face and feel his joy circling around the seal, who is now barking.

"This is so amazing," I exclaim.

"Yes," the man says softly. "He wants to live."

I feel the tears starting, so I get up and turn my back. I whisper, "Thank you," and make my way down the beach.

The Pacific Ocean rests in front of me, gentle and warm as if nothing wrong has ever happened in the world, as if I can trust that there will be no more loss or suffering. I wade in up to my knees and stand filled with gratitude for this moment of kindness, of relief. The gulls swoop down in search of breakfast, and I see a sailboat coming around the curve of the far cliffs. It's a perfect moment to drift without any worries. I am going to imagine being that sailboat, unencumbered and free.

6

WHICH WOULD YOU CHOOSE: THE LIBERATOR OR THE HEART THROB?

It's margarita time once more and I'm sitting on the little lanai, reflecting on the sight of that native gentleman blowing life back into the animal's body. How absolutely natural it appeared, and yet it was a miracle—not at all like the medicine I practice. I wonder where he comes from, how he knows what he knows. This is my first encounter with "mystical" medicine, except for watching John of God on Oprah and visiting a few psychics back in the day. It's not that I do or don't believe in these things. It's that I am naïve and inexperienced and somewhat afraid. Let's just say I am curious but cautious, like any good American girl.

I take a long shower and thank whomever it is that runs things for the warmth, the soothing of the water. I guess watching that seal pup come alive has made me feel more conscious of my own aliveness. I check my breasts even though I know they are strong and healthy, the same way I know that being happy and feeling loved helps keep people healthy. I think of letting my hand move between my legs and go with it.

One of my least favorite moments during a gynecological exam is talking to women about their atrophied vaginas. They almost always look at me totally shocked as if they had no idea it would happen. Well, of course they don't know, nobody ever talks about this stuff until it happens and they are forced to face old-ladyhood.

Atrophied. What an ugly word. Sounds dry, prunish, vacant. Exactly. Vaginas are all of this when they are not loved and taken care of. Unfortunately, for most women, if a man doesn't do it, it ain't gonna get done. I make sure I'm in there a couple times a week, because I love my sex and there's no way I'm going to shrivel up.

In the cabinet behind the desk in my office I keep a tool kit for demonstration purposes. Here I store The Rabbitizer, Holy Moley, Big Boy, The Liberator, and The Heart Throb. It's a smorgasbord of vibrators, all made from different materials, in different sizes, shapes, and colors. Next to them sit bottles of silky liquids with names like Awaken, Thrust, and Sultry Beginnings. Who does the marketing for these things? If it were me I would choose names like Open, Relax, or Trust. But maybe that would scare people. Never mind.

Depending on who is sitting in my exam room, I put on a pretty good show, turning the cigar-like wands on and touching my patient's hands with them so she can feel the makeshift thrill. I am the Duchess of Dildos, the Goddess of Goop performing for her. But I gotta say, not many of these women are thrilled or excited. Mostly I get responses like, "Too artificial for me," or, "It smells funny," and "That's WAY too big—it's built for a cow!"

There is so much fear and anger that comes with aging, with being without a partner. Sometimes women would rather just resign themselves to letting their vaginas shrivel up. Others tell me they will visit the Good Vibrations shop and purchase something that feels right to them, but I know they are fibbing to make me feel better. So I pull out my child-sized speculum and we proceed into silence and denial.

I used to really be into sex. I had several wonderful lovers in medical school at Stanford, long before I met my husband. I was mad about this Algerian guy, Akli. He was the most amazing shtuper. I remember those endless forays from twenty-some years ago as if they were happening right now, his wide, pillowy soft lips searching for the girl inside me. He asked me to marry him, but I knew an independent career-minded woman like myself could never function, let alone thrive, under the rules of his country, so I let him go. That was my first real heartbreak.

Then there was Mike, who had no ambition but a great tongue. He was into tantric sex, and together we re-invented the Kama Sutra. Oh my God. Unbelievable! He was followed by Jeff, a chef at La Fleur du Printemps, who painted me with béchamel sauce and devoured me. I may not have been sure of my beauty, but my sexuality had an outrageous esteem all its own, husband or not.

But after David's first affair I went underground. We still have sex, but we don't make love any longer. I don't allow it because I know he won't stop being with other women no matter what I say. He has to do it, it keeps him feeling young and vital. And me, well, I've been half desirous, half asleep. Keeping the emotion out of it is the only way I can show up at all. And besides, I think not having the distraction of a romantic sex life has energized my work in a big way. I have escaped the worry and distrust of my crumbling marriage by showing up for those who need me, who I can trust, who value me. And I'm okay with that. My life is about helping women get free of their fears. I only wish I could find someone like me out there to work with. In the meantime I keep my fears packed and ready to go, right next to that fuchsia sarong.

7

EVERY WOMAN WANTS TO FEEL CHOSEN, CHERISHED, AND CHAMPIONED

Who the heck *is* that? The sound of that undulating, native-sounding flute has penetrated my evening snooze and interrupted my erotic dreams. Actually, it's quite beautiful and hypnotic, so different from the more classical, uptight tone of my own instrument. Or maybe that's the flautist.

Whatever the cause, the sultry music seduces me from the couch, and I decide to check it out and trudge outside. I follow the music down the path through the bushes, toward the shore. This little piece of heaven, Seal Cove, is empty; winter means isolation and solace and my own semi-private little beach. The moon keeps breaking through on the sand, and its light leads me to a kind of temple that looks like it was designed to evoke a civilization from long ago. I stand by the side gate next to a massive palm. The moon goes into hiding.

Inside, in a room filled with flickering candle light, the healer from the beach walks slowly in a circle, his elegant fingers caressing a long flute that reaches from his lips to well beyond his waist. I assume I am watching some kind of ceremony. Trails of smoke drift through the window...it smells like pot. I back off a little because I am the lightweight of lightweights around any kind of intoxicant. I can get ripped on an Excedrin. And...brilliant! I am also aware that I am a little scared.

The man's persona is haunting: part sorcerer, part aborigine, moving gracefully through the smoke. He puts down the flute and picks up what looks like a brass bowl, and begins striking it with some kind of mallet. With each ringing of the bowl I become more aware of the overpowering darkness of this night, but when I look up into the purple sky the moon suddenly breaks through. The whole thing is unnerving. Just as I turn to go, the wind comes up, sending the outside chimes into motion. He comes to the window and looks out, then stands there watching me. To my relief, he says nothing.

I go back to the house and pour myself a glass of wine, and then of course I have a massive hot flash, followed by another migraine light show. What was I thinking, to go out prowling in the dark? I'm not twenty-one anymore, or even forty-eight. So what am I? No matter what society tells me about how I should feel at forty-nine, I feel like I'm in my twenties...besides the migraines. I feel strong and grounded, and one other thing...I feel disappointed. Not just with my husband, but with what I have not created in my life. And I wish I could get to the source of who inside me does not want to create it and why. Part of it is the "feeling chosen" thing. I want that, but not enough to leave the "settled for" thing.

What I notice in my practice is that nearly every woman who gets sick is waiting for some man to come along and choose her, so she can feel like she matters. Or if she already has a man, she's waiting for him to wake up and start treating her like she matters. Like my patient Jane Jacobs, a very attractive social worker who is good at taking care of men. The minute she meets one who is interested in her she starts overdoing, at which point the man takes advantage, gets turned off, and leaves. Jane gets depressed and angry and calls him a bastard. And so the cycle goes. Whatever happened to the days when a woman felt secure enough within herself to let a man show her what he had to offer—*before* she started showering him with attention? I remember my dear friend Michelle recounting to me how, in the older courting traditions of Europe, a woman would invite suitors into her chamber to display their gifts. Each one would bow down and present her with a display of trinkets, gems, or even recite poetry. The woman would listen and look, then tell the man to be on his way. Later she would reflect on the various offerings and decide who and what she was most drawn to. She got to do the choosing.

Wow, where did that scenario go? Now all I see are women being afraid they won't be chosen. Or cherished. Isn't that a wonderful word? *Cherished.* Like I hold true meaning for someone, and they are going to prove it to me in every way they know how. Oh, the longing to feel chosen and cherished...championed. It's all-consuming, that wish. I totally get it. It's like a big gaping hole inside, aching for someone to come along and fill it up. The thought of feeling altogether loveable makes me come alive! And then I feel lost, because in my well-educated brain I know that I'm the one who's supposed to cherish me, who's supposed to make myself feel loveable. When I notice that scared kid inside who's waiting for a man to do it for her, she embarrasses me so I shut her up.

Maybe I want a man to cherish me so I don't have to do it for myself. But how can he think I deserve it if I don't believe I do? I guess I believe it...sort of. Maybe eighty-eight percent? Nah, more like sixty-nine and a quarter—on a good day seventy-five. The truth is I don't know what I would have to accomplish in order to feel I deserve to be cherished. It would have to be *big*. I should have been a brain surgeon. Or a saint. Or had better teeth. Maybe if I get that bunionectomy. Who am I kidding? I've got a long way to go before I get my act together enough to be chosen by someone wonderful.

Max watches me from the corner, resting against a standing lamp. I wonder how courting works in the cockroach kingdom. I wonder why I have made him into a male when he could very well be a huge female. This is yet another perception of mine that has little to do with reality. I have projected onto this insect what works for me, just as I tend to do in most situations in my life.

8

A PHOENIX IS RISING IN ME

It's been a good day—the second in a row with no pulverizing migraine! I spent most of it exploring tide pools, and lounging in the sand watching the turtles paddling around in the distance. I fell in love with the Pacific all over again. This evening I am on my second gin and tonic. I can feel the surf pounding in the distance. The night comes down in clear violet and I wrap myself in the gorgeous afterglow. I am lonely but I am not needy. Sure, kiddo.

I want to check my answering service messages—and then again I don't. I know I should at least make the necessary callbacks, but I can't raise the phone to my ear. Instead I put it in a drawer and walk away. Every time my mind wanders to David and who he might be choosing for the night I change the subject. I am high and I'm relaxed. Perhaps staying off the phone is a way to take care of myself. What a concept.

But old habits die hard. I resist calling my service, but I retrieve my phone and dial my personal voicemail, dreading and hoping for a message from David. I am rewarded for both. His voice is as cavalier as usual, telling me he has made his reservation to go to Scotland to race in the next event at Knockhill. I dial his number so I can pummel him with the several reasons why another race in Scotland is a bad idea. By the second ring I resolve not to mention the likelihood he'll spend his evenings in the arms of some redheaded Scottish lassie. By the fourth ring I realize I'm actually relieved he's going. On the fifth ring he picks up.

"Hi, darling. You don't mind do you?" he begins. "It's only for a couple weeks. You having fun out there? I bet you're bored as hell."

"Not at all. There are some interesting folks in this part of the world."

"In Nowhereville? I guess if you find hippies stoned on ecstasy scintillating.... Have you been drinking, darling? I'm surprised you're not already checked in at the Four Seasons. You know you won't be able to stand it there much longer."

"Actually I kind of like it here," I say way too defensively. "It's very peaceful and I have my own little beach to myself. There are only a few other neighbors and it's really quite charming." Max is scurrying faster than usual back and forth on the floor board.

"Well, if you like it there so much, why don't we buy something? You know...one of my business partners wants me to go in on a development in Hana. There's a lot of money to be made up there."

"I like it on this little cove."

"What? You're cutting in and out. I'll call you from the track. It will be a few days. Enjoy your stay at the resort. Aloha, darling."

And then, as always, he is gone already into his next death-defying experience, speeding down the track of another town in another country, full of adrenaline, his insecurities keeping him warm and far away. This isn't what I want. Why can't I leave? I'm like every patient that stays with a man because she doesn't want to be alone. I am those women that I counsel. They will soon see through me and witness the weakling that I am, the fucking phony co-dependent. I will be left once more.

I feel the faint echo of a pulsing blood vessel behind my right eye, so I head to the bedroom, open the window, and stretch out across the bed. I close my eyes and drift off into a sweet dream about the monk seal. I see his mom and pop swimming up to greet him, and I pick him up in my arms and hand him over. The four of us dive deep and disappear.

The sound of drumming pulls me out of the dream. I have always been mesmerized by native drumming, and my pulse aligns itself to the hypnotic beat. The deep resonance echoes throughout the cove so that it feels like there's nobody here except a semi-drunk, half-delusional Pisces gynecologist and a bowl-gonging, know-it-all shaman who drums like he owns the joint.

I move closer to the window because I am being called, summoned to an ancient feeling inside myself that feels uncomfortable and prickly…altogether outside of my normal existence. The steady rhythm of the drum pulls me to a gateway of fantasy. Somewhere inside I am opening and entering, fortresses are falling down, rivers are being crossed, and I am breathing from the center of my belly. I feel faint and giddy. My legs are shaking and my heart is beating out of time. I am scared that the booze has opened up an emotional place in me that I can't control…or don't want to. I put on a shawl and begin my evening walk in the direction of the temple-like structure.

I lose all track of time, hiding outside his window, watching as he walks around the room fanning massive black feathers through the thick smoke. Then his voice rises and he speaks matter-of-factly toward the ocean as if he is deepening a kinship. I move in closer, maybe twenty feet away.

God, he's gorgeous. He's maybe around forty, long black shiny hair that falls straight to his waist, brown skin, limbs artistically sculpted with long muscles like a swimmer. His body moves effortlessly in old blue jeans and a red sleeveless shirt, unbottoned. The way he moves in those jeans...elegant, commanding, connected.

And then for no apparent reason he throws off his shirt and turns, exposing his back to the candlelight. I am stunned by the work of art that emerges from his waistband and covers his spine and shoulders all the way up to the nape of his neck. At the base of the tattoo, flames rise up in fiery oranges, golds, and reds. Out of these soars a magnificent bird, a phoenix, I guess, adorned in golds, peacock blue, and multiple shades of purple, its tail trailing in vivid golden tones. The proud head is pointed toward a starry cosmos. It's absolutely masterful...and believe me, tattoos turn me off. Way off. As the man bends to pick up an instrument, his musculature ripples, and the winged being shimmers in the flickering light. I am transfixed.

The night wind stirs the chimes and he looks up, sensing a presence, just like the other night. He goes to the window and finds me standing there, no longer in camouflage.

"Aloha" he calls out.

I turn and flee.

9

SHAMANS SHOULD NOT LOOK LIKE JAVIER BARDEM

For two days now I have been bombarded by clusters, the relentless stream of headaches that earns us migraine aficionados the red badge of courage. Or raw fortitude. I lie in bed with an icepack over my eyes and another under my neck, and steady doses of the best meds I can write a scrip for. Still, my temples feel like they are going to explode. I am honestly feeling a little scared.

The experience has given me a renewed appreciation for what my patients go through. I could weep for them. Desperate to connect, I try to find David, but he is not answering his cell. I don't have a way to reach Jess.

Finally I call Barb and confide in her about my head and my fifth lollapalooza mind-bending temple stomper.

"Uh, hello, there's a healer right down the beach. Haven't you noticed? Not that a traditionalist like you could take a risk like that...."

"Well, I did notice the smell of marijuana and the attitude."

"I've never had a session with him, but the gossip in town is that he's the real thing. I doubt that he smokes weed, it's probably sage you're smelling. Shamans use it to cleanse their space. He certainly is easy on the eye, don't you think? More movie star than medicine man."

"I didn't notice," I say in my professional voice. "What does he do? I mean how does he do it? I'm at the point where I'll try anything."

"I have no idea what he does, I've only had a couple of conversations with him. He's a loner, but really very nice. You'll just have to take a risk and go with it, won't you? You're always telling me to trust. I guess it's your turn."

I'm not so sure.

Late afternoon I walk the length of the beach both ways and meet no one. I tell myself I am releasing insecurity, walking in my strength, blah blah blah, hoping I'll heal myself without need for said shaman. Deep down I feel myself wanting to meet up with him without having to plant myself on his doorstep. I also want to kneel beside that baby seal again and make sure he knows how loved he is...and I'm well aware that particular longing is easier on my brain. So I walk so far, for so long, that the sun sets and it is night again. But, alas, the seal is gone.

For a moment I am the abandoned pup.

On the way back I stop and look up at the flute player's home, with its lush, well cared for entryway. As I stand there, a pot-bellied pig comes running to the landing and stares me down. He's a dwarf, but daunting— and determined to protect his property! I throw him a Trisket from my fanny pack. He grabs it and runs.

I've worked up an appetite and I'm out of Triskets, so I stop by the cottage just long enough to pick up a shawl and car keys, ready to find a softly lit veranda in town where some young waiter will serve me a late dinner and a glass of wine. Or two.

I lean into the bathroom mirror and run a comb through my hair, and there is Max, watching me. The creatures are certainly showing up for me in Mauiana. I guess this is our private ritual now...whenever I prepare to leave, Max the Roach appears. Every single time! He drags himself up on the wall and pauses as if to say, "Leaving so soon, Katherine? When will you be coming back? I'll be waiting up for you." He looks kind of pathetic there, alone, braced on those three legs.

This is a tough one for little old co-dependent me. I don't like leaving anyone out or alone. Ever. So as I look down at his massive shell and spindly appendages I begin to wonder if there's something I am supposed to be doing for him. Me, an M.D. who spends a lot of time each day washing her hands, killing bacteria. I know the terrible reputation cockroaches bear, and I have disposed of many in my day. When we spent one Christmas in Miami the place was lousy with them, and we'd all scream when they would rush out of the garbage can. And then David would perform a massacre. We were all greatly relieved until the next onslaught.

But this is different. Maybe because I have given him a name, Max feels...well...soulful. Besides, it's kind of comforting to have him here like a friend along the path. How needy is that?

I decide to try an experiment and leave a couple of raisins and a tiny chunk of cheese in the tub. My inner critic rises in protest, and admittedly I feel a little nuts. But then a scene from the film *Castaway* flashes before my eyes and I see Tom Hanks in an intense conversation with the volleyball he'd named Wilson. So there you go! I feel exonerated. Almost.

I move real close to the wall and count the spindly legs, checking to see that it is really Max. Of course, how many three- or even four-legged cockroaches can appear in one humble abode? But still.... No doubt about it, it's him. So I place my index finger over my upper lip to feign a French moustache, then announce in a lousy French accent, "This evening, Monsieur Max, you will be dining on a succulent morsel of our best cheddar garnished with several juicy raisins." Oh my God, his right antenna just moved.

As I open the door to leave I see his damaged body willing itself down the hallway like Quasimoto headed toward his castle, dragging the twisted bit of orange behind him.

I manage to extricate myself from this drama, drive into the little town at the edge of the cove, and dine on a small portion of snapper that costs forty dollars a la carte. I am struck by all of the drugs being sold on the street right in front of me, just below the veranda. These kids look like they're in their late teens, surfer types, dreadlocked and smiley. I am so blessed for my Jess' good sense and groundedness, and I toast her with a glass of pinot grigio.

The migraine is back with a vengeance, accompanied by the requisite dizziness. I drive to the small emergency clinic, but it's closed. The nearest hospital is on the other side of the island, and I know what that will be like— hours of waiting to get a drug that will knock me on my ass and I will miss my vacation. I refuse to start that pattern.

Riding home in the car I almost decide to pay the seal healer a visit. But then I get scared again that he might be a real wild card, maybe a mass murderer who killed the people whose house he is staying in. After all, shamans don't have money like that, or ooze sex appeal a la Javier Bardem. Shamans live in caves and huts, hidden away from resort towns and, as I learned from the gods of Google earlier today, they often don't have any contact with civilization at all for long periods of time. I realize I know nothing about this guy except the gossip that Barb has shared, and, ahem, I am greatly aware that he has way too much personal magnetism to be doing any laying of hands on me. And now to get my boundaries in place….

I take a hot shower and let the gentle spray wash over my head. This is obviously not the right move, because in a minute my head is throbbing and I am feeling nauseous. I walk outside to get some of that soft cool air, when I see the healer approaching. Jesus! Can't anything be simple?

He says, "Aloha," and walks toward me.

I feel nervous and put up my shield.

"Kaimana," he says, offering me his hand.

"Dr. Katherine Jamison."

He nods, not really listening, or so I project. "You're in pain," he says, moving in closer, placing his warm hand on my forehead. "You're on fire."

Is this where the mass murdering begins? There is a definite calmness in those eyes. Perhaps he is a great actor….

"Come, let me do some healing. You need not suffer like this."

"Oh, I'll be alright. I'm used to it."

"To suffering?"

Oh no you don't! You're not getting into me that way! I take control of my suffering self, shake my head, "No," then turn and walk without looking back.

An hour later I realize I should have taken that risk. I wish he was a mass murderer who would lop off my head with a nice swift movement of his axe. I have consumed so much medication I am now nauseous, dizzy, inebriated, and panicky. It dawns on me that Barb mentioned to me about her secret stash of marijuana in the fridge. And there it is, a small, Chinese-looking box just like she said! I open it and find three marijuana cigarettes.

"Where are the fucking matches?" I yell way too loudly. Like a madwoman I thrust open the kitchen drawers and find nothing. In the living room I desperately fling open cabinets and search the bookcase. Every sound is amplified fifty times in my head, but onward I pillage into the bedroom and find nada. Finally, at the top of the medicine cabinet I see a small matchbook. I begin to ask myself why she would have put the matches here, but then I remember her own chaos, her illness.

I light up and inhale a tiny bit. Feeling sicker than ever, I suck it back and cough myself silly. Soon I realize my body is drifting far above the couch I am supposed to be lying on...in fact I really don't have a body anymore. I am air. Headacheless air. Wow, I am incredibly relaxed and high and happy. I am happy! I get down on my hands and knees and blow some smoke in Max's direction so he can share in the moment. He's definitely not into it and hobbles toward the kitchen.

The ocean seems most appealing, out there, under the clear, starry sky. I picture myself on the beach alone, but somehow that makes me feel paranoid. I look over at my flute and re-paint the picture. Me, marijuana, moonlight, and music...Maui magic! Wow, pot has brought out the bad poet in me.

I head out the door, plop down on a beach towel on the sand, take my flute out of the case, and blow lightly. I know what I want to play, that great song by Van Morrison...Moonglow. No, MoonSong, that's it! Immediately I feel the rhythm of it and my body starts to move. I snap my fingers and hum that sexy melody, and in a couple of bars I break into a scat. Soon I'm scatting for all I'm worth, until I break down laughing at how elated I am.

I tell myself to calm down but I can't contain myself, so I bring my flute up to my lips and breathe. The notes echo out clear and soulful over the quiet Pacific. The sky is still and lavender. I am playing to an audience of humpbacks and spinner dolphins.

And oh, look, over there to my left I spy a curious little pink pig and a squatting shaman. What the hell. I play on, super stoned and submerged in the sound.

"Beautiful," he calls out when I have finished. "You are feeling much better. I am happy for this." I turn and he bows to me.

"Thanks," I call back, smiling. I gather myself and leave the scene. I wish I knew what I am so afraid of.

THE NEXT MORNING my head is worse than ever. I resort to weeping. There are rays of lightning in front of my right eye, flashing neon. My left temple is so tight and sensitive that I cannot touch it. I am now officially in hell. Fortunately, the lightning does not last long, so when it subsides I gather my stuff and walk out to the car. That little pig is lying down right behind it. I try to shoe him away but he doesn't give a shit, and rolls over in the sun.

"Jesus!" I shout. "What else can possibly happen?"

In the distance I hear, "Kanoa! Kanoa!" and then a trail of words in Hawaiian.

All I can do is lean against the car with my eyes shut.

"The headache has come back to you?"

"Yeah," I manage to say, "with a vengeance. I am going to the hospital."

"There is no need. Come with me and we will release it."

I have no excuses left and my headache is overwhelming me. I tell him a shaky "Okay," and we walk down the little sandy path in silence. There is heat in the space between us...palpable heat. No bells, just heat! The little pink pig trots next to us.

I realize that my heart is beating very fast and I feel like I could pass out. This guy Kaitana, or...Kaimatra...

takes hold of my arm as we move through the iron gate. Every nerve in my body wakes up to his touch. He continues to support me until we are inside.

This is no cave. This is a home that has been consciously architected to embody the landscape of Hawaii. He leads me down a long, curving hallway into the room I have seen on my surreptitious nightly reconnaissance. The room is filled with musical instruments of various sizes and shapes, and there's a wide velvet divan and matching armchair. He leads me to the divan, where I lie down. A standing Buddha with breasts smiles at me.

I am shaking...no, quivering. Vomit rises in my throat. I swallow it back. Kaimana places a cold cloth on my forehead and under my neck. This room is so serene. He takes my hands in his hands...they smell like lavender and cinnamon.

"Breathe," he whispers.

I look up into his green...no, gold eyes, and attempt to inhale a deep breath.

"No, like this. Effortlessly."

He begins to breathe in a certain pattern and I do my best to follow along, though I feel way out of sync. My mind is bombarding itself with a torrent of fearful thoughts, but I keep trying to concentrate on my breath.

Then something shifts, and I become aware of a river of energy moving from his warm hands into mine. My hands feel really hot. I keep telling my mind to calm down, and after a while it begins to listen.

For some reason I turn my attention down into my body and see purple light flowing through my bones and coursing through my blood. It's as though I'm standing under a waterfall of purple light. I can see my cells drifting in a sea of purple...I let go a little more and I'm floating in the sea, totally free. I feel nothing but softness and light. It's so peaceful inside of me. No headache at all. No reality at all.

This purple experience goes on for what seems like forever. I open my eyes and look at his face. His eyes are closed and he is whispering a prayer or invocation of some kind. In this light he looks like a young warrior.

His well-sculpted face has one of those really cool clefts at the chin. He's all cheekbones, an aquiline nose, thick eyebrows, long dark eyelashes. Exquisite pale lips. I see now that he is wearing a little pouch around his neck, hanging on a dark cord. I notice, too, that he has no hair on his chest, which is very well developed, as are his arms. It's not that worked-out looking chest that guys at the gym have. It's the chest of a man who comes from a lineage of physically strong people, a man who inhabits his body and uses it well.

His skin is the color of a walnut shell, with a slight sheen to it, the sun's patina. This one isn't scared of Maui's sun! The veins in his arms are wide and blue, with a deep scar on his right forearm. I have never seen hands as beautiful as these...so sensitive, so expressive.

I attempt to sit up, but he gently signals me to lie back down. He stares into my eyes for a long time and then takes my hands again, but more intensely this time.

"I see where your emotional blockage is, Katherine. If you want to get well you will need to express your fear and your sadness."

"I've tried," I say, holding back tears. "It's overwhelming."

"It feels like this for many reasons. First, I see your sadness. In your aura I see a black hole where disincarnate souls are draining you...you are feeling their pain as well as your own. This is why you feel so much sorrow."

How do I respond to that? Running out the door would be good. But my desperation has a hold on me and is actually listening to what he is saying. I am a three-year-old now and I will do what I am told.

"Can you help me?" I whisper.

"Yes. But for now you must rest."

He smiles so sweetly that I actually smile back.

"Come here the day after tomorrow and we will continue your journey."

I hang my feet over the edge of the divan and ease my weight onto them. I am wobbly, but again he holds on to me until I feel more stable.

"Thank you, Kai—"

"-mana. My name is Kaimana."

"Okay," I say, having totally given in. "Thank you, Kaimana."

"Here in Hawaii, Katherine, we say, 'Mahalo.'"

"Mahalo, Kaimana. Please call me Kate."

I move toward the door but then catch myself. "I'm sorry—I didn't bring my wallet. Will it be okay if I come by tomorrow to pay you?"

"Pay me what, Kate?"

"Pay you...money...for tonight. For your...um... services."

He smiles what might be the kindest smile I've ever seen. "There is no payment. After all, it is not me who provides this 'service,' as you call it. Your healing comes from a source that contains both you and me. I am only here to help you find what already exists within you. No, Kate, there is no payment for this."

I'm too woozy to digest what he's saying, let alone argue. I let him guide me back down the long hallway and out into the fresh night air.

As he opens the gate I notice that the ironwork is a montage of turtles and dolphins swimming in all their reveries. He walks me down the path to Barb's place, and bows to me in a simple way. I watch his body move easily into the night.

My headache is gone.

10

I RETURN TO MYSELF, SCENE ONE

B ut two days later my temples are throbbing again. Even so, I can't seem to stop procrastinating. It's almost time to head on up the path to the shaman-on-the-hill, and I know it's either that or the hospital.

I drag myself out of bed and slather on a glob of Barb's special lotion. Leave it to her to find one that smells like peaches and roses. When it comes to pure sensuality, she sure knows how to take care of herself. I guess the sweet fragrance has turned Max on, because he's perched closer to me than usual.

"You know," I confide out loud, "I'm having a hard time trusting that going to Kailana's, or whatever his name is, for a healing is going to stop these migraines. I have no idea what kind of protocols or sorcery he might use!"

Max skitters a few inches up the wall, falls on his back, then wiggles his three legs in the air and rights himself.

"Okay okay, you're right, that's a little harsh. I guess I'm just scared. A part of me sees that he is a sensitive, intuitive man who seems to have good intentions. But I know nothing about where he learned his art, or if he's certified or has a degree. You live next to him—do you know? Do shamans actually follow a curriculum, or do they study with some kind of shaman mentor? And who is his mentor, anyway? In one moment he looks like he emerged from the rainforests of Brazil, and then he opens his mouth and speaks the king's English like a Rhodes scholar. I don't know what to think! Maybe I need a second opinion."

Max raises his feelers. I have come to understand that this is some kind of cockroach acknowledgement. I am also aware that I have swapped my loose fitting pants for tighter jeans.

"I really don't know what to wear to a healing," I say naively. "So I guess anything goes?"

Again Max raises what I feel is a concerned antenna.

He's not the only one who's concerned. I have that scared feeling in my chest, but I think it's more about the healing than the healer. I am nervous about what he will find in me, whether it's healable, how long it will take to heal, how I will be different in the long run. After all, it's been a decade of migraines. I am a pro at not letting them overcome me. I have run with these bastards, made love during them, taught with them, attended weddings with them, driven cross country with them; they've accompanied me to the symphony to hear Rachmaninoff, for Christ's sake. And lest we forget, my migraines have occasionally helped me gain distance from my marriage.

"You know, Max, maybe it's not such a good idea that I refer to the migraines as mine. Sounds like pride of ownership."

Both antennas sway to the right.

These migraine marauders and I have been in partnership for a very long time. I notice an eerie fear of loss. How crazy is that? New Agers talk about the gift of an illness, and I agree that you do learn a lot about yourself when you are struck with something dramatic. I see it every day in my practice, women finding gratitude for their precious lives after losing a baby or their uterus and living through it. I guess my gift is that I learned that I can endure pain alone. But now I am incredibly sick of it.

Okay, I'm dressed. Earrings? Or would that be too much? Perspiration drips down my arms and I check to see if I should have shaved. I am fucking nuts right now.

FOR THE THIRD TIME in as many attempts to walk to Kaimana's house, I turn around and head back to mine. I don't know if I can handle this. I'm pretty sure I can't. But if there's a chance I can get a break from the pounding in my skull...I head back one last time to either my doom or my salvation.

As my sandals crunch against the gravel on the path, I see there is a lovely pale yellow flag mounted on top of his mailbox. I'm sure I haven't seen it there before. When I get closer I can see it has the outline of a phoenix on it, hand stitched in lavender thread.

Kaimana appears at the iron gate just as I do, and opens it before I have a chance to turn the handle.

"Aloha, Kate. I am ready for you," he says.

"Thank you," I say, not yet able to meet his eyes. "This flag...it's beautiful."

"Yes, it is. It was a gift from someone who came to see me many times. She had great courage, and was able to release a great deal of sorrow...very much like you. I place the flag here so people will know this is a day for healing, and that all are welcome."

I nod and touch the flag. It's incredibly soft. Then I straighten up and hand him my business card. Maybe I am safer if I keep things professional. He takes a quick look and puts it in his pocket.

My cell phone rings. I check the number and see that it is a friend. No matter.

"You will have to leave that outside. No technology once we go in."

Perfect. I am entering the abyss with no way to call for help.

I turn off the phone and slip it into his mailbox.

In the daylight his home is a joy to the senses...creams and sea-foam greens, celadon and fuscia. There's a magnificent stained glass window of a whale and its baby breaching in turquoise waves. Overstuffed chairs and thick pillows are placed thoughtfully around the living area. In the center of the pale pink tiled floor is a massive peach Indian rug that looks very old. I take off my shoes and feel its silkiness beneath my toes.

"Please have a seat, Kate, while I finish my last appointment. I will only be a moment." He smiles, then slips silently away down the hallway.

I sit down. Then I stand up. My feet are sweating on his gorgeous rug. I look around the room nervously for something safe to sink into. I feel like nothing is safe, so I go to the bookcase and pick up *The Life of Buddha*. I hear voices and footsteps coming down the hall and I quickly place Buddha back in his place on the shelf. Kaimana passes by with a young woman.

"I am proud of you, Kyra," he tells her, and she leaves smiling.

He probably says that to everyone. Here he comes with that beautiful face, that face that is hiding God knows what. His innocent-looking eyes look deep into mine, and he asks, "Are you ready?"

I don't have an answer. Even so, he turns and I follow him back down the hallway. The energy and light in this room where he does his alleged healing work is, I confess, wonderful. Somehow, for one minute, my heart takes it in and settles back into a normal rhythm. I breathe in the pale peach walls, the large abstract watercolors, and the fascinating array of instruments. I sit down.

"You'll need to take off your watch. There's no need to be concerned about time."

I unbuckle my Tank and he places it on a nearby table.

"Before we begin, I would like you to choose an instrument you feel would be healing for your heart and soul." Kaimana runs his hand across several instruments, touching each one in such an honoring way. None of them is the sort of thing you'd find at the San Francisco Symphony. We're talking instruments that must have been played by Bedouins, gypsies, and the like.

My heart starts pounding again. Man, do I feel out of my element!

"This one is a kalimba from Africa. It's a thumb piano." He plucks the silver prongs of the lovely lyrical wooden box and lets me give it a try. "How does that feel to you?" he asks.

It's absolutely lovely and sweet, but it isn't going to heal my sadness. That will take a fleet of grand pianos. I shake my head.

"And these? Do these brass bowls from Tibet resonate with you?"

He walks around me, touching the rim of each bowl, creating a series of different tones. Each bell is more beautiful than the last.

I feel them in my spine, but none of them really feels like me. "I love these, but they don't go deep enough," I tell him. Maybe they don't make them deep enough for my sorrow.

He tries other relics from Morocco, Russia, Mexico, and China. Each one is unique, but I am feeling like a failure. Could it be that, of all the people who come here to see him, I am the only one he cannot heal? Wow, what an ego. How's that working for you, Katherine?

"I have an idea," he says, and leaves the room.

I get up and pace. I can't even imagine what kind of shenanigans have gone on in here. I am full of fear and becoming full-on negative. He returns with a six-foot-long, tubular instrument.

"Let's try this," he says, grinning, and then he blows the most primal sound toward my heart. The low vibration resounds around the room. There's a lamp with a dancing goddess painted on it and, I swear, she actually moves.

"Whoa! I've heard that instrument before, but it has never affected me like this."

"This is a didgeridoo from Australia. Does the vibration resonate with your soul?"

"Yes...yes...I believe it does."

"So. I will begin with bells and chimes and some special bowls. Then when you are deep down in the dreamtime, entranced, I will accompany you on your journey with my didgeridoo, here, as your ally."

"Entering the Dreamtime?" I say, even more clueless. "Not sure I know what that is or how to get there." Oh, brother.

"Here. Hold this spirit animal. She will lead you." He places a wooden sculpture of a lizard in the palm of my hand. "This is a fetish of a Hawaiian lizard, a gecko. In Hawaiian mythology she is called 'mo'o.'"

Mo-oh? Fetish?! I roll the small, carved wooden sculpture around in my hand. I don't know what I am supposed to feel or how this will help me connect. "Actually I'm feeling a little nervous," I confess.

"A good sign," he tells me.

Really? For whom? Kaimana motions for me to lie down on the divan, then places a silk covering over me. I look up at the ceiling, which has a lovely painting of a night sky with hundreds of stars. This is crazy! What am I doing? I can still leave. I'd better leave now. Sit up, Katherine!

Kaimana lights a stick of sage and spreads the smoke around the room. The air is thick and I cover my face with my hands. I feel very claustrophobic, and my throat is closing up on me. I put my feet down on the floor.

"I don't think I can do this. I'm just too nervous."

"Lie down, Katherine," Kaimana tells me quietly. "Relax into your breath."

What breath? I am so panicky I can hardly take in any air. "Are you sure?" I say pathetically.

Whatever he answers doesn't matter now because I am outta here! I get up from the divan and grab my purse. "Please—I'm sorry—please let me pay you for your time."

"Kate—"

"No...no. I can't. I—I've got to go to the bathroom," I stutter. "I think I'd better go back to the cottage. I'll be back later."

"Kate, if I did not believe you could handle this I would not be here with you."

"Thanks," I say racing down the hallway. I slam the gate behind me, working hard to keep myself from breaking into a run. Finally I slow down and consider returning, but fear keeps me moving away.

Inside the cottage I pace up and down the hallway. I'm into my breath, alright, but I'm sure not relaxing into it. What did I expect, anyway? Here I am in Maui, land of self-proclaimed saints and sex-starved gurus who have been kicked out of their native countries only to prey on vulnerable runaways! And lonely gynecologists who don't have their shit together! Just hearing myself talk reminds me I am a major drama diva and I can dredge up a horrific tale at the drop of a hat when I need an excuse to escape.

For some strange reason Max decides to cross over my foot, and this totally freaks me out.

"Jesus! I yell out. "It's time for you to go," I say meanly, grabbing a broom from the kitchen. I sweep him out and slam the front door. And then I sit down and weep, but then it dawns on me that this dangerous healer dude might come up the path to find out why I haven't returned. And—*shit!* My cell phone is confiscated neatly in his mailbox.

I change my clothes and drive into town where I can yell for help if I need it, and where I will be unrecognizable among all of the other white tourists.

11

MANGO TANGO
AND MEN AS MIRRORS

I walk the narrow streets and see something I haven't seen in light years. There on the corner of Paradise and Ma'a'a'hela'ana'ana Avenues—seriously!—sits a red phone booth with an actual pay phone in it. I dial information and get the number for the Four Seasons. Just hearing the sound of the reservations person eases my heart.

"Hi there, I'd like to make a reservation. I'll take anything."

The sweet female voice gives me the devastating news that they are completely sold out. "It's like that everywhere on this side of the island. It's convention time and there's a film festival going on. Try us again next week."

Sure, if I'm still alive.

I slam down the heavy black phone—the panic has dissipated; now I'm just pissed off. It's an improvement.

I decide to get something to eat while I figure out my new plan of escape. I choose the Hana Café and take a seat inside. It's a very exotic menu, a vegan menu. I am so out of my element, but I am incognito and that's what counts. A young man with many, many nose rings and blonde hair dreadlocked into thick tentacles comes to take my order.

"I'm new at this," I explain. "What would you suggest?"

"The seitan is fantastic, better than the tofu."

That's a hard one for a chicken lover to fathom. I go for it anyway, and find myself gnawing through some kind of brown, leathery, non-meat concoction. My God! It's a true culinary experience if you are into munching on penny loafers. I am very much for healthy food, but come on. I can honestly say that the Special of the Day Savory Seitan Stroganoff is absolutely disgusting. I apologize to my taste buds, pay the bill, and excuse myself.

A Jerry's Ice Cream sign lures me down the block. Two cute teenage Asian girls recite for me all the flavors. There are only five, but they are all handmade. I choose two scoops: Coconut Macadamia Nut Java and Mango Tango. They are incredible. I lighten up. The power of ice cream. I swear, I could be lost in the most traumatic funk and just one scoop nestled in a homemade waffle cone dipped in chocolate and crushed almonds can render me hopeful. I lick away my troubles and all of the leftovers around my lips, then drive down to the beach where half a dozen muscular male bodies are windsurfing across the waves...and I cannot help but think of my husband. This is the kind of thing he would salivate over—and be an instant champion at. I can picture him, first time out, finding his balance and heading toward the big waves.

I wish I was his big wave. And then I don't.

I walk the beach and picture myself walking away from my personal life—not just the medicine man debacle, but my relationship. I can't even really call it that anymore. It's just a dead marriage, inanimate like that mesh of cold seaweed lying in the sand over there. When we were first together we traveled a lot, and everything was new. I liked that, but I liked coming home and just hanging out even more. I wanted a baby, wanted to build a tightly bonded family. Not David. He gets bored and moves on very quickly, like there always has to be something new to keep him distracted. Nice man...well, sort of...but there's no juice left between us. It all went underground after his first dalliance. As I see it now, it was all my fault—the choosing, I mean. I was so unsure of my beauty and insecure in my body that I picked a quixotic stunner as a mate. A champion on the racetrack but never a champion for me. A magnet for younger women.

How stupid was that? I chose my worst fear because unconsciously I thought I'd appear more attractive by being with him. After all, he chose *me*, and that was the big message I wanted the world to see. Except that wasn't what was going on at all. The truth is, after our seventh anniversary he hardly even noticed me. Once the heavy romance wore off I became an appendage. And believe me, I tried my damnedest to create a lifestyle that supported his every desire, just so he would stay. It's the old Prostitute Wounded Healer archetype that graces my office every day. For *him*, I became a first class chef, learned Spanish and French, and let him beat me at tennis. What that got me was a perpetual C.E.O. racecar champion who respects his wife and thinks it's great she's an M.D., but who will entice another woman at the drop of his racing helmet...someone who will make him look better and feel younger, faster, and more on top of things. These women never last long, they come and they go. It's just how he survives. He's very adrenal...six espressos a day and counting.

I'm a Pisces woman who is slow and deep in my relationships. On the surface I'm not thick, but thoughtful. But underneath it all I am thick with longing. If anyone knew how much love is bottled up inside of me they'd run—scared they might touch me by mistake and watch my body explode into a million pieces. Still, it's been a long time since I let myself relax with my husband. I haven't wanted to because I've known all along that he can't handle anything that resembles bonding. Or is it me who can't handle it? After all, I chose him as much as he chose me. Why would a juicy woman choose a man she could not surrender with? It's a long, tricky story. One that I thought I was going to begin to unwind and maybe heal today. So much for that idea.

As the late afternoon sunlight warms my skin, I realize I'm feeling like a grownup again. I say a little affirmation to myself: "With each step I am letting go of all my fears. With each step I am trusting myself." Someone inside me likes this and agrees.

I glance at my naked wrist and guess that it's probably around five thirty. I head back to my car and make the short drive along the winding two-lane road to the cottage.

12

THANK GOD
FOR AUNTIE GRACE

The air is purple and dusky as I pull into my narrow, covered parking spot. I have left something behind on the beach near the village, and I'm feeling much freer. But the first pangs of guilt return as I put a wedge of cheese away in the fridge, a thick piece of provolone that Mr. Max would've gobbled right down. I realize I have done something wrong, an action brought on by careless emotion.

I can't resist the deepening sunset, so I wander all the way to the beach. At the far end of the cove I suddenly remember that I could run into Kaimana out here...and a wave of confusion about him washes over me. But the last rays of the sun are warm and nurturing, so I decide to take my chances. I sit down, stretch out my legs and lean back on my elbows, and let myself absorb all the healing rays I can.

Something distracts me from the rhythm of the waves, and I turn and see his elegant figure at the far end of the beach, standing over an elderly native woman. She is sitting in a wheelchair with her head tilted back, resting against the headrest. Kanoa lies at her side. Kaimana bends over and touches the woman's shoulder with what looks like reverence. He gently pours water over her head, then pours something from a bottle into his hands and massages her long white hair into a foamy lather. He does it so lovingly that I can practically feel her sighing. He massages her neck and shoulders for a moment, then uses another bottle to rinse the sudsy shampoo away. He dries her off just as gently, and wraps the towel around her head. Then he begins massaging her arms and hands, her legs and feet. The woman is either blissed out or has fallen into a restful sleep. Kaimana stands and leans over her, and takes her hands in his. They exchange words and then he kisses both of her palms. She puts her hands on the sides of his head and pulls him close. She kisses his forehead.

These are not the actions of a bad man. I am such a frightened fool, scared of my own shadow.

He sees me and waves, then motions for me to join them.

"She does not speak English," he explains, "but she would like to meet you. This is my Auntie Grace...well, everybody's Auntie Grace. Auntie, this is Kate."

She nods. The woman's face is glorious, golden with deep creases, wings of light, all around her eyes. She smiles in the loveliest way, as if she can see the lovely me. I want to kiss her hands, too! They are big and strong and peaceful. I want an Auntie Grace.

Kaimana touches my shoulder and says, "I wonder if you would help me wheel Auntie up to the house. I want to carry her inside so she can lie down and rest. Could you help us with that?"

"I'd be honored."

I balance the wheelchair as Kaimana lifts it over the rocks onto the path. He pushes the chair up toward his house, and Kanoa and I walk beside auntie Grace in the silky warm evening wind. Kaimana carries her through the gate, and I leave the wheelchair next to the divan, where she will rest. He walks me to the door.

"I am so sorry for my behavior this afternoon," I tell him. "It's those demons that I'm scared to confront."

"I understand. We all have them. But each of us is doing the best we can."

"Yeah, I guess so." It feels like maybe he really does get me. "I would like to come again. Would that be alright?"

We agree to meet tomorrow, and I turn to leave.

"Goodbye, Kate," he says, looking kindly into my eyes. I retrieve my cellphone from his mailbox and head down the path toward home.

I AM NOW FRANTIC to find Max. I go from room to room.

"I'm so sorry," I call out. "Please come back." I cut up many pieces of cheese and leave a trail outside into the house, well aware that I will most probably attract many strangers. Oddly, no one arrives, not even those tiny ants that besieged me on my arrival.

Barb's little television flickers in the darkness of the room. I can't stand the drone of bad news, but that's all there is except for one wonderful story about an eight-year-old girl named Tina, who saved a puppy who ran out into the busy street outside her home. And with that I descend into serious weeping.

Internally cleansed, I turn off the set and do my nightly renovation: wash, brush, oil up and down, spray, and smile. This was a day and a half...I can't take anymore. I have nothing left. And then up the left side of the wall limps my Main Man.

My eyes well up—again—as a wave of gratitude overtakes me. "Goodnight, you!" I whisper, and turn off the light.

13

LOOK AT KATIE JAMISON NOW

I'm up early with a migraine, what a surprise. Still, I had such beautiful dreams, a series of floating, drifting, free-falling scenarios. Not at all like Dr. Jamison, San Francisco M.D. Today feels different.

I dress in loose-fitting pants and leave my shirt untucked. Kaimana is again at the gate when I arrive.

"Aloha. How are you feeling today?"

"Well," I say, smiling vulnerably, "I'm here."

"Yes, you are, and courageous, too."

"It was Auntie Grace, I think."

"Is she not wonderful? She is my queen."

"Mine, too."

"I worked with her late into the night. You'll be immersed in her energies."

"Well, that's good news." My voice is trailing because that old devil fear is drifting in.

In the center of the healing room floor, Kaimana has arranged several soft blankets, with the edges folded under so it looks like a large nest. He motions me to lie down, and I feel like I'm settling into a cloud. Like the other night, he wants us to begin by breathing together in a slow, steady rhythm.

The first three breaths are no big deal, but then my heart starts to race, and waves of anxiety begin to surface. I keep breathing. Oddly, my body wants to move. It wants to dance—no, now I'm furious and I want to pound my fists on the floor! Wait...everything's softer now, as though I'm falling into a trance. There's a stillness around me...but it feels like I'm alone on a boat headed for the rapids.

"You are doing very well, Kate," Kaimana whispers. "See if you can let go a bit more. I am right here with you."

I emerge from the trance and realize that I'm rolling on the floor like a toddler having a full-on tantrum. I can't believe this is me! My body is rocking from side to side. I feel my arms being raised and pillows being placed underneath.

"Go ahead and pound if you want to. You will not hurt yourself."

I've always wondered what would happen if I just let myself go...who I'd find behind the iron-clad control-freak Katherine. Am I really a screaming rageaholic? Maybe I'm more like my mother than I care to know, and that's why I've kept my anger under wraps.

"That is right," Kaimana whispers in a tender voice. "Let go. I am here right beside you."

And so I pound. Hard. And scream. Kaimana places a pillow over my chest that also covers my mouth.

"Here," he says, "scream into this."

I am on a jet taking off for Frustration City, spewing out futility from every pore.

"Yes, let it all go now."

Then this most unattractive sound emanates from my throat that is part gurgle, part moan. Perspiration is streaming down my forehead and my back, and my mouth is so dry it feels like it's stuffed with cotton. For a moment the room goes silent except for my rocking body and occasional whimper. I still can't believe this is me! Perhaps it isn't. This must be Rhonda, Sybil's daughter.

Kaimana picks up the didgeridoo, aims it directly toward my heart, and blows deeply. It sends me off on another journey—there's no turning back now, even if I wanted to. Inside my mind I follow the sound in and out of circuitous hallways and doorways, and eventually it leads me to a profound stillness. I'm not even sure I'm breathing. A little later I feel Kaimana walking around my body, and he's making this awesome sound like there's a family of wild geese flapping their wings all around me.

"Kate...," he whispers next to my cheek, "open up your lungs as you would open two doors. Open them and let the sorrow fly out of you like a million blackbirds."

I do as instructed. I look down inside my body and envision each lung with a large, heavy door, and both doors are swinging wide open. The flapping sound begins again. I open my eyes and see Kaimana waving two huge, shiny black feathers all around my body. He stops and brings the wings down directly on my throat, then walks and waves some more...then he uses the feathers like big brooms and brushes me up and down and back up again, like he's sweeping away a lifetime of debris.

I feel all of this weight rising to the surface now...the anger, the sadness...my heart is opening and pounding and I am ready to scream again. Kaimana places his open palms under my head and the energy comes rushing to the surface, wave after wave after wave. Finally it all calms down and my body goes limp, resting in his nest of pillows.

"Breathe, Kate, breathe. That is good. That is very good. Now I want you to walk down into your body."

"You mean like I'm walking down stairs?"

"Yes, that is good. See ten stairs in front of you. I will count as you walk down. Every time your foot touches one of these stairs, you will relax even more. Do you understand what I am saying? Can you see the stairs?"

"Yes," I mumble.

"Number ten, watch your foot coming down."

I see my sandaled foot going down the first step of a lovely staircase.

"Nine, going further down."

I feel my heartbeat slowing even more.

"Eight. You are relaxing one hundred times more deeply."

Oh my God, I am so relaxed. I hardly hear his voice...it sounds like he has moved to another room.

"Are you here with me?" I slur in his direction.

"Yes, Kate. I will not leave you. You are now very relaxed. "

Yes indeedy.

"Envision a sacred space where there is an altar. "

"You mean like a religious table?"

"It doesn't have to be religious. This is an altar to your soul. Do not force a particular image, just relax and let it appear in front of you. Let me know when you can see it."

After a while I manage to look through a purple fog and envision a forest where there is a simple pine table with a vase of white roses on it.

"Akay...."

"Wonderful. Notice what is on your altar. Perhaps you want to place something on the altar today that signifies your healing."

"There are white roses and pictures. Pictures of myself at different ages. I can't really make them out."

"Perfect. Just let them be there. If there is a prayer you wish to say, go ahead and say it to yourself."

"What should I pray for?"

"You tell me. What do you want to change? What do you want to heal?"

I'm so relaxed I can hardly form the words. "I want to come back...back into my life...into my body. So I can feel safe...free...."

"Alright. Now make a prayer, ask for what you need. How about something like this: 'Please, Spirit, help me to return to my body so that I am fully here, feeling safe and free.' How does that feel?"

"Feels beautiful."

"Okay, then. Make your prayer."

I do.

Kaimana announces the next part of the journey by gently striking a large brass bowl. I go deeper.

"Now, Kate, invite toward you the parts of yourself you abandoned a long time ago. The ones you left behind because they were challenging or hurt or frightened. Invite these lost parts of you to this healing ceremony."

"Okay," I say timidly, not really knowing what he means, or what to say. "Please come to me now, you hurt parts." My heart starts racing and I feel like leaving again.

Kaimana gently strokes the bowl, invoking their presence.

To my utter amazement a small figure appears out of nowhere. It's a toddler in blue-jean overalls, and she's running toward me. She's a sad little towhead with wonder in her eyes. I notice how she wants to please me...there's a neediness in her I immediately recognize. She's me. Somehow I'm greeting the lonely little kid I was a few decades ago. I can't believe it's happening, but I know it is.

"Come here, little one!" I say clapping my hands together, happy to remember how cute I was.

I put my arms around her. I can feel her little heartbeat next to mine. At the same time I feel her fear, her immense loneliness, and it's in my heart as much as hers.

"I'm so happy to see you," I manage.

She looks deep into my eyes.

"Tell the truth, Kate. Open up a little more." Kaimana instructs quietly.

"I'm trying. It's very emotional. I don't know if I can do more."

"This little girl has waited for a long time to reunite with you. See if you can reach out and tell her how you are going to take care of her. You are very intuitive. Tell her what she needs to hear to trust you and not run away."

I brush back her bangs and look into her lake green eyes. It's as if they are saying, "I'm so scared right now. Please don't leave me."

"I love you, little one," I tell her, and she grabs on to my neck and presses her head against my chest.

"Are you letting her know how important she is to you?" Kaimana asks gently.

"I need to stop. I can't do anymore," I reply.

"Try and stay there with her just a moment more. She has been an outcast for a very long time."

His words spark something hidden somewhere deep inside me.

"I feel someone else coming," I whisper, "and I'm feeling really scared."

"I can see her coming, too," he says tenderly.

Kaimana invokes the brass bowl again, announcing the arrival of a second figure. This one is larger and older than the toddler, but moves with a youthful arrogance. I sense that she's another part of me.

I feel the tears welling up as she comes out of the shadows and shows me her radical self. This is me at seventeen in a mini skirt with a Camel cigarette hanging out of my flashy red mouth. I want to throw her a tube of Clearsil, but I know that would be highly inappropriate. She is Ms. Resistance, all fired up with no place to rebel, and I feel just as resistant as her fury rises up in me again. She's scary and she has a secret. I want nothing to do with her.

"Okay, I'm done," I announce, opening my eyes. "It's just too much!"

"I understand," Kaimana says. "Let us stop for today. You have done very, very well, Kate. Now you must go home and rest."

He kneels down beside me, and I sit up in the middle of my now rumpled nest and look up into his golden eyes. I see so much kindness there, as though he can contain all the hurt and anger I'm so afraid to turn loose. But still...it's all just way too much.

He puts a gentle hand on my arm, and tells me, "Go home now and take very good care of yourself. You may find that many emotions arise, and you may want to cry— a lot. That is all perfectly fine. Drink plenty of water. But please do not drink any alcohol during this time. Allow your mind to be clear while you process all that you have experienced."

Kaimana stands up and extends his hand to help me to my feet. He picks up the didgeridoo and leans it against the wall, places the bowl back on the corner table, then turns to me with his warm, encouraging eyes. "This was a good healing, Kate."

Not really. I want out. In no way is this the vacation I had envisioned or the downtime I was lusting for. I brush the hair out of my eyes, straighten my shoulders, and pull my checkbook out of my purse. After all, business is business.

Kaimana takes the checkbook from my hand and places it back in my purse, then gently drapes the purse over my shoulder. "Let us work together again, day after tomorrow."

"Okay," I lie.

FOR A FULL TWENTY-FOUR HOURS now I've been trying hard to run from my tears, but they overtake me. I feel like one of the shattered shells from the tide pools, a battered fragment that has been tossed and tossed and then dumped recklessly in the constantly shifting sand.

Can it possibly be that I am more exhausted and upset than when I arrived? How can I have done this to myself? I thought I was doing the right thing. What was I thinking? I am particularly jumpy because I will have to tell Kaimana that I don't want to go any further, and this will be very uncomfortable for me.

I pour myself a gin and tonic. And then a second. I tumble into bed. Soon I am in a strange landscape where I have lost my glasses and my keys. What's worse is that my teeth are falling out and scattering all over some remote highway. A young girl is walking toward me and I shout, "Get away from me!" I am sure it's that same girl I experienced at the healing. She looks hollow and starved, and her lower stomach area is all pooched out. She looks at me with total disdain and then I feel it, I feel how deep the well of her sadness goes. Just like mine. There is much more to this story, and I know now that I will have to return to it, like it or not. It's the only way I will ever be free.

14

BACK TO THE WOMB

I open my eyes and realize I've slept eleven and a half hours. It's mid-morning, but I still can't drag myself out of bed. I bury my head in the pillows, vacillating between anxiety and depression with a shot of despair. With all of this baggage, how have I navigated through life as well as I have? Oh, the power of denial.

But enough is enough—I finally get myself up and into the shower. I stand in front of the mirror and notice how the left side of my face is youthful and the right side is turning the corner to ninety. I'm definitely emotionally lopsided. All the more reason to keep my appointment with Mr. Shaman.

"Okay, Max, wish me luck. Actually, lend me some courage to hang in there through this, can't you? I don't want to go! Do you think all this misery will end those freakin' headaches, Max?"

My cockroach pal stares off into oblivion. He's right, it's all up to me.

I walk down the path and trip on a wayward miniature coconut. "Damnit!" I yell out. "What else can happen today?" Probably not the best question to put out to the universe.

Again Kaimana knows to meet me at the gate. He bows and smiles. I look down and walk past him down the hallway to the healing room.

"How are you?" he asks, knowing exactly how I am.

"Not too wonderful. Been through a lot. Talked myself into coming back."

"That is very brave of you. Shall we take a few moments and have a cup of tea before we begin?"

"I'd like that."

"I have a lovely lavender and rose petal tea. How does that sound?"

"Sounds amazing. But hold the hallucinogenics...just kidding."

Kaimana smiles. "No LSD for you today? That is excellent, because we only distill whole herbs and flowers here."

Yeah, but it's going to be a heavy trip anyway. I take a deep breath and watch him glide toward the kitchen.

He returns and we sit across from each other on two large pillows, sipping our aromatic elixir from delicate teacups with hand-painted flowers on them. I am convinced they are bone china.

Finally I have to break the peaceful silence. "How long have you lived here?" I ask.

"Nearly twenty years. I came here from Delhi when I was twenty.

Ah-ha! He's in his late thirties. "It's a beautiful place. Did you design it?"

"Yes, but I had the help of many wonderful people, many Hawaiians...my mother's family."

"So you have native Hawaiian ancestry on your mother's side?"

"Yes, that is correct. I am a half-breed," he says, smiling and pouring me a bit more tea.

"Have you always been a healer?"

"Ever since I can remember." Kaimana pauses, and even I can feel a shift in the energy. Then he brightens again and says, "But this session is about you, not me."

He gets up, pushes his pillow back, and gathers the instruments he will be using. I hand him my teacup, push back my pillow and lie back on the floor. He places the little gecko fetish in my hand.

"Here we go!" I say nervously.

"Yes," Kaimana says, leveling me with a touch on my shoulder. "Here we go."

Soon we are in our breathing adventure together, but this time I feel my shoulders coming down as I begin to relax. I look down into my body and once again see my feet touch down on each of the ten stairs. I breathe more fully with each striking of the brass bowl. But this time my mind is very active, bombarding me with very important thoughts, things like, "What should I have for lunch?" and "What's the name of that pig?" I tell Kaimana what's going on.

"Sometimes, when the mind is anxious, it uses mindless chatter as a diversion. It is a way to try to avoid getting lost or losing control. Just allow your thoughts to drift by like leaves in the wind. Do not respond to them. Allow them to express themselves, but try to stop caring what they mean. Just let them be."

I picture myself as a tall aspen with lots of falling leaves floating away on a breeze, out of my brain. My mind asks if Kaimana has ever been married. I do not answer but let the yellow leaf drift away. This is nice.

Next he directs me to envision walking on the beach, looking out at the turquoise waves.

That I can do.

"Each wave," he tells me, "relaxes you deeper and deeper."

Whoa, my breath is coming in so slowly, rolling over me like these small turquoise waves. As I walk I feel a soft wind soothing my nervous system.

"With each footstep, let go a little more."

And so I do. I walk slowly amid palm trees swaying softly, the feeling of warm powdery sand caressing my feet. I'm a happy camper until I feel a force coming toward me that casts a shadow over the distance between us. My heart starts racing and chills run up and down my arms.

"I feel her coming again," I tell him, my voice quivering.

"Which one?"

"It's the angry one. I feel her rage, and she's not even that close. What do I do?"

"Welcome her. Her rage is really fear. She is as frightened as you are."

She comes toward me like the first swirl of a tornado, sweeping up air and sand as she moves. As she gets closer I see her red lipstick and chipped red nails. Cigarette smoke curls around her.

"Welcome," I call out. "I'm so glad you are here." Liar!

"Bullshit," she asserts her face contorted. "You're not glad at all." She throws her cigarette on the sand. "You're scared of me like everyone else. Why the fuck did I bother? There's nothing here for me." She turns and walks away.

"Wait," I yell. "At least tell me why you're so pissed off. Come on. I really do want to know. Maybe I can help you get through it."

"You? I doubt it. You're nothing but a people pleaser. A prostitute. You'll do anything for love, even sleep with a douche bag like your husband who doesn't give a shit about you. How can *you* help me?"

"Look, I know I've made bad choices for a lot of the wrong reasons. I know I overdo, overgive, overfeel! I've chosen false security and insecurity over true love. I know that. But I am changing. That's why I'm here. Now tell me why you are so angry and scared, so we can get to know each other."

"It's about the abortion, stupid!"

"Don't call me stupid!" I shout out loud indignantly into Kaimana's face.

"Let her call you whatever she wants," Kaimana interrupts adamantly. "Stop censoring. Let her have her say." Then his voice softens. "Do not be afraid. I am right there with you."

The teenager spews on. "All Mother could think about was how embarrassing it was for her, and that made me feel like crap. I was so humiliated. She never even asked me how I was feeling, and I was completely wacked by it all! You didn't stick up for me, not once. You were like a deer in the headlights, all victimy and weak. You let her treat me like shit and then you dumped me. How do you think that made me feel?"

"Alone," I say, remembering the terrible isolation and sadness I endured. "My God, I'm so sorry for whitewashing your feelings like they were nothing. That was a hideous time for you, and I slammed the door on my emotions, split myself off from you, and moved on. I felt so helpless and ashamed and completely overwhelmed by it all, so I just followed Mom's lead. I didn't know what else to do. Please forgive me. Do you think you can?"

Tears stream down my cheeks. She stands there in silence for the longest time...the damage I have done to this beautiful girl.

"The pain of the whole abortion thing was really bad, but the pain of having to face everything alone was worse."

"Oh my God, I'm so sorry, Kathy," I say out loud. I open my eyes.

"Keep going, Kate. Close your eyes. Tell her you love her."

"This is so painful. I don't know if I can keep going. Maybe I should stop?"

Kaimana shakes his head and takes hold of my hand. My heart turns over. I feel a surge of energy that allows me to go back in. Kathy is right there, meeting me face to face.

"I remember the pain now during the abortion," I confess. "You were so strong, doing everything on your own with no support. Actually, I get it now...that because of what you endured I became a doctor, a gynecologist. How could I not have seen it before? I realize now that I've been trying to find you through all my patients." I feel a huge space opening up inside my chest. It's filled with love. "You are one amazing girl. I'm so proud of you."

There's a very long silence, except for my weeping. I can see that she is crying, too. I willingly open my arms and she walks in. I hold her tight and stroke her curly head of hair. Simultaneously I hear Kaimana lift the black condor feathers and begin dusting off our sorrow. He whisks them over our shoulders and spines, and it feels like he's cleaning out our nervous systems. I am sobbing from a place I have never been before...and now I see why. I know I am feeling real grief.

I open my eyes and see that Kaimana, too, has tears in his eyes. My suffering is moving through his body, being transmuted through his massive shoulders and elegant hands. I watch him processing me, and then I get it. This is what being felt by another is all about. This is compassion. You don't sit back feeling sorry for someone, you actually feel her pain with a loving heart. And then you let it go. Whew.

Kaimana sings to me what I feel to be the sweetest Hawaiian lullaby, and strokes my head the way I always wanted my mother to. I feel safe and seen and scared to feel it.

I close my eyes once more. In a matter of minutes I am out there again sinking into the great subconscious.

This time there's a silvery liquid all around me and I am floating like a fetus still connected to the mom who never wanted me. I notice her green-brown soupy self-loathing coming through the umbilical cord into my tiny innocent form.

"Get out!" I yell and yank the cord out of me. I see a satiny light above me and I swim toward it, feeling totally detached from my mother's judgment and suffering.

I find my way into that light and find the precious, hopeful little toddler me waiting there. "Swim to me, little one," I call out. She swims to the teenager, who wraps her arms around her. Then the three of us embrace and merge into one person.

This is enough! I can't take any more! I am exhausted. "I can't process anymore," I tell Kaimana, and open my eyes.

"Fine. Let us stop for today." He sits down beside me and takes my hand. "Tell me, how do you feel?"

I close my eyes and try to connect with my feelings and realize I don't want to. I mean what I said...enough is enough. I switch into rational mode. "It was very interesting meeting those parts of myself. I'm not sure what they have to do with my migraines, but I'm glad I tried this anyway."

"You are not finished, Kate. I will see you in two days. And Kate, please continue to rest and be gentle with yourself. There is a very real possibility you will feel a need to cry again."

Ya think, medicine man?

Kaimana walks me to the gate and smiles with such sincerity. He reaches over to give me a supportive hug and I quickly move away. Sincere or not, it's just too much!

THE SUNSET IS extra beautiful, so I prop myself up on the lanai to watch the show. Suddenly I realize that once again I have left my cell phone in Kaimana's mailbox, so I walk back to get it.

When I get close to his house I see a group of boys teasing the little pig. One of them kicks him in the rib cage and he starts to squeal.

"Get away from that pig!" I yell. "Kaimana!" I scream. I push the kicker and he pushes me so hard I fall to the ground.

"Take the pig!" one of the little bastards says in a macho tone.

"Kaimana!" I scream again.

In that instant a threatening wind rises in the road. Dirt scatters and palm leaves fly all around us. The boys run off and I pick up the pig and run toward the house. I hand him over to Kaimana, who has shed his gentle countenance and stands like a warrior.

"They were going to take him," I say out of breath.

"I would never let that happen. I gave him the name Kanoa, which means 'the free one.' It is my responsibility to protect his spirit." He scratches Kanoa's belly. "Besides, he is my friend. Those children do not understand how one can have a connection of that kind with an animal. I have compassion for their ignorance. Thank you, Kate. Today *you* have become my friend."

"I just didn't want anything to happen to this wonderful little guy," I say, scratching Kanoa's soft pink ears. "I'm glad I was there to help."

"It was meant to be. Now we have helped each other."

He reaches over, and this time I let him hug me full on. In the silence that follows something is happening, something is swirling around me. I cannot name it, not because it is too distant, but because it is intimately close. I could say it feels like déjà vu, but that wouldn't even touch the intensity. Inside me lush landscapes are emerging on foreign soil. This sudden connection feels very, very unsafe.

I know now that this is what I have been unnerved about all along.

15

WHO AM I REALLY?

Kaimana wasn't kidding. For the next thirty-six hours I gush non-stop, all night, all day, and all night. Honokohau Falls, the sixteen-hundred-foot waterfall nearby, has nothing on me. Childhood memories rear their ugly heads, and I feel the sadness I did not feel back in the day.

I definitely am not going back for another session. It was fascinating, and I love the journeying with sound—but I feel a migraine coming on and I am so disappointed. Obviously shamanic healing doesn't work for everybody. I'm not discrediting Kaimana, I'm just giving up on the process.

The morning sun is burning through the thick wet air next to my skin as I walk the beach alone. Every few steps my feet get sucked into the gooey sand and pull me off balance. I feel grossly uncentered and out of my body. All this emotional processing has launched me like sputnik, and I am orbiting the earth feeling disconnected and isolated.

I decide to drive to one of the five-star hotels on the other side of the island and have brunch. It takes me sixty grueling minutes to get there. The whole way my mind is bombarded with self-mutilating thoughts, like, "If only I had gotten help after my abortion I probably would've chosen a more healthy man to marry later on," followed by a wave of mega judgment. And, "Who would I have become if I hadn't rebelled against my parents and just accepted them for who they are?" It's the kind of monkey-brain head-spinning that dumps your ass in the gutter and leaves you emotionally nowhere.

I walk the shoreline in front of the massive resorts that line Ka'anapali Beach, and watch the graceful bodies of young men on their surfboards, gliding effortlessly ahead of the breaking waves. For the first time I feel a bond with Seal Cove, and wish I could yell to them to go around to my side of the island and try surfing that beautiful coastline. But I am too selfish for that. I don't want to lose my privacy.

Up ahead I smell something burning. It smells like leather. I ask a young Asian groundsman what is going on.

"Luau," he tells me. "Bake pig."

"Really," I mumble, suddenly totally repulsed. I turn around and walk as fast as I can, because those torrential tears are coming again and waves of remorse are welling up in my chest, like the waves crashing against the sand. For a moment I see Kanoa's gentle face and I lose my balance. I'm overcome with confusion and feel like I could pass out. I hold on to a palm tree and rest my forehead against its bark. The sobs completely overtake me.

"Poor pig, doesn't have a chance. So sad. It's all so sad."

I manage to regain my pseudo composure and get myself back to the parking lot, where a young couple is propped up against my car making out. The girl turns, and I see that she is pregnant. The boy bends down and kisses her belly. She holds his head against her with her eyes closed as if for the first time she is being acknowledged and loved by a man who wants her and the whole experience of their life together. Or is this just another one of my lofty projections? As I get closer, they smile shyly and walk away.

I'm very spacey again as I travel the back roads, wondering what happened to Tom Stevenson, the father of the child I aborted. Why didn't he come forward to support me? Even though Tom was plagued with acne and smelly feet, I manage to lament his detachment. I should be joyful that I escaped that prison. But instead I obsess on how, most of my life, I have felt unsupported by the opposite sex. My head feels like it will explode as I realize how much of that I have continued to create, keeping young Katherine's sad story alive for some twenty-three years. As I drive through the areas where the rainforest blocks the light, I put out the call to all the versions of me who have felt unsupported, and ask them to join me in the car. I envision the car packed with females of all different ages. "Listen up, everyone." I tell them. "Don't lose hope. I promise we will figure this out." And then the crazy crying starts in again.

Maybe it's just that the information coming up in this work with Kaimana is presenting itself in a way I never expected. I certainly don't know how I'm supposed to be feeling after all this. And still that demon migraine peeks around the corner in back of my right eye. When the road takes me through a town big enough to have a drugstore, I stop and pick up more caffeine-stoked headache medicine. I take two in the car without water, hoping they enter my bloodstream before the Fourth of July firework display begins over my right temple.

I CLOSE THE CAR DOOR and stop to take in the beautiful tangerine light that so often fills the sky over Seal Cove at dusk. I walk out and sit on the black lava rocks and breathe in the fragrance of fresh, salty ocean. My headache is on the back burner. I hear a few notes of Kaimana's flute, and turn to see him playing just a few hundred feet away. He looks up and I wave to him. I may be tormented by what's going on in my own brain, but at least I'm more relaxed about him now.

He continues to play awhile, then gets up and heads in my direction. Now that I'm moving beyond my apprehensions, I can admit that this is one stunning specimen walking toward me...it's hard not to swoon. Where are all the women who pursue him night and day? Holy shit—maybe he's gay. Nah...possibly a hermit, though. I read once how highly evolved beings like the Dalai Lama channel their sexual energy up into their higher chakras, into the spiritual realms. I wonder if that's Kaimana's scene. Well...this inquiring mind will never know.

He leans his big fine torso up against a rock just a few feet away, and gives me a big warm smile. "Why don't you get your flute? Are you feeling up to it?"

"I'm not that good." Oh, brother.

"Come on. You are good enough to have fun. And the sensual tone of your instrument going out over the water is quite powerful."

My God, what a smile that man has! "Alright!" I say, scrambling to my feet and heading toward the cottage. "But let's keep it simple!"

On my way I key in to how different this feels. I don't play much at home because I'm afraid of being judged. In fact, sometimes I hide out in the upstairs bathroom playing out the window into the San Francisco skyline, the way Robin Williams played his sax out into lower

Manhattan in *Moscow on the Hudson*. What a great scene that was...and, oh, I know it well. But now, the idea of playing with someone who isn't here to judge me feels pretty damn exciting.

As I get close to the rocks I almost drop my flute, and realize I'm running. I slow down, brush my hair out of my eyes, and try to act nonchalant...sort of. "What are you into?" I ask breathlessly.

"Pick something you like and I will play around you."

"Okay, how about 'Blue Skies'?"

"Of course. Willie Nelson lives right down the road."

"Very cool." I place the flute next to my lips and blow. Kaimana lets me play on my own, then starts circling the melody with his own very far-out counterpoint. The resonance between his Native American flute and my nickel version is fascinating...almost intoxicating. I feel totally inspired, and lose the last vestiges of my self-consciousness.

We sound so lovely with the waves collaborating in the background. Afterward, as we sit in silence watching the waves, I have the fleeting feeling that I might indeed be making a new friend. My only wish is that he wasn't so devastatingly sexy. Okay, that's not really my wish.

"Are you ready to begin again tomorrow?" he asks me, back in his healer mode. I guess he has picked up on my ambivalence. "The worst is over. Now it is time for your soul to journey into the mystical."

Well, now, how can I turn away when my soul is on the line? "Okay," I tell him. "But I was really disappointed when I got a migraine after all that."

"You westerners are often in a great hurry. True healing at the deepest levels takes time and devotion."

"Okay, okay!" I say, well aware that I'm the embodiment of Western impatience. "What time, then?"

"Night is a stronger time to travel shamanically, especially with a full moon guiding us. Auspicious. Come about 9 p.m., and eat only a light meal before you come."

We say goodbye, and I my feet feel light on the path as I walk home to have dinner with Max.

At bedtime, while I'm washing my face, I notice the wrinkles under my eyes. What a bummer the mind is! I was having such a wonderful evening until my tricky, tricky brain had something it just had to tell me to pull me out of peace and throw me into insecure misery.

"Fuck off!" I tell it, flicking off the light.

Max follows me down the hallway to the tiny turquoise room and positions himself on the wall by the open window.

But now my mind has me in its clutches again, and talking to myself—out loud. "I wonder if Kaimana wears underwear to bed. He's certainly not the type to wear a nightshirt. Maybe just one of those Paul Newman undershirts...the sleeveless ones? My guess is he sleeps in the raw." Now there's a glib answer for you. Geez, Kate.

Can we at least class it up a bit and say he sleeps in the nude?

I am trying to hold my ground, but each time I see him that ground gets more shaky.

Finally I find a way to end my ludicrous apprehension. "What does it matter, anyway?" I ask Max. "He can't be more than forty. A man like Kaimana is never going to go for an aging broad like me. Never in a million years. Jesus, Katherine, get a grip! You're a physician who would never get involved with another doctor! And I have to believe that healers with integrity do not get involved with their patients...I don't think, anyway. I'm sure they have a set of standards like medical doctors do. But who knows whether they keep their integrity?"

As I fall asleep I see Kaimana's dark eyes watching me, his full lips framing my name..."Kate...." My Pisces mind likes to play at the deep end of the pool in dangerous waters even though it scares the doo-doo out of me. And so my dreams continue to unfold with Kaimana playing the leading man in my nonsensical nonstop melodramas.

16

ROUND THREE

Late evening...something new. Kaimana and I bow to each other at the gate and head for the healing room that is all set up for me to take my place.

"What, no mango tea?" I say kiddingly.

"I would like to take tea after our session, when we have finished our work."

"Okay," I say, sensing a sternness in his voice that makes me nervous. "We don't have to have tea." This is how I cave to people I care about when I am scared. I give up what I want.

"I grew up in India, land of tea and honey. I would never turn down a 'cupper.' I don't have mango tea, but I do have passion fruit. It enhances the big moon."

Groovy, he's warming up. I forgive my weirdo self.

"That sounds wonderful. Mahalo."

He motions for me to sit down in the nest of blankets. "Kate, I know you have not had the results you expected. But I ask that you let go of expectation and allow your soul to lead you to its own healing."

What if it's my soul that's trying to lead me to the door? "Hey, showing up is still a big deal for me. Isn't that what counts?"

He goes to the table in front of the window and picks up a rattle made from a flesh-colored gourd. "Showing up is the first important step. Trusting the journey is the second."

I lie back and Kaimana begins to chant, and I feel the vibration of his rich, supportive voice. Already I'm going under. The rattle is moving above my head in a steady rhythm, and I'm in front of my altar.

Out of nowhere an enormous mountain lion shows up. She appears as shimmering gold light, with eyes like polished, faceted citrines. Holy shit.

"There's a big cat here," I tell Kaimana.

"I can see that. What a powerhouse you are to call in such an elegant animal. Tell her you are happy to see her. She comes to protect you."

I look into her endless amber eyes. I am still unsure of myself, so I say out loud, "I am happy you are here. Thank you for coming here tonight."

"Good, Kate."

"You are welcomed," the big mountain lion tells me. She moves in closer to my body.

I'm a little scared, but at the same time I feel the strength of her body supporting mine. And anyway, her voice sounds more like a big, rumbling purr than a roar.

She speaks again. "I come because there are many souls around you who need to go home. Most of these entities were your patients. But there are others who have left their bodies, and yet they hover in the field around your body because they are drawn to your light."

"Really?" I say, dumbfounded and more than a little freaked out. "Why would they be?"

"Many reasons," she rumbles. "They do not know how to find their own light. This is not healthy for you. It is time to let them go."

"Tell me what to do."

"Call in your guides."

"What?"

"Call in your allies on the other side," the mountain lion says in a commanding voice. "I am one of your guides. Now you must call in the others. A true healer depends on his or her connection to her teachers for support. You need us in order to bring through the highest healing frequencies. Otherwise you have only your ego to guide you. Now, call your teachers."

"She is asking me to call in my teachers," I tell Kaimana with a worried voice. "What do I do?"

"Call out to the universe as though you are calling for your most beloved friends so they can find you. Go ahead. You can do this."

"Okay," I say. I still don't know what the heck to do, but I just take a deep breath and say, "You beautiful ones who stand by me, come to me now so I can release the souls who are stuck here around me." Oh my God, that was awful. I almost laugh because I sound so tenuous, so free of conviction. I am a physician who depends on her expertise from years in medical school and everyday experience. It has only been under dire circumstances that I have stopped my work, closed my eyes, and prayed for help from who knows where. Never in a million years would I have guessed that anyone was looking after me from other dimensions.

But what do I know—in they come. First a light purple, angelic form appears, then a rather somber Native American looking dude walks forward. Then my dad walks in. My dad!

This must be my imagination again! But does it really matter, if it heals me?

They come to me and we all walk arm in arm toward a waterfall of light.

My father gently touches my face. Then he takes a step back and makes a big sweeping gesture with his arm, and commands, "It's time for you all to go home now. You cannot stay here any longer. There are many waiting to reunite with you over there." And then he points into the waterfall.

Is this my dad, sad-sack Jerry Cohen who scrimped on almost everything so his darling daughter could give his life meaning by graduating Stanford Medical School summa cum laude? This can't be that same little man who could not stand up to his wife's addiction and abuse, who was afraid to protect me and allowed that crazy woman to haul ass on me whenever the scotch took over! My father was the ultimate definition, the epitome, the very embodiment of the term "passive aggressive." Pretty amazing what a little death experience can do!

To add to my amazement, my father's newfound conviction and his commandment awaken everybody out of their half-deaths. One by one the stuck souls materialize out of what I guess I would call my aura...anyway, it's this colorful field of light encircling my body. They drift out of their semi-comas and blink their eyes in the newfound light.

I can't believe what, or I should say "who," is materializing. Good Lord! There's Bonnie Rutherford, my patient who died of ovarian cancer last year. And Annette Barnes, whose breast cancer just took her out. Streams of unborn babies rise out of me into the different frequencies of light. It's beautiful to see them soar like this! Many other patients I've worked with pass before me. I feel almost stupefied. I had no idea that subconsciously I've been acting like a lighthouse for these lost souls.

Kaimana raises his rattle and shakes it strongly all around me. I feel a great weight releasing out of my head.

And then the weirdest thing happens. My mother materializes. I am stunned. She looks incredibly, refreshed. I stare at her in disbelief—A, that she was stuck in this aura thing, and B, that she actually has been hanging around me since she left. Bitterness and anger are spiraling up and out of me.

Kaimana sees this and starts drumming.

My mother turns and looks straight at me and asks, "May I speak, Katherine?"

This is the only time she has *ever* asked for permission to come into my space.

"I know you don't want to hear it, but there is something I need to say...want to say."

Oy. Here it comes. Judgment time.

"I'm sorry I have been such a burden to you," she says, looking straight into my eyes.

The words "I'm sorry" have never passed her lips before now. I'm stunned...and humbled.

She goes on. "I'm sorry I had so little to give. You know that's the way it has been in our family for generations. My mother was a drinker, her mother was a drinker. We dealt with a lot of depression. I'm not blaming them, it's just that I want you to understand. I've done a lot of thinking about our relationship and why I never really connected with you. I think I reacted to you so badly because I got jealous when I saw how special you were and how lovely your life was going to be, because I didn't have that same chance."

"So you tried your damnedest to ruin it?" I say out loud.

"Please forgive me for being such a headache in your life. I have been constantly trying to communicate how sorry I am after I passed, and I think I just caused you pain."

It feels like I'm getting sucked into a whirlwind of confusion, gratitude, relief, rage, disbelief, and God knows what else. "Kaimana, what am I supposed to do with that?" I'm pleading for a lifeline.

"Repeat after me," he instructs. "Tell her, 'Mother, I love you and I know you love me, and I want to heal this condition between us.'"

I obey...grudgingly.

"Now," he continues, "say, 'Please forgive me for any lifetimes in which I have caused you any suffering, as I forgive you, and close this karma with you now.'"

I look at him in disbelief. "But...."

"Go ahead. Just say it. 'Please forgive me....'"

I say the words, though I can't force myself to sound like I mean it.

"'Ho, it is done.' Say it."

"Ho, it is done." Something deep in my bones tells me he's right, that this is exactly the right thing to say. But after all the years of trying to bury the guilt trip my mother heaped on me, I never thought I'd be asking her for forgiveness. But ho...I guess it's done.

My mother turns to me, smiles a toothy grin, and tosses me a little red heart.

"What should I do with the heart?" I ask Kaimana.

"Well, how does the heart feel?"

"Joyful."

"Then make a space within you where you can treasure it."

I shake my head, but I can feel my disbelief fading away. There's a warm energy flowing through my veins and into my heart that I'm sure I've never felt before.

Kaimana strikes the gong and off Jane Ann Williams strides, with ten or twelve other souls, through the waterfall. I see Dad coming to get her. I guess codependents are codependents even on the other side.

Those professing to be my guides are standing a breath away. I feel their strength surrounding me, holding me upright.

"Thank you," I tell them. "Thank you for being here for me. I believe your presence here today will help me complete this journey to reunite with myself."

The angel steps forward in her cloud of purple light. "Just remember to keep your heart open to give and receive love."

"Be well," the Native American says in a deep voice. "Remember me. We will find each other again."

For some reason I want the Native American to remain, but he and the angel fade out. The mountain lion walks up to me, then sits and stares intensely into my eyes.

"That big cat is back again."

"So I see. She wants you to learn how to protect yourself. I will teach you. For now, let her transmit her strength and groundedness through her eyes into yours. "

An amber light so pure and warm flows from her eyes into mine. I feel my cells drinking in the yellows rays and a sense of wholeness and confidence anchoring me into my body. For the first time I feel I am here one hundred percent. The mountain lion bows down, and then vanishes—just like that.

I open my eyes and Kaimana is in a trance himself, chanting in a voice that sounds like it comes from ten thousand years ago. He places my hand on his heart and holds it there so I can feel his powerful heartbeat. I have no thoughts, no agenda, no story to hold on to. I am being taken care of by a medicine man who is channeling the love of the Creator into my soul. And now I am aware that I, too, am an intimate part of creation.

We are both drenched. I reach up and put my arms around his neck and put my head against his wet chest. He smells like the ocean, salty and earthy. He doesn't fight me in this. We rock together now, very slowly, with a slight chanting sound coming from our throats. The sound comes from somewhere deep inside my body, resonating with his. "Ah...ah...ah...."

And then the energy fades and we are done.

"I don't want to move," I whisper from my little girl part.

It is in this moment that, for the first time in my life, I trust my place in the world completely...I don't question anything that is happening. I just let go.

17

FRIENDS

Kaimana gently removes himself.

I lay back, eyes open, more alive than I can ever remember. "That was remarkable." I look up at him, see him watching me with that gentleness in his eyes. "I cannot thank you enough...for everything...."

"Thank you for allowing me to experience that with you. We will see how you feel in the next few days."

There's a long silence. The moon is flooding through the windows. Kaimana gets up to leave the room, explaining that he needs to be alone for a few moments and that he will return with tea. I walk around quietly, looking for that rattle. Out of all the instruments Kaimana worked with, this time it was the rattle that took me under its spell. I finally find it lying inside the big crystal bowl. It's big and heavy, and just the slightest movement elicits a powerful sound of dried seeds striking against the skin of the gourd. I begin to shake it, and imagine myself walking as Kaimana did, sending out energy to an invisible patient. I know this sounds crazy, but deep down inside I feel I have done this before. That Native American gentleman is around me again, encouraging me to dance as I shake the rattle. I hear his invocation again and again, and drumming in the background. Am I losing my mind? I have my eyes closed when I hear Kaimana enter the room. I turn to see him lowering the tea tray onto the pink tile floor.

"It is a tradition that no one touches a shaman's instruments except the shaman."

"Oh my God, I'm so sorry!"

"But since we have done very deep work together, and you *are* a healer yourself, it seems that this has happened for a reason." He passes me tea in another beautiful cup.

"Thank you for not being angry. Again, I am so sorry!"

"Not at all. And even if I were angry, you could handle it now…you whose spirit animal is the mountain lion!"

"That was amazing, the way her eyes sent me so much love."

Kaimana arranges two tufted, maroon pillows on the floor, and sits down on one of them. I settle onto the other.

"You know," I venture, "there's something I want to ask you about that...but I'm kind of embarrassed about it." I look up at him, and I can see in his eyes that nothing I say will disturb that ancient steadiness of his. "Since the day I arrived, a three-legged cockroach has been hanging out with me in the cottage. At first I was grossed out and felt really weird about it, but then—I know this is ridiculous—I started to feel connected to him. A few days ago, when I was really going through a rough time after we did our work, I took my feelings out on him and swept him out of the house. When I realized what I had done I got really emotional and searched for him everywhere. For some odd reason he returned. Could it be possible that he's my real spirit animal?"

Kaimana's face lights up. "It is interesting how a cockroach is misconstrued, is it not? In the native beliefs, this creature is an emotional and spiritual shape shifter. He comes to teach fortitude, and how to adapt to changes in life. The fact that this particular animal does so well on three legs demonstrates his medicine. We say that the main lesson cockroach teaches is how to survive no matter what is going on in your life."

Gulp.

Kaimana's smile grows wise and big. "You could develop a lot of affection for a teacher like that."

He pauses, then reaches over and picks up his rattle. "Since you have been drawn to experience some of these instruments for yourself, let us go a step further so you can begin to understand what I do. Perhaps you will take your new self-knowledge home with you to the mainland...that is, if you still have the energy to do a little more work this late into the night. "

"Me? I'm a night person anyway, and right now I have more energy than I know what to do with."

"Good. I, too, feel energized." He places the rattle in my hand. "I would like to help you become open to using this instrument as a tool for healing. Does that interest you?"

"It sounds fascinating—and of course I'm afraid I won't be very good at it."

"Why would you think that when you derive so much joy from playing your flute? That must feel healing to you. It is certainly healing for me."

"Really? How so?"

"Well," he says placing his hand over his heart. "Your beautiful, heartfelt notes enter right here and make their way down into my blood and bones. That way I can feel your intention through the sound. It heals me.

"You see, Kate, before I play an instrument I become conscious of my connection to the Creator. I see that presence as light streaming through me. That way, I know that neither I nor the instrument is the source of the sound. When I am connected to the Creator, that is the true origin of the sound. In that state, love flows through me effortlessly, abundantly, and the instrument makes a deep, rich sound that emanates from an infinite source. Does that make sense?"

"I think I understand what you're saying. But I don't know how to connect, or even what I'm connecting to."

"Well, close your eyes and think of the ocean and the energy that moves through it. Let yourself become the ocean, and feel yourself being fed by the Creator's energy the same way the ocean is fed by it."

I close my eyes and think of the waves hitting the black rocks in the cove. I envision myself as the ocean, and see streams of light from the moon pouring into me.

Kaimana takes a long, deep breath as though he is breathing the ocean into me. Then he waits. "So?" he asks.

"Okay. I feel the rays of light, like you said...feeding me."

"Now feel that same light stream through you. Let it pass through your cells, into your hands, and then into the rattle."

I envision a lush white light flowing into me, and I shake the rattle. Slowly I feel a stronger vibration coming through into my hand, a different flow.

"Now move around me and notice where the rattle wants to take you. Your intuition will tell you where my energy is low, or where it needs assistance."

I open my eyes. "My mind thinks I shouldn't be doing this. It's not correct for who I am. What an ego, huh?"

"Be kind to yourself. It takes strength to move beyond an old archetype, even for a moment. Take a deep breath and start again."

I get to my feet and walk around Kaimana, waving the rattle in his general direction. I envision the light that creates everything, and right away I feel a sense of freedom coming in. The rattle is really shaking now, and my hand is moving more purposefully, in all different directions. Am I shaking it or is it shaking me?

I need validation. "I know this is crazy, but I want to go to your heart."

"Please do."

I bend down and let the rattle move numerous times toward him and away, toward him and then pulling back. I can actually sense the sound entering his body and going straight to his heart. I am delighted at how easily I seem to move around his body, like I want to take off into some kind of mystical dance. I feel the Native American part coming through.

Kaimana encourages me to keep going. "Now let go and let the rattle carry you into its energies."

This is becoming too much for my ego again, and I plop down on the floor across from him.

He looks startled. "What happened?"

"That was just a little too free for me."

His pale lips broaden into a smile. "The more you practice, the more you will be comfortable with the dance of your soul."

"May I come again and practice with you?"

"Of course, Kate." He looks deep into my eyes for a long moment, then gets to his feet and opens the door. "But for now," he says, "aloha...until next time." He stands silently while I gather myself and head down the long hallway.

As we walk toward the gate I am aware of that familiar longing rising in my chest. I stop and turn toward him, but I can't quite look at his face. "Soon?" I ask.

"Yes," he tells me, and turns back to the house, leaving me at the sandy path.

I wait and watch him through the window, bending forward to blow out the candles. He looks out the window and sees me standing there, gazing at him from the darkness.

I wave.

Mercifully, he waves back.

MY LITTLE PLACE IS DARK and quiet except for the waves in the distance. I really don't want to turn on any lights. Electric light feel so confrontational compared to candles. I am candle-ized! Kaimana-ized! One thing's for sure, I'm not afraid of him any longer. In fact it's quite the opposite. I feel drawn to our friendship. I am full of this evening's healing and our connection—and that feels so good. I'm not saying I'm not shaky or feeling a little whacky. That's there, too. But I like him. I really do. I feel drawn to him.

Finally I give in and light the tiny oil lamp because I want to find Max. I have lots to tell him. I stroll past my cell phone sitting on the centuries-old straw rocking chair, and feel a twinge of guilt. I take a seat and speed dial my voicemail. The first voice is David. His message is the one that, a few days ago, I thought I wanted to hear...he wants to come back early from Scotland and fly over to join me at a resort. I feel my mouth form the words, "Oh, no."

I sit with my hands folded in my lap trying to make sense of my feelings. I'm relieved when I see Max crawling along the baseboard of the living room wall.

"I don't want him here," I tell my steadfast pal. "I'm really beginning to enjoy who I am. I'm making great strides. Have you noticed?"

I swear his antennae are twitching, confirming my growth.

"Thank *you*! I've worked so hard to integrate these nutty parts of me. I don't want to have to explain any of it. He wouldn't get it anyway. I know what I have to do, I just don't want to face it. Not yet! I'm actually starting to feel peaceful, and I feel very protective of that. Know what I mean?"

Within seconds I am dialing, and to my surprise the call goes right through. That hardly ever happens. "Hi, darling," I say in my most charming voice. "How's it going?"

"I'm a little bored, actually. I haven't been doing great competitively speaking, so I thought I'd get outa here and come join you."

"I think you would be bored here, too. It's been raining a lot, and it's very muggy. Why don't you go in to Paris for a few days? Or even better, head down to Monte Carlo? A lot more action for you there, right?"

"Oh, I don't know. I feel a bit lonely."

Shit.

"What are you up to then, my darling girl?"

"Actually I've enrolled in classes, so I'm on a pretty tight schedule."

"What kind of classes? Hula? Lei-making?"

Witty white mainland boy. "No, dear, nothing like that. I'm learning new techniques to incorporate into my practice." *Oooooh*, treading into treacherous waters here....

"Oh, yeah? Who's teaching?"

"Kaimana someone. He's a specialist. You wouldn't know him." That's the understatement of the century.

"Sounds utterly tantalizing. I think I'll pass this time."

Thank you, Great Spirit. "Good decision. Like I said, the weather isn't the best, and you'd be bored silly up here in this little cove."

"Okay. See you at home, babe." Click.

Now Katherine, what was that all about?

It's about something I'm not ready to face yet.

And so I turn down the lamp and head for bed. Before I make the big voyage into dreamland I practice envisioning connecting to the light, to the Creator. I look down into my body and watch every cell filling with light. I see myself in a boat throwing flowers to my cells, telling them how much I love them, blowing them kisses. And then I drift into a new kind of serenity. I believe they call it nirvana. I feel utterly boundary-less and connected to everything.

18

THE WISDOM KEEPERS

omewhere in the middle of the night I wake to heavy footsteps marching down the path past my house. I duck down and head to the window just at the moment the first warrior passes by. I blink my eyes several times. Am I still dreaming? I look over to the bed, but I am not in it. I am a woman crouching in a camisole and silk trousers, watching ghostly warriors parading into the night. Whatever this is, all I can do is go with it.

There must be ten or twelve of them, Hawaiian spirits in full regalia—feather capes, shining helmets made of gourds, moonlit shields protecting the warriors' massive oiled bodies, with glittering spears fixed at their sides. I can feel the energy of these souls, and the consummate, innate sovereignty they hold over this land. Their psychic power reverberates in my chest next to my skipping heartbeat. Nobody would mess with these folks unless he was mentally ill or tripping. I must be in a dream! Why would ancient beings like these show up here, right in front of me?

I know I'm not tripping, but maybe I've slipped into some kind of psychosis? No, I am awake and fully here and have opened myself to the spirit realm, and now I must stop panicking so they don't pick up on my fear. They are unbelievably powerful. *Nobody* could come within a fifty-foot radius because their protection is so thick, vibrating like a wall of dark mirrors around their wavering bodies. My hand is trembling as I close the window and they trudge out of sight. I reach for a sweater and pull it tight around me.

I'm not sure I like what is happening to me. I feel I am losing any control I might have had to begin with, and the previously "unseen worlds" are becoming a little too visible. I wish I could call David or Jess or any of my friends and tell them what is going on. But they would never believe me. Hell, I can just hear the jokes they'd be making for the rest of my days.

A newly emerging part of me pushes me to be courageous and open the front door. She knows there is something important going on and doesn't want to miss it. The old me is quaking. I can almost hear her demanding, "*Are you crazy??!*" as I put my hand on the doorknob.

Suddenly the Native American materializes before me. "Go now," I hear as his eyes look intensely into mine. "I will stand with you. Do not be afraid."

It dawns on me that I am about to be a witness to some kind of ceremony. I tentatively open the door and take a step outside. The shadow of the Native American walks alongside me. A moonbow forms an arc over the ocean, casting turquoise, emerald, purple, and opalescent hues above our heads. Everything appears to be shimmering. My legs are shaking, but we walk toward the ocean where Kaimana already sits cross-legged. He sees me coming and motions for me to sit down next to him. The Native American stands to the side. We watch as the warriors walk to the edge of the black rocks. They raise their arms, and the waves begin to build and crash against the rocks, blasting this little cove in a wild crescendo. The most ferocious-looking of the spirits turns and stares at us. I take Kaimana's arm. The chieftain stares for the longest time, then slowly they all begin their trek across the ocean into the incoming fog...and disappear.

"I am so grateful that you are here," I tell Kaimana. "I was thinking I was in an outrageous dream, but then I couldn't wake up because I was already awake...."

Kaimana holds my clammy hand. "I know you do not understand—and I do not fully understand the significance of this either—but believe me, the moon and this tribunal passing through at this time means something profound is going to occur soon, something that cannot be planned for or stopped. It will change everything. And you and I have just been initiated into that destiny."

"What do you think it means?"

"I am sure it will all be revealed at the right time. But I have no doubt there is a karmic reason the two of us have been brought here to experience this together."

If only I understood what "karmic" really means…. "I guess so," I tell him. My pounding heartbeat settles down a little. I remove my hand from his hand because it feels way too good. "I'm such a neophyte in these matters, a neophyte and a sometime non-believer."

"I see your guide is watching over you."

"He was the one who told me to come outside."

"Thank you," he calls as the Native American turns to leave the scene. Kaimana gets up and turns away from the ocean, back toward his house.

My fear takes over again, and this time I can't hold it in. "I feel totally unnerved by all of this, Kaimana. I'm sorry to ask this, but…." I swallow hard and gather my courage. "Would it be possible to sleep on your couch tonight, in the healing room? I just really don't want to be alone."

Kaimana pauses before he answers. "Yes. Of course." He extends his hand to help me up.

We stand for a moment looking out at the now gentle Pacific. It appears that nothing really happened here, except that a shaman and his student saw it all. Yes, his student, his friend, and in my fantasies something deeper.

I've decided to learn everything I can from my medicine man. I'm in too deep now to have it any other way.

19

PRIVATE EYE JAMISON
ON DUTY

I wake up to the light of the setting moon pouring in through the window. I look out to see it hanging huge above the horizon to the west, and the whole scene is bathed in that magical light just before dawn. It must be around 6 a.m., but it feels so safe here I don't want to leave.

Everything in Kaimana's home has become of great interest to me, so I clip on my P.I. Jamison badge and proceed on an official search. I'm a touch ashamed to be checking out his sacred residence with such an intrusive eye...but just a touch. Mostly I'm on a mission.

I cannot get over the feng shui of this house. Everything sits in divine order with exactly the right light and space supporting it. But something feels strange—I could swear there's some sort of shadowy figure following me. Never mind, that's just silly. No, wait...there it is again. I check in and ask myself if it's the Native American gentleman. I know it is not. No matter, it must be those annoying floaters I've been getting in my eyes for a while now.

Everywhere I look there's a lovely moment, a treasure...like the bamboo cabinet that holds hundreds of little bottles and glass jars, with labels handwritten in red ink. They say things like "Frankincense," "Elm," "Lemon Blossom," "Gold," "Rosemary," and "Myrrh." Next to them sit maybe forty smaller bottles marked "Peony," "Pink Lotus," "Gardenia," "Calendula," "Pure Rose," and on and on. I love his love of flowers! I have no idea how these potions work, but I want to try them all! What a difference from the medicine cabinet in my office, crammed with mass-produced free samples of estrogen, birth control pills, and expensive creams...some of them reliable, some of them unpredictable at best, all of them with a list of side effects a mile long.

It dawns on me that in my exploration I have not encountered one phone or computer or television. Perhaps they're hidden away somewhere. I don't see any patient files, either. I check the cabinets beneath the bookcase and find more animal fetishes wrapped in bark cloth, and anatomical illustrations of human and animal bodies.

At the other end of the hall there's a spiral staircase. I go up. At the top there's a small tower where I assume Kaimana meditates, because it just has that sacred feeling. Silk renderings of mystical gods and goddesses and female saints hang from the walls. One of them is Guadalupe. I know this because my housekeeper, Concepción, wears a medal of Guadalupe around her neck, and extols her many virtues. Beside her silken image sits a gigantic statue, half elephant, half man. I bet it's Ganesh, some kind of East Indian elephant spirit I've read about. I've never seen an image of him before, though. In a way he's kind of sexy. Moving right along....

I make my way back to the healing room, and browse around the condor feathers, rattles, and drums. I spot Kaimana's medicine bag hanging over the corner of a chair. I want to open it, but stop myself. What is it that I really want to find out??

I wonder what a shaman eats...broiled eye of newt with a side of squid ink? Uh, nice, Kate. He's probably vegan. After seeing his relationship with monsieur piglet, I can't imagine he would eat any kind of meat. I head back down the hall to the kitchen and take a peek in his fridge. All the normal stuff is there: bags of almonds and pumpkin seeds, a bowl of fruit, all kinds of greens. There are four tins of coffee beans. And chocolate, chocolate, and more chocolate! Each shelf is organized methodically. There's even a bottle of pinot noir. Pinot!

"Aloha," he says, entering the kitchen.

I whip around. "Aloha," I say, not knowing how to explain my presence.

There's a long silence that stems from awkwardness on my part and probably on his, too. I avoid his eyes and search for something to do with my hands.

"That was excellent healing work last night, Kate."

We both stand there wondering what to say next.

He thinks of something first. "I am still trying to understand the auspicious introduction we had to the royalty. It was very powerful."

"I'll say," laughter ripples out of me in a nervous stream.

Again, terrible silence.

"Please excuse me, Kate. I am not one with a lot to say. I am even more internal in the morning. I guess it is because I have lived alone for a very long time."

"I understand. I'll get going and give you some space."

"Wait." He's quiet again, just watching me. "Before you go...did you enjoy looking at my home?"

Shit. "Yes, I did. Very much." And then, as I grab my sweater and head toward the door, "Lots of interesting pieces. You designed all this on your own?"

"My vision was to design a healing sanctuary. So that is what I have been pursuing since the nineties. I had a good deal of help.

"I like this Buddha."

"Actually this is a statue of Quan Yin, who is known as the goddess of compassion and a protector of women. She is a beloved bodhisattva who gave up her own Buddhahood because she could not leave the earth with all of its suffering. She moves in the middle realms, somewhere between the earth and the other side. About one-third of people all around the planet pray to Quan Yin every day."

"I'm sorry to ask so many questions, but I really am curious. What the heck is a bodhisattva?"

"A bodhisattva is a student of enlightenment. Basically, they are friendly souls. I think you are one."

"I love that! It's so simple. I love her eyes and her kind smile. I love how she looks right into you."

"She can take on any form...the wind, water...a mountain lion...whatever she needs to be to get the healing done. She is often represented as an energy of purple light. In fact...I believe you have met her before."

"I've met her? What do you mean?"

"I'm quite certain she came to you as one of your guides for your healing journey last night."

"Yes—the purple angel. Yes, I remember. She's the one who told me to keep my heart open."

He smiles.

We both start to relax, and Kaimana walks me through his home, introducing me to things that hold special meaning for him. It's as if he hasn't shared anything personal in a long time. He's definitely breaking through his era of internal solitude!

"What's in that building over there?"

"Come, let me show you."

We walk out behind the house to a long, narrow, wooden shed. He opens the door and we enter a dark space with shuttered windows. At the far end of the shed there are windows open to the ocean breeze, and sunlight drenches shelves of lush greenery. But my attention is pulled back to a delicious scent that's both delicate and complex, surrounding me and inviting me to stay in this dim little corner. I am completely seduced...oh, the fragrance of damp orchids! As my eyes adjust to the darker interior I am blown away to see hundreds of them, blooming in every nook and cranny, on every shelf.

"A few members of my extended family," he says, spreading his arms open very wide. "Would you like to meet them?"

I nod yes.

"These are my African toddlers, over here, and next to them are their sisters, phaeleonopses. Over there, drinking in the sun, are their cousins, cymbidiums, and starts for my flower and herb garden. Most of them are indigenous to the Hawaiian Islands. Right behind you, on that table, is where I create my tinctures."

The place is screaming with color. Even his straw gardening hat is hot purple. I am so overwhelmed that I can no longer hear his words. This is another ocean to swim in, so many textures and shades, so much love and nurturing gathered in one space. I want to be quiet and just take it in.

Finally we're back outside, and we walk down the path to the gate.

"I have a favor to ask of you, Kate. I expect to see many patients this week, and there is one in particular with whom I do not feel I am making progress. She is a young Hawaiian girl, perhaps fourteen, who is pregnant. She will deliver her child soon, and I have a strong feeling that this delivery will be difficult for her. Something is incorrect. Would you be open to seeing her? I am sorry to impose on you while you are on your vacation, but I feel compelled to ask."

"I would like that very much. I'd love to be involved somehow with the Hawaiian people here."

Kaimana's smile is broad. "Great. Tomorrow, early afternoon?"

I am needed. I am jazzed!

"Yes, okay," I say, trying not to grin like a happy schoolgirl. "Actually it's perfect, because I was thinking of asking if you would be my teacher. I'd like to learn as much as I can from you—learn to open to my intuition, about healing energy, or anything you're willing to teach me. If I can assist you in some way...maybe I can return your kindness and learn from you at the same time—that is, since you seem unwilling to take cash," I add with a wink. Even I'm impressed with how bold I'm getting.

He laughs. "Well, although your cash is not accepted here, your assistance will be very much appreciated. But you, Kate—*you*, learn to open to your intuition? I believe you mean you want to learn to trust the powerful intuitive nature that is your gift. And yes, I would be honored to be your teacher."

"Great! I'll see you tomorrow, then!"

Inside me the little girl is skipping down the path.

INSIDE THE
HEALING ROOM

I roll over in bed, open my eyes, and smile at the sun filtering through the leaves outside my window. It's a novel experience. I usually wake up and promptly bury my head under the covers to stop the throbbing. But this morning I am headache free. Kaimana lives!

I decide to take full advantage of this rare day of freedom from pain, so I pack a light brunch to enjoy out where the rocks meet the turquoise waves. I linger till the sun is almost overhead, then head back for a quick shower. I pull on a silk blouse and dab on a touch of mascara and head to Kaimana's to play apprentice to the medicine man.

The yellow flag is perched on top of his mailbox—the medicine man is in. His front door is open, so I walk in and hear him talking to a woman. I try to intuit what's happening without making a disturbance. Quietly I walk toward the healing room, but as I pass an alcove I see a petite young Hawaiian girl on the floor, curled up in the corner in a semi-fetal position. This girl can't be the fourteen-year-old he spoke of! She has the face of a ten-year-old, and her belly is growing. She's well into her second trimester. Her hands look so delicate resting on that big belly. She doesn't look particularly happy to see me. There are tears in her eyes, and black eyeliner smeared around the edges.

"Hi, there," I whisper, bending down. "How're you doin'? I'm Dr. Jamison...please call me Kate. I'm here helping Kaimana today. Actually, he asked me to come spend some time with you. Would that be okay?"

No response.

"What's your name, honey?"

"Ilima."

"What a beautiful name. What does it mean?"

"It mean flower," she tells me, looking down at the floor.

"How are you feeling, Ilima? Your baby is almost here."

"Soon. I think she come early. I worried. No place for her to be."

"Where is your family? Do they live near here?"

"They don't want us."

"Where's the boy?"

"No boy." She turns her face away.

Kaimana and his patient, an elderly Asian grandmother-type, walk out of the healing room. He smiles at us as he walks her to the door, and then comes right back.

"Aloha, Ilima. I see you have met Dr. Jamison."

"Kate," I tell him.

He bends down, too. "Let's see how we can help you feel better. Will you come with me, Ilima?"

Kaimana holds out his hand and she takes it. With his help she hoists herself onto her feet, then reaches into her pocket and digs out a small, luminous blue stone, the kind that are scattered throughout the sand in the cove. She offers it to Kaimana.

"I bring this for you," she says.

Of course. That's the proper way to pay a shaman. Now I get it.

He takes the stone from her small hand and holds it very carefully, admiring it like the precious gem that it is. "Why, thank you, Ilima. It is very beautiful."

She nods, and the three of us make our way down the hall to the healing room. It's no easy task for this mother-to-be to maneuver herself onto the divan, so Kaimana takes her elbow and gently supports her until she's comfortable.

"Kate is going to take good care of you, Ilima. She wants to make sure your baby is healthy and ready to come. I'll be right outside, okay?"

Reluctantly Ilima lets go of his hand, and Kaimana exits.

I have no tools, not even a stethoscope—just my hands, my experience, and my budding intuition. "May I feel your tummy?"

She nods yes, and I begin poking gently, feeling the position of the child. Both seem to be doing just fine from a physical perspective, but it's obvious this girl is depressed and freaked out.

"What hospital are you having your baby at?"

"No hospital. I come here." And then, in the most vulnerable voice, "You help me?"

"Yes, of course, I would love to help you, Ilima. I'm only visiting Maui for a short while, but I'm staying just down the road, and I'll be helping Kaimana while I'm here. Between the two of us we'll make sure you and your baby have everything you need. Okay?"

"Okay." The girl can smile!

Kaimana knocks on the door, then reenters and asks the girl if she and her "keiki" would like to listen to some healing sounds and rest awhile. She nods and turns on her side.

Kaimana chooses that beautiful Native American wooden flute. He places the instrument very close to Ilima's belly and plays a simple melody. Tears cover Ilima's cheeks. I hope they are tears of gratitude—but then I realize that whatever they are expressing, they are welcome and good.

Soon the tears stop, and the mother-child's breathing becomes slow and deep.

After her nap we walk Ilima slowly to the path leading to the road where, Kaimana tells me, a girlfriend will pick her up.

Back in his house we sit down for a cup of green tea.

"Ilima has experienced a terrible trauma," he explains. "She was raped in Lani Lanakila, a tent encampment up country. It is a very rough place. Many kind-hearted people live there, but it is also home to some who are living in their darkness. Now Ilima needs nurturing and softness. She needs to be around a woman like you."

"I told her I would help her in any way I can while I'm here."

"That is good news."

"I was wondering, Kaimana, could I sit in and watch you do your work some time? I'm fascinated with what you do, and I feel like there's so much more to experience. I promise I will stay in the background."

"Actually, I would be honored to have a medicine woman at my side."

"I'm hardly that!"

"Well, then, what are you?"

"I'm a woman who is a traditional medical doctor practicing western protocols."

"I think you are much more than that. You will be surprised to see how you naturally understand the ancient ways. I will be receiving patients again tomorrow, and I expect that many will come. Would you like to come and assist me? You can work with the Tibetan bowl and help me to ground the energy of the room."

I'm sort of flabbergasted, but I agree. And I have absolutely no idea how to ground the energy of anything.

"Ten o'clock, then?" He asks.

"Ten it is."

I GRAZE MY WAY through a salad of fresh greens and mangos, but the silence starts to be a little much, so I flip on the six o'clock news. I can stand it for five minutes, then I quickly turn it off. I need all the good chi I can muster because, after all, I don't want my newfound aura to deflate! I pick up my flute and ease into "In a Sentimental Mood." It's one of my all-time favorites.

A warm shower before bed, and I'm still humming the melody. Never mind sentimental—I'm in an ecstatic mood!

I set Barb's alarm clock so I won't oversleep, and breathe myself into a calmer state.

I LET MYSELF IN the front door at 9:58, and Kaimana and his patient are already talking in the healing room. He introduces me as his assistant, and I learn that James, this elderly gentleman, is suffering with chronic inflammation in his hands and ankles.

"Is it osteoarthritis?" I ask Kaimana.

"We do not name these things. It tends to make them stick around."

Interesting. He speaks of illness like it has a personality.

James lies down.

"Kate, if you will work with that large brass bowl over there to help balance the energies in the room, we can get started."

I'm confused because I don't know the first thing about balancing energies. That doesn't seem to worry Kaimana, though, so what the heck. I pick up the cool brass bowl and strike it gently five times. The resonance is deep and clear, like it is announcing the beginning of a ceremony. Amazingly, I can feel the whole place becoming calmer.

"Mahalo," Kaimana tells me, smiling. "If you would do that intermittently I would be very grateful. In fact, before we begin, I would like you to walk around us, and invite the bowl as you do."

Uh-oh. Even when he tells me how to do it I don't know what he's talking about. "Invite the bowl?"

"Touch the bowl gently with the mallet," he instructs, picking up on my insecurities. "Invite it to offer its voice."

I walk slowly, touching the lip of the bowl with the mallet. Okay, I can do this. It feels really great, like I'm part of something very important. I circle Kaimana and his patient, then stand to the side.

Kaimana rubs his hands together and then takes James' hands in his, and begins to chant. His chant sounds a little Native American, a little Hawaiian. Maybe he's making it up as he goes along. Or maybe he's been possessed by some kind of multinational, cross cultural medicine man. Focus, Kate.

He begins to rub James' right hand, giving it a vigorous massage. Suddenly James cries out, but Kaimana tells him in a soothing voice that it will soon end. Sparks begin to fly out of the hand, and soon little arrows of light are darting around the room! Little arrows of light! I've never seen anything like this! Kaimana moves on to James' left hand. Again the patient cries out, energy flies around the room again...and I am freaked!

Kaimana takes both of James' hands lovingly within his own. "The inflammation in your hands is due to sadness in your heart," he says with compassion. "What makes you so sad?"

The man begins to sob, and tells us about his wife's family in Japan. They lost everything in the big tsunami.

His wife has been very depressed and he has no way to help her.

"It sounds as though you feel your wife's happiness is out of your hands. Is that so?" Kaimana asks.

"Yes," James weeps. "I have no way to fix it. My wife is suffering."

"And you feel what?"

"I feel guilty because she goes through so much and I cannot help her."

"So you create your own suffering. How does that help your wife?"

"It does not. Is that what has caused the pain in my hands?"

"Yes, my friend, you have been holding your loved one's pain in your hands. How are they feeling now?"

James takes his hands from Kaimana's grasp, turns them palms up then palms down, and says, "They feel pretty good." He opens and closes his fingers, then gives both hands a good shake. A smile spreads across his face as he looks at me, then back at Kaimana. With a chuckle he says, "They feel fine." He smiles broadly and laughs, gazing at his hands with an amazed look on his face.

Kaimana watches and nods. "Good. Very good. Now let us take a look at your ankles."

He rolls up James' pant legs, inspects both ankles, and pushes into the edema. Both of his lower legs are bright red and hot. Kaimana stands at the end of the table and pulls the redness out of the sole of each foot like he's removing heavy boots. Within moments both ankles are normal in size and color.

How did he learn to do this? He does it with such confidence.

He returns to his patient's side. "My dear friend, repeat after me: 'No matter what others experience, I am willing to move forward in my life.'"

James repeats the affirmation several times.

"Now try out your new ankles," Kaimana says, and helps him up off the divan.

James grins. "How do you know me so well, Medicine Man?"

"Because you and I are one and the same, James. For the most part we have the same desires and the same inappropriately guilty responses. Now you know that if you continue to create guilt, the inflammation will return. I think you are learning that your wife must heal herself. It cannot be your responsibility. It is part of her evolution. Bring her here and we will help her let go of her suffering."

James gets up and they shake hands. When it is my turn to say goodbye to him I feel I am holding the hands of a very young man. I want to question Kaimana about everything, get inside his head and find out how he knows to do this stuff.

"How are you doing with all of this?" he asks drinking a glass of water and blowing into his hands.

"I'm out of my mind enjoying every second—and of course I have a million questions. Like why are you blowing like that?"

"I am blowing away any residue of James' suffering that I might have retained. It is a simple technique taught to me by my teacher. I must be vigilant about not collecting other peoples' energies. If I am not fastidious, I get overwhelmed and my energy collapses. So...," he blows into each hand like he is blowing out a candle, "this is one way of letting it go. Sometimes it is particularly difficult to maintain my focus and remain within my own energy field. But it is always important."

"All of this is so new to me, but so valuable. Every doctor should practice these techniques. Maybe then we wouldn't get so burned out. We'd actually have more compassion for our clients."

"You are exactly right. I knew you would understand quickly."

"Well, I'm starting to find my way. Do you want me to stay?" I ask Kaimana as he spreads a fresh towel over the table.

"No, I think that is enough for today. We will do more work tomorrow, if you wish."

"I just want to make sure I'm helping. I guess I'll get better as I spend more time around you, working with you."

"Right now your job is to connect with the Source, to allow the energy to circulate through you and into your hands and flood the room with universal light. This is what heals people."

There are no more patients waiting at his gate, so we head for the kitchen and he pours each of us a huge glass of water, then floats cucumber slices and sprigs of mint in each one. It's refreshing and soothing all at the same time.

Between sips I confess, "Part of me still has a hard time taking in what you accomplished with me earlier, and today with James. Your methods challenge everything I've been taught—and yet I see miracles happen because of them."

"Just try to keep your mind and heart open, Kate. That is what will allow the healing energies to flow through you. There are many ways to use that energy. With you we did shamanic journey work. For James, we infused him with universal light and then released the negative emotions that were causing him pain."

"You're amazing—part angel, part Electrolux!" This is the second time I've seen him laugh. Beautiful.

"It is not me, you know. I am only the conduit. When you are ready to assist me, I will ask that you make a deeper connection with the Source."

"Yes...it feels like I'm working superficially. I keep looking for those guides of mine."

"There is no need to look for them, Kate. Simply call them in. Invoke them. Be patient, you will get there. I have been doing this since I was a little boy. I committed early because I knew that surrendering to that kind of faith would save my life. "

I help Kaimana freshen the blankets and pillows in the healing room. I love doing things for him and with him. Is this the easy companionship I've heard patients and friends allude to?

He asks me about my office, who helps me, how many hours I work. How do I feel about my practice? How do I release all my patients' problems at the end of the day? David and I have never met each other this way. I don't even know if he likes what I do. Once in a great while when I've been exhausted and he realized I was withdrawing from him, he's questioned me about my patients in a detached sort of way. Once I tried to tell him how difficult it was to see a patient struggle with a terminal illness. His version of support was, "Maybe she should get another opinion." *Duh.* As hard as I've tried, there's never been any real connection between us unless we were talking about his world. Just thinking about it now makes my belly ache.

ALL WEEK LONG, patients come with their fibromyalgia, allergies, macular degeneration, AIDS, diabetes, domestic abuse, and despair—my diagnoses, not Kaimana's. They also come with beautiful stones and shells, flowers and fruit, baskets of sun-dried seaweed, hand-woven scarves...all manner of offerings that, as Kaimana explains, represent an exchange of energy in return for the healing he offers them. They have slipped getting out of bed, been bitten by a centipede, or overdosed on crack, but all come back to life on Kaimana's table. I'm convinced I have pretty much seen everything.

And then it's time for Steven to arrive. I know something's up, because before he gets here Kaimana sits me down in the healing room, and very solemnly tells me I need to prepare myself for the next patient. He describes Steven as a young boy who is in pretty bad shape. The doctors have diagnosed him as schizophrenic and bipolar and have dosed him up on various high-powered medications in an effort to assuage his violent episodes.

"In my experience this kind of behavior comes from an entity or a group of orphan souls who are lost," Kaimana explains. "All they need is to be directed home. Or," he says and stops, looking pensive, "or this could also be a child who has imagined that he has been overtaken by a demonic entity. I pray that this is not the case because those beliefs are very difficult to dispel. I won't know what is really happening until I get in there and see.

"More than ever, I will need you to keep the room peaceful and filled with light. Do you feel you can handle this?"

He reaches over and touches my hand. I let his touch in.

"Kaimana, so much of what I have experienced here is utterly mind-boggling. I can't believe what I'm seeing case after case. You're changing the way I think about medicine, healing...about life. I'm a bit in awe of the work you do.

"I won't lie to you, though—what you tell me about Steven does scare me a little. But if you think I'm capable of supporting your work with him, you know I'll do my best."

"I am no miracle worker, Kate. My patients put their faith in me, and that faith is actually the realization that they are connected to the Source. Ultimately it is their own healing ability that works the miracles. It is my wish that each one of them—and you—know that the miracles are waiting within each of us if we believe it is so."

Kaimana's eyes look so deeply into mine that I know he sees a part of me I haven't even met yet. With just his gaze, he fills me with so much warmth and peace that I begin to feel that connection to the Source that he talks about. It's as though any boundaries that once existed between me and him, or the baby seal on the beach, or the ocean itself, have dissolved. I have never in my life felt this kind of energy, radiating from somewhere deep in my soul, healing every hurt I've ever had and filling my heart with more love than I imagined I was capable of. There is nothing in the world but this moment.

And then the screaming begins.

A WAYWARD SOUL
GOES HOME

Someone is pounding on the gate, and there's a maniacal sound coming from what seems to be a human voice. I hurry down the front hallway, but then I remember how emphatic Kaimana is about staying calm no matter what happens.

Breathe, Kate. Relax and breathe....

As I open the front door I hear a woman's voice yelling, "Stop that! Stop it right now!"

Behind the gate I see a child who appears to be seven, maybe eight years old. His fists are locked around the iron bars of the gate, and he's shaking it as though he's determined to tear it down with his bare hands.

"Let go, Steven!" the woman screams. *"Let go, damn it!"*

I open the gate and the boy swings toward me, his blue eyes fiery and fixed.

"Hello," I say offering my hand to the woman.

"I'm Bridget. This is my son, Steven," she blurts out.

The boy lurches forward and attempts to bite my hand. I quickly get out of his way.

"Please come in," I say, doing my best to sound calm.

Bridget tries to grab Steven's hand, but the boy runs past her and darts into the house. Suddenly he stops, then turns and very quietly comes back to the doorway and looks at me with an innocent, almost sweet expression. I bend down and try to make contact, and he spits in my face. I am grossed out—and quite pissed—but I persevere.

"Follow me," I say wiping off my face. "Kaimana is waiting for you."

"I've heard good things about this guy." It's a statement, but the look on Bridget's face says she has plenty of questions about him.

"Kaimana is a true shaman. I'm sure he will do the best that he can...with the help of the universe." I cannot believe these words are coming out of my mouth.

Bridget shakes her head. "Shaman?"

Steven is screaming again. The sound is nerve-shattering.

"Healer...he's a great healer." I'm trying not to shout. When it's quiet again I go on. "Kaimana is a remarkable healer, but he won't tell you that. He says it all comes from his connection to what we might call God. He calls it the Source, that which creates everything." Well, listen to me!

"We shall see, won't we?" the woman mutters. She makes no effort to hide her skepticism.

"Yes, we shall," I say as we enter the healing room.

Steven has already arrived, and the space is filled with his venomous spewing. "Son-of-a-bitch," the boy shouts at Kaimana. "Fuck you! Come near me and I'll kill you! *I'LL FUCKIN' KILL YOU!*" He picks up a large brass bowl and hurls it.

"Calm down, son." Kaimana says gently, walking around the boy the way a mother wolf would circle a wayward cub. "I know that you are very angry."

"You're a fucking moron."

"You are afraid, too."

The boy pounds on one of the drums.

"Even though a part of you is very angry and afraid, I know there is someone else inside...someone who is calm. Someone who is peaceful and innocent."

"Shut up, motherfucker! Cocksucker! There's nobody here but us chickens...cock-a-doodle-doo!!! COCK-A-DOODLE-DOOOOO!!!!!!" The boy becomes his version of a rooster clucking and strutting about the room, kicking things out of his way.

Kaimana follows close by. "Who are you?"

"None of your fucking business."

"Are you Steven?"

"Not on your life."

"How long have you been in this boy?"

"Long enough to slurp up his stupid sweetness!"

"Yes, he is a very sweet boy. Is that why you chose him?"

"Shut the fuck up!"

Kaimana puts his hand on Steven's shoulder and Steven runs in the opposite direction.

In a hideous voice the boy says, "He's a weak, weak boy, that little Stevie."

"You like that weakness, do you?" Kaimana asks. "It makes it easy for you to use his body and control him, I imagine."

"You betcha, sweetheart. He's so weak, all I had to do was show up in the middle of the night and take over."

"While he slept, right?"

The young man shoots Kaimana a murderous look. "What's it to you, fuck face?"

"Well, I like the boy. And probably if you told me who you are and what happened to you, I would like you, too."

"I doubt it, asshole."

"Why would I not like you? Did someone tell you not to like yourself?"

He laughs derisively. "You don't know the half of it."

"I imagine that you have seen it all."

The boy picks his nose and scribbles mucous on the wall, spelling out DIE!

"Is that what you would like to do? Would you like to die?" Kaimana is very close to the boy again. "That's what you want more than anything, right? To die? It seems so easy for everyone else, right? But not for you."

Steven begins to slow down.

Kaimana pushes on. "For you there is no death. You are stuck in a half-life, are you not?

The boy stands in the middle of the room and shoots Kaimana a devilish look.

"My heart goes out to you, son, for your suffering."

The kid runs over and spits in Kaimana's face.

Kaimana grabs him and attempts to pin him down. Bridget just stands with her hand over her mouth. For a fraction of a second I'm not sure what to do, but very quickly it becomes clear. Operating totally on instinct I move into the fray, crouch at the boy's head, grab his wrists, and help Kaimana hold him down. Steven shakes his head violently and kicks his feet.

Finally the kicking stops, and Kaimana slowly lies down on top of the child and puts his head on his chest. The boy spits and sputters until there is nothing left inside him but his heavy breathing and big, wet tears that slide down his contorted face.

Silence returns. All four of us are trying to catch our breath. The boy closes his eyes, exhausted at last—for the moment.

"I want to talk to Steven now," Kaimana commands. "Now!"

A little voice replies, "I'm here. Can you help me?"

"Yes, that is what I am going to do. But you must help me, too.

"How? I don't know what to do."

"Does the boy have a religion?" Kaimana calls to his mother.

"Not really," Bridget shrugs.

"Is there anyone he loves more than anything?"

"I don't know. Not really."

How could you not know? Quiet, Kate.

Kaimana keeps going. "Steven, what is your favorite thing?"

The boy is quiet for a moment, then suddenly he knows. "My dog, Jack."

"Oh, that is very good, Steven. What kind of pup do you have?"

"He's a Jack Russell."

"I bet you love him very much."

"So much."

"And of course he loves you so much, right?"

"Yes."

"I bet you miss him a lot."

"I do."

"Well, you do not have to any longer—he is right there with you. Look over to your right. Can you see him, Steven? Can you feel his energy?"

"Yeah, I can!"

"That is good, Steven. Now listen very closely. You are a very good boy. In fact, you are a great boy. Do you understand what I am saying?"

"Yes."

"Wonderful...now I want you to take a deep breath and remember a time when you and Jack were very happy, a time when you were free. And strong...you knew you could do anything. Can you remember a time like that?"

Steven tries to breathe, but it's shallow and tight. "Yes."

"Tell me where you are and what you are doing."

I see Steven's face beginning to contort a little, and I'm concerned that the angry one will push through and take over again. I remember what Kaimana asked me to do before Steven arrived, and try to fill the room with peaceful light. Right. Peaceful light in the middle of all this? I breathe, and remember that incredible loving energy I felt just a short while ago.

Steven's face softens a bit. "I'm building a playhouse in the backyard with Daddy," he says. "Before he goes inside he tells me he loves me. He says I'm his little hero. Then Jack and me run around and have a lot of fun."

"Perfect. Now, in a moment that other boy who has been living in you is going to try to take over. When that happens, I want you to become Daddy's little hero again. Do not pay any attention to the other boy. Just see yourself holding Daddy's hand and running around with Jack, free and joyful. Alright? I know you can do it. Your Daddy told you so. So you tell me, can you be Daddy's little hero and just stay where you are joyful, no matter what that other boy says or does?"

"Okay. I think I can."

"What a great kid you are, Steven! There is one more thing: If for some reason you start to feel frightened, I want you to look at the rays of light all around you. Just look and you will see them. They are magic, and they will protect you. Look now. Can you see the rays of light?"

The boy's face is starting to revert back to the self-destructive personality. "Yes," he says tentatively.

"Steven, look into the light!" Kaimana says vehemently. "Can you see the white light?"

"Yes, I see it!"

"Okay. Here we go." Kaimana moves closer to Steven's face. "I want to talk to the other boy. May I?"

Steven's face twists into a whole other façade, one dripping with disdain. "What the fuck do you want? I was sleeping!"

"I want to help you go home."

"I don't have a home."

"Every soul deserves a home, and so do you."

"Don't fuck with me." The tone of this boy's voice is changing. He almost sounds sad. He looks up at Kaimana, and the fierce expression has the faintest tinge of hope.

"I am not. I know you do not trust me. I understand that. I know you feel like a piece of garbage. You believe you do not deserve to pass over into the light." Kaimana looks deeper into his eyes. "There are many new friends and family members waiting there for you with outstretched arms. They do not care about your past. I see them. I promise. I am telling you the truth."

"They don't want me, so don't tell me that." The boy's voice breaks. He's starting to thaw.

"Tell me, son...you are not Steven, are you?"

"No," he says. "I'm Billie."

"Okay, Billie. Now, please help me understand. What makes you say no one wants you? What happened, son?"

Billy turns away and makes a move to free himself, but it's a half-hearted effort.

Kaimana tries again. "Let me help you cross over. I know you are tired of this hell. Let me help you get out of here."

"God won't let someone like me go through. I'm so tired," the boy says. Tears begin to well in the corners of his eyes.

"That is not true. God is waiting for you to come. He holds no judgment, Billie. How old are you now?"

"I'm eighteen. At least I was when I crashed and died."

"Where did you crash?"

"I crashed on the highway."

"Were you alone?"

"What does that matter?" He is angry again, then sullen. "I was drunk and it was late. I lost control of my van and it crossed over the highway and crashed into another car."

"You must have been terrified."

Billie's voice sounds panicky. "There was this guy and girl in the other car...they were just married. I killed them. I mean...they died right there. I killed them." The tears overflow his eyes, and his chest heaves.

"Oh, son, how painful for you. I am so sorry."

"When I saw what happened I just left my body and I couldn't get back in."

"That is understandable. I might have done the same thing."

"My father was sitting next to me when I was dying in the hospital. I heard him say I was always a bad kid, that I was one of Satan's children. He thanked God that I was dead!'"

Billie starts crying violently. Steven's body shakes.

"Hold on, Steven. Look into the light!"

I cannot contain myself, because I'm scared Steven will slip away. I speak calmly into the boy's ear. "Remember, Steven, you and Daddy and Jack are safe and happy in your playhouse. Right?"

Steven nods, and there's a hint of a smile at the corner of his mouth.

Kaimana continues, "That is good, Steven. You can relax now. I need to talk to Billie."

"Yes, I hear you," says Billie.

"I want you to look over to the right, Billie. There is a beautiful waterfall. Can you see it?"

There's a long pause.

"Yes."

"That is the gateway to freedom, where we all go to pass over and to be forgiven. It is time for you to go through that waterfall into your new life."

Billie sighs, "I don't think I can."

"What if I were to go with you and guide you? The truth is, I would like very much to help you. Because, Billie, I feel your innocence, and I know the universe wants you to come home—to your real home—where you will be loved the way you have always wanted to be loved.

There will not be any more worry or sadness or fear or shame, only many opportunities to learn to love yourself and to be loved."

Another long pause.

Finally Billie speaks. "Can you come with me now?"

"Yes, Billie. I can and I will."

Then Kaimana slowly loosens his grip, eases his body off of Steven's, and sits beside him. I let go of the child's hands. He appears to be nearly asleep.

Kaimana whispers, "Steven, would it be alright with you if I hold you in my arms?"

Steven nods, with a barely audible, "Yes."

"Sleep deeply now," Kaimana says with his hypnotic voice, and then lies down next to him on the floor. Ever so gently he wraps his arms around the boy's small frame.

Steven is in another zone, far away and safe. Kaimana looks up at me and motions to the drum. I reach for it and begin drumming.

"Billie, are you ready to let go?"

"I...I think so."

I quietly hit the drum. Kaimana holds Steven's body close into his and takes in a long breath. They are cheek to cheek, melting into each other.

Mask after mask of intense emotions pass over Kaimana's face. At one point he breaks down sobbing, at another he shakes violently. There is a period of peacefulness and then terrible shaking. It's mesmerizing and exhausting and terrifying and sacred all at the same time.

I watch Kaimana fight for Billie's soul for well over an hour. All the while Bridget is curled up in a corner...she appears to be entranced, just like her son. I remember that I have a job to do, so I turn my attention back to the drum, and fill the room with peaceful light. I envision myself walking with Kaimana and cutting through Billie's torturous existence and guilt, being a second sword, if you will. I visualize Kaimana walking Billie to the light and watching him being greeted with kindness and love.

After the long journey Kaimana quietly lets go of Steven and sits in silence. His face is as calm as the planet Venus resting outside in the night sky. Steven opens his eyes.

"How're you doing, kiddo?" I ask the boy.

His eyes are filled with wonder as if he is seeing life again after a long illness. I open my arms to him and he reaches over and lets me hold him. This is the sweetest boy.

Kaimana bends down and hugs Steven too. Then he stands up and, without a word, leaves the room.

Steven gets up and walks over to his mother. "I want to go home, Mom. I'm tired."

Bridget picks him up in her arms and holds on to him really tight. Tears of gratitude stream down her cheeks.

We walk to the door and she takes my arm. "I don't know what to say. Please thank Kaimana for us. I will find a way to re-pay him."

"No need. Just love your son and hold him close." I watch as the monster who raged at the gate, just a couple of hours ago, passes through now as a normal kid.

I'm exhausted, too, but I want to find Kaimana and thank him. Finally I find him upstairs in the meditation tower.

"Leave me alone," he says sternly. "Not now."

"Is there anything I can do to help?"

"I said leave me alone."

I walk outside and sit against an old palm tree for a while. I admit I'm a little hurt, but I manage to talk myself down from that. Kaimana went through a lot with that boy. He's got to be wiped. I need to give him lots of space and go home. As I gather my stuff I hear a whooshing and tapping sound above me. It's coming from the meditation room. I climb the stairs and find Kaimana turning in circles in the middle of the floor, faster, faster, faster! Turning to the right, then turning to the left. How can he do that without passing out?

As he twirls, his aura casts out shards of energy that hit the walls like dark spears of lightning. Finally he falls to the floor. I know I must leave him alone and not interfere with this process. As I turn to leave, I am honestly freaked out when a parade of spirit people exit through his open mouth. As they head toward the light they look like interconnected bubbles with faces peering out of them. I'm frozen in my tracks as Kaimana continues his release...first there is moaning, then his body goes into labor and expels another group of souls with nowhere to go. It seems to go on forever. I wait. The birthing ends. This is way too much for my heart and mind to handle, but I stand in the doorway determined to help him if I can...if I don't pass out.

Kaimana begins to weep. From where I am standing I can't see his face, so I move closer. It scares me to see him so depleted. I kneel down and wipe the tears and perspiration off his face. At first he protests by turning his head away. I feel his immense suffering as if he is that tormented boy, as if he is Billie.

"Is it alright that I'm here with you now?"

He nods yes, but he's very far away. I sit cross-legged with his head in my lap. He stares out into the distance.

"Something very bad happened to you, didn't it, Kaimana?"

Kaimana just stares at the wall, but his expression has the vulnerability of a child.

"I feel your suffering. Like you've told me so many times, breathe and let go, and just for now let me take care of you. Can you do that? Can you let someone take care of you?"

I lovingly lift his warm, damp hair away from his neck. He begins to cry again and covers his face with his hands. I am feeling someone's shame. Is it his or the boy's? In my very core I search for a way to penetrate his pain. I close my eyes and rub my hands over his back. I think in some way I am calling out to the phoenix for help. I feel guided to look more deeply into his face so I turn his head toward me and gently wipe his tears away. I see a circular redness above his eyebrows.

Somehow I have a sense that the area above his eyebrows that he calls his third eye is absolutely plugged with emotion, like a cork in a bottle of wine. I visualize such a plug, and make a gesture as though I'm pulling it out, envisioning the cork sliding out as I do. Damn if that red circle doesn't disappear, and the muscles in his face begin to relax!

I'm delighted and mystified by the part of me that is beginning to trust my intuition. In a way, I am in labor, too.

I watch his breathing slow way down until he enters sleep. I will never get over how beautiful his face is, so dark and erotic. Even the scar on his arm turns me on. I can't help myself and run my finger over it. Too much, Katherine! I gently set his head down, and he turns over on his side and continues to rest. I slip silently out the door.

As I walk on the beach in the late afternoon sun, I am angry at myself for overstepping our carefully constructed boundaries. I sit on a rock where I can see the mist gathering at the edge of the cove, and the wise woman inside reminds me that none of these boundaries has actually been discussed. They are totally illusory, kept in place only by our fears. If either of us could ever dare to surrender and trust again...but then a wave comes crashing against the rock and brings me back to earth.

I return to the cottage and drift off on the couch, restless with images of the incredible day. I get up to turn the light on, and before I can repress it I realize that in my half-asleep nap I dreamt I was kissing Kaimana's sensuous, generous lips...and he was beginning to respond.

I splash some water on my face, run my fingers through my hair, and grab the car keys.

22

HUNTING FOR MY TRIBE

I drive into town, past head-shop windows filled with pipes of all different sizes. I smile, just a little smug because I've been traveling to other realms without help from weed or any other substance. There's a long line in front of that awesome bakery, and as I open the car door the smell of pineapple upside-down cake is overpoweringly in my face. There's nothing like the scent of brown sugar and butter to bring me back to the real world.

I decide to skip the sugar and get some real food. I'm starving, but I don't think I can handle a heavy dinner, so I order an omelet with goat cheese. The waitress asks if I'd like bacon with that. Just as my habitual "Of course" is about to pass my lips, I am horrified that I almost fell into the dissociative trap—bacon isn't just bacon, it's a pig. A pig with a soul. Like Kanoa. I've looked in that little guy's eyes and believe me, he has tons of soul. I ask for fruit salad instead.

I finish my meal and stroll idly past the shops. Something is definitely happening to me...it's like the whole scene is different from what it was a few days ago. That deep connection to Source that Kaimana somehow transfused into my cells stayed with me through the whole ordeal with Steven and Billie. Now I feel as though I'm floating on that energy, and I'm connected to everything I see. I stop at the window of a European boutique and stare at a pile of leather purses on sale...and they become a stack of animal skins dishonored and thrown in a heap. I feel a wave of sadness when I think of the skins being stripped off the carcasses of cows.

I turn away and see a little flower shop and cross the street and buy myself a beautiful bouquet of white roses. They're just like the ones I saw on my inner altar during my first healing session with Kaimana. They make me so happy I start to cry.

All at once I realize I'm completely and utterly exhausted. I drive myself home, put the roses in water, and head straight to bed. As I close my eyes I feel totally at peace. I know without any question that I'm exactly where I'm supposed to be, doing exactly what I'm meant to do.

23

THE HEALING POWER
OF HANA

I sleep late into the morning, then spend the entire day alternately sitting on the beach, staring at the waves, and dozing on my couch. When I sleep it's that deep, drugged, dreamless sleep that only comes from utter exhaustion. In my waking moments I entertain the idea of checking on Kaimana, but my gut tells me to let him have his space to heal himself the way he needs to.

In the middle of layering my late-night repast of moonfish and wasabi, the weird doorbell buzzes. Max skitters past me down the hallway. I'm shocked to open the door and find Kaimana's beautiful face gracing me with his presence. Actually I'm a little unnerved seeing him here...feels like change is in the balmy evening air. He seems a little nervous, too, or maybe I'm just projecting. Again.

"Good evening, Kate. I trust I have not disturbed you."

I've never been quite this pleased to be disturbed. "No, Kaimana, not at all. Are you okay?"

"Yes, I am well." He smiles that delicious smile. There's no trace of the other-worldly ordeal he went through just a day ago. "Tomorrow morning I will drive upcountry into the bamboo forest to gather some herbs for tinctures and the like. I believe you have not yet been there, so I thought I might invite you to accompany me. It is quite incredible there…lush, green, with many species of flowers and plants…you will be amazed. That is, of course, if you wish to join me."

Those amber eyes reach into mine, so I look down at the sandy floor. Kaimana on my doorstep is a vastly different experience from Kaimana the medicine man in his healing room.

"Well…I…I…I…." I am stuttering like a schoolgirl! I feel the blood rush to my cheeks.

"I would like to show you some of the most beautiful landscapes you will ever see. There is a garden that is a favorite of mine, where the flowers bloom in the most innocent of colors. We could have lunch there, if you like."

He pauses. I can hardly hear what he's saying because my heart is pounding in my chest. "I don't know if I can," I manage. "I mean…it sounds lovely, but…I have client files to update and phone calls, and...." Jesus, Katherine, how lame are you?

"I see. Well...if you are able to postpone your work for one day, I believe you will find it most worthwhile. There are some sacred places on the island that I would like to share with you as well."

And I deserve to go there because?

His expression darkens. "But, of course...if you are unable to leave your work...."

"No. Yes. Okay. I mean...it sounds fascinating. Sounds like an adventure! Yes, sure. I'd love to go. What time?"

There's that smile again. "The earlier the better. We will have a very full day, that is for certain."

We agree to leave at 4 a.m. from his house. I'll pack a lunch. When he reaches over to close the door, his hand grazes mine and a bolt of lightning ignites my nervous system. I stand motionless until the door closes behind him, then maneuver my wobbly knees to the bed and sit down, close my eyes, and try to begin breathing again. And try to remember the last time I felt this giddy.

Then someone inside me sounds an alarm. Watch yourself, Kate. This is what you do. You run away from your husband instead of facing your problems. Now you're hoping you can distance yourself even further through Kaimana so you can escape it all. Why can't you ever just be alone, on your own, and be happy with yourself?

It's a valid point. Running away, escaping into some other distraction has been my m.o. my whole life.

But I really believe there's another side to it. This is a different kind of man and a totally different kind of experience. I feel like he gives more to me than I give to him. I've never had that before. Doesn't that show that I'm making some kind of headway? Heck, if nothing else, I've chosen to run to a different *kind* of relationship. What if, this time, I choose someone who actually values me?

No matter who or what he is, Kate, for you he is an escape.

Really? Which side of the story is true here? They both feel right.

And wrong.

This is where my schism lies. In this moment I can't tell if the voice of caution is coming from a place of wisdom and speaking the deepest truth, or if I'm just beating myself up the way I've done since I was a kid, anytime I grasped at a bit of freedom. And the fact is it's damn hard to believe I could be appreciated just for being me.

Sometimes I think I should stay out of relationship for a while, spend some time in relationship with me, until I figure out how to operate from strength instead of fear. But this man...Kaimana. Somehow he seems to know my own strength. That's the part of me that he sees, and when I'm around him I can see it, too. Is that so bad?

Actually, isn't that what love is supposed to do?

When I'm finally able to quiet down and listen to the benevolent voice inside, I feel an undeniable sense of certainty in it. After all, I'm learning just like everyone else, trying to relax and pay attention to my life without all the fears. What would happen if I started treating *myself* with a little more love and acceptance? It's what I've told my patients a thousand times. Maybe I'm finally starting to walk my talk.

I WAKE UP APPREHENSIVE, not letting myself feel excited, just a bit scared. I can't seem to make a simple decision like what to wear or whether I should put on eye shadow. Anything positive feels like seduction. I realize I am projecting, so I just keep moving.

When I arrive at Kaimana's he is loading his jeep. I add my Igloo filled with fruit and crackers, and a thermos of jasmine tea. As we climb in the car and head down the road, away from familiar turf, I am very aware that something has changed. We are no longer patient and medicine man, or even student and teacher. We are a man and a woman alone together, away from Seal Cove for the very first time. I wonder if he feels any of the nervousness I feel. If he does, he shows me nothing,

Kaimana's jeep grips curve after curve on the hair-raising route that winds along the edge of the moody Pacific. I feel as though we could crash at any moment, but I don't seem to care. I pull out my iPod and introduce him to Bill Evans and Wayne Shorter, two of my favorite jazz musicians. He seems to be loving it.

We arrive at the sacred land Kaimana told me about, park the jeep by the side of the road, and begin the long climb up. It's been raining, and it's muddy and slippery. Kaimana walks behind me in case I miss a step. It feels like my shoes have suction cups on their soles, grabbing the viscous earth as though they don't want to let go. We stop and lean against a grandfather banyan tree. His arms spread above us like long, gnarled, arthritic fingers reaching into the undulating forest. Exotic creatures screech, water pings on leaves and flower petals, wild swine grunt, and bees the size of small black golf balls buzz through the breezeless forest. It's steamy in here. I watch a trail of sweat trickle down Kaimana's suntanned neck and my equilibrium momentarily abandons me.

We resume our climb, and finally reach level land. There's little sunlight here, and as the forest deepens I begin to hear a steady Click!Click!Click! just ahead. We keep moving, and with each step the sound grows louder, until it's a cacophony of clattering that sets every cell in the forest to vibrating.

"Clickclickclickclickclickclickclickclickclickclick!!!!" It's the bamboo announcing its sovereignty, as if to say, *"You are entering a very private place...walk lightly!"*

We do. And as we enter the dark forest a shiny cool breeze ushers us into a nation of giant bamboo trees that clatter against each other in and out of unison. These bamboos are two and three inches thick, and some must be at least forty feet tall. We walk quietly, honoring their majesty. Once in a while Kaimana connects with one of the grandfather bamboos and nods or casually bows. Every sense is heightened, and I'm completely immersed in the moment. Kaimana catches my eye, and I look up at him in wonder.

He smiles. "I see that the forest speaks to you." He says it so quietly that I'm not sure if I hear him with my ears or read his thoughts. It doesn't matter. "Close your eyes so you can experience everything the bamboo has to share with you. Take my hand...I'll be your guide."

I slide my hand into his, and it feels exactly like I hoped it would. It's happening. Maybe it's the old pattern emerging in me or maybe this is me breaking through the pattern. It's too soon to tell.

The wind blows into my shirt and I shiver. I'm not sure what stirs me more, the wind, the bamboo, or the way the skin of Kaimana's hand feels against mine. He's right...with my eyes closed I inhale the aroma of mint, rosemary, and damp rocks that still carry the sweat of last night's warm mists. Now I feel a breeze, and with it the smell of something lemony, tart, and fresh. And now it's all about the pure erotic scent of wet Maui red earth under my hiking boots.

A chorus of bees, frogs, and winged ones zooming around us resonates through my whole body. And the air—well, with my eyes closed I feel like I'm swimming in a sea of honey thinned by lime that's been mixed with a jigger of dark rum. Exotica!

Kaimana's gentle voice breaks through the sensory intoxication. "Open your eyes, Kate."

We're in a grove with trees that are younger and smaller. We walk a while longer and then the energy shifts once again, and we enter an ancient gateway lined with bamboo some eighty feet high. These are the ancient ones.

Kaimana drops my hand and turns to me. There's a reverence in his eyes that reflects the sacredness I feel in this place. He says, "I have brought you here so that you can choose the right bamboo for the flute I am going to create for you."

My heart turns over. "Really? But I thought it was against Hawaiian tradition to take anything from the land."

"Not if you use it in a sacred way that heals the earth. We only choose bamboo that has ended its life cycle and seeks to be of service."

"I see. But how will I know which piece to choose?"

"Quiet your thoughts, open your heart, and let the bamboo choose you. Of the many who have fallen to the earth, you may find one who reaches out to you."

I wander among the bamboo, and soon spot a small, light green wand that seems to be set apart somehow from the other stalks and leaves that carpet the ground.

"This one feels like the right one."

"Alright. Ask her for permission to take her."

"Is it okay if I bring you home with me and make you into an instrument?"

"Now listen to your heart."

I do my best to trust what I feel.

"I feel it's okay."

"Good." he says. "Now make a prayer of gratitude."

"Thank you for your special gift. I promise to honor your spirit by bringing beautiful sounds to the earth. Amen."

I pick up the bamboo, and Kaimana pulls a cloth from his knapsack and wraps it carefully around the stalk. I hold it close to my chest. Already I can feel the sacred music resonating in my heart.

"It's exciting to think of playing such a sacred instrument," I tell him. "I promise I will get good at this."

"I have no expectations. I just want you to have something that will help you feel more empowered, to deepen your connection to the land."

"Thank you, Kaimana. Mahalo. I...I'm very moved by this honor. I hope you will teach me how to play it with the kind of joy you bring to the music you make with your flute."

I feel happy and I feel sad...at the same time deserving and scared that I will somehow be found out. Like a kid who got an A on a paper she wrote but really deserved a B. This spiritual connection with Kaimana throws me into such emotional turmoil. I don't feel like I deserve it yet. I'm just a beginner, a novice...or is this just a story I'm making up so I can hide from my own sacredness?

Back in the jeep his leg is so close to mine in the front seat that it would only take the smallest gesture to brush against it, to touch his thigh for the very first time. Fortunately the radio separates us, and we sit in our separate seats gazing in opposite directions as the Hawaiian landscape rolls by.

On the way back we take a different route. Kaimana wants to show me Hele Aku, which he tells me is a tiny town whose name literally means "go away"! It's an un-populated village where the ocean is so dark it undulates jet black. In the past week I have seen pink, black, and yellow beaches, and an ocean that's peacock blue, lime, white-crested, and, after the rain, bark brown. A black ocean feels foreboding, filled with shadowy dark forces.

As we enter Hele Aku I can see right away what he means about it being tiny. It's a village where there's hardly any there there. For me there's something overwhelmingly eerie about the place. Maybe it's the high surf, crashing angrily, ominously against the rocks.

Kaimana senses that something is bothering me.

"Maybe I'm just projecting," I try to explain, "but I feel like there's some kind of dominating power breaking through the water onto the beach. The surf feels almost too powerful. Overpowering. Do you feel that?"

"Go on," he urges gently, a look of quiet concern on his face.

"I feel like we're being warned not to stay too long."

"I can see why you would feel that way. This is a power center. Many battles were fought here a long time ago. That may be what you feel."

But I feel much more. I feel anger...fury, really. My gut feels upset enough that I know I want to leave. I tell Kaimana, but he is insistent that we remain a while longer.

"I want to show you a heiau. It is a sacred place that no one knows about. When I first moved here from Delhi I was in very bad shape. Akahi, my teacher, brought me here to heal. I believe you will find it very powerful and moving. But it is imperative that you never tell anyone about this place. Can I trust you, Kate?"

"Absolutely," I say. My heartbeat quickens, and I swallow deeply.

We drive down a very primitive road covered in driftwood...it's very hard to navigate. No wonder no one else knows about the sacred place. No one would ever suspect that what lies at the end of this road is a secret healing chamber.

Again, I am overcome with a panicky gut.

Kaimana touches my arm. "Many years ago, ceremonies were performed here that involved dark magic. You are very intuitive, Kate, and you sense those energies. But please do not worry. No one can harm you. You will see.

I take a deep breath, jump out of the jeep, and swallow my fear. We climb over craggy black lava rocks and into a large opening in the side of a cliff. We weave through a narrow tunnel. There's barely any light, the air is warm, and it's difficult to breathe. Claustrophobia swirls around me in dusty patterns.

"There's no air in here," I complain nervously.

We turn a corner and enter a large circular room, where light pours in from the far side. Kaimana tells me the space was used as a clandestine meeting place for tribal activities eons ago. I can hear the ocean waves in the distance, and fresh air seems to be wafting in from the same opening that lets the light in. I feel relieved. I always need an escape route.

Hundreds of petroglyphs cover the walls, apparently depicting an ancient story. Faces of warriors glare fiercely in my direction, male figures carry women on their shoulders, scorpion tails rise, shark gods bare their jagged teeth...and, in a bewildering change of mood, families pray in circles beneath stars that gleam in cobalt skies. The energy expressed in these simple carvings is so dramatic I have to sit down.

Kaimana sits down beside me. "This is where I come to do my own rituals and prayer work," he tells me. "I find solace here on this sacred ground. Sometimes I even sleep here. It is my private sanctuary."

"What kind of rituals?" I ask.

"One day, if you decide to continue on this path, I will show you. For now, just experience this place and take what it offers you. Try not to ask for more."

I stand up and trace my fingers over the symbols and pictures on the cave-like walls. I find myself wondering what the petroglyphs of my life would look like. I picture a woman riding the back of a giant cockroach. Or maybe I'd be a warrior-gynecologist poised between the open legs of a pregnant female pulling out a new member of her tribe.

Suddenly I have to pull away because I feel something burning my fingers—it's almost as if the figures are coming alive! As if their story wants to be told out loud. Shaken, I sit back down and try to quiet the noise in my head, but the vibes in here are too strong. None of what I'm feeling makes any sense to me. It's almost like there are ghosts in here...or maybe just some kind of ghostly hunger in the air. Whatever it is, it makes me feel damned uncomfortable!

"Kaimana, it's too much for me in here. I'm feeling afraid. Can we go?"

We gather our things and make our way out, climbing carefully over the piled rocks. I have never been so relieved to feel the sun on my skin.

On the road again, Kaimana is compassionate about my fears. "As I have told you, many battles were fought on the Hele Aku peninsula," he explains. "We have worked very hard to clear the energy, but there still exists a resounding battle cry echoing through those caves. Your fears probably arose because you were aligned with those cries of war. But also, there are many powerful Kahuna— that is the Hawaiian word for a priest, or a magician. They visit the heiau from time to time from the spirit realm. When you are still, they have many things to tell you."

"Yes, I think I felt them," I say. I'm not sure if I'm relieved to know what it was, or panicky about the idea that spirits were trying to talk to me.

Kaimana continues. "The peninsula was also a safe haven for many families and tribal leaders. They went to the heiau, sat in circles, and wove the dreams for their tribes. Lovers went there to speak their vows."

Suddenly there's a pause that seems to linger forever, and again I feel a panic rising in my chest. But this time it's not spirits that I'm afraid of.

When he finally speaks, Kaimana looks at me with a tenderness I haven't seen before. "Is something wrong?" he asks.

"I guess I am still scared from the experience I had in the heiau." No, Katherine. You are scared because you are unraveling. Or maybe it's just that the world as I know it is unraveling. But I fake it. Sort of. "I actually felt the hieroglyphs speaking through me. I don't know what to do with that."

"Yes, to someone who has not experienced the power of the Hawaiians, that kind of communication would be astonishing. But perhaps it was your fear that depleted you. Frightening thoughts can drain anyone. Many troubling things have happened to the Hawaiian people, and I can see that you are very sensitive to dark emotions...."

And to romantic ones. Heck, I feel safer talking about warring spirits than about what's going on in my gut. But I've got lots of practice hiding from that sort of thing. "It wasn't just the sacred gathering place, either," I tell him. "It seemed like the whole Hele Aku peninsula had a scary, haunting energy. I felt that way from the moment we headed onto the land. I don't like the kind of angry energy I sensed there. The ocean felt angry, and anger is something I avoid as much as possible."

"I understand. I can feel that too. But I learned a long time ago that no matter what kind of emotions or actions are being expressed in the outer world, I must remain calm and stable in my inner world. This is one of my teacher's most important lessons. 'Just notice life,' he would tell me. 'Live as an observer, try not to react.' By practicing this non-reactive way of being, I find that I am not at the mercy of what I cannot control. I just accept what is happening and let it move through me."

I shake my head. "But isn't life boring without engaging more than that? We've gotta have a little drama in our mundane lives, or what's the point?" I think of David and his reactive, dramatic life. How once upon a time his racing, diving out of airplanes, gambling at Baccarat was a turn-on for me. Now I just watch him do his thing and I simply don't care. There must be a middle road between being a passive observer and freaking out, but I'll be damned if I know what it is.

The terrain changes as we head away from the ocean, past tiny towns with names I can't pronounce. We pass acre after acre of pineapple fields. Then, around another bend, the sun casts a shimmering white glaze over a field of sugar cane. No camera could ever capture this light...it is otherworldly. But I'm a rich white tourist from the mainland, I want to try anyway. I ask Kaimana to stop, and I take some pictures of green leaves bathed in the white light.

We drive for another half hour until the road begins to curve uphill, and giant, fragrant eucalyptus trees tower over us on both sides of the road. Once again the landscape has changed completely.

"Where are we?" I ask.

"I would like to surprise you." He smiles.

We travel through very hilly terrain, and then arrive in the center of a Monet painting, the luscious gardens Kaimana promised he'd show me. Before us, acres of pink, white, and purple lavender flowers reach their delicate blossoms into the warm wind. It's a heavenly surprise. What a difference between this delicate world and the Hele Aku peninsula.

I walk the narrow paths between the rows of lavender, humming occasionally and plucking a leaf or two, taking in the various fragrances. Kaimana is busy gathering different varieties to make his herbs, salves, and teas. He takes off his shirt and I try not to stare, but when I feel it's safe I watch as he bends to choose the right buds, his phoenix ascending in the afternoon sun. He must feel my eyes on him, because he looks up and waves. His face is so innocent that I see him as the young Indian boy walking the streets of his homeland.

We let ourselves merge with the sweet scents and visual beauty as we share a quiet lunch on the terrace of a little café overlooking the gardens. We're the only guests, and it feels like the whole scene was created just for us. As we sip lavender tea and eat warm lavender scones, I'm entranced by a pink blossom caught in his hair, resting just over his left temple. I want to reach over and pluck it off.

I want to touch that warm brown skin.

But instead I intensely butter another scone for the road...and devour it on the way to the jeep.

ON OUR WAY HOME, Kaimana turns down the slack-key guitar music and asks, "Would you like to have dinner with me tomorrow evening, Kate? I will create something delicious." He says it so charmingly. "Or would that have us spending too much time together?"

"Well, since it will be *delicious*," I say, surprising myself with a confident wink, "I would love to. What can I bring?"

"Nothing. My garden and I will take care of you."

"I think you've already done that."

24

THE ROAD
TO KAIMANA

I have bathed and shaved and brushed and slipped into a lovely white blouse and really snug jeans. Max has parked himself on the back of the toilet. I look at my ass in the mirror—not bad.

Then in a flash I see myself as the seventeen-year-old girl who felt disconnected from everybody, especially from herself. I say to her reflection, "You are my darling girl. You are perfect just the way you are."

Max is watching from the windowsill.

"So, do I look okay?" His feelers move a little.

Who am I kidding, anyway? This man knows what I look like. It's what I feel like that matters. And who is this woman who blows a kiss to a gigantic cockroach as she floats out the door?

KAIMANA IS OUT behind his house setting a colorful table. I walk over and give him a small hug, and he returns it. This feels big already.

"Would you like something to drink?"

"What are you offering?

"I made some fresh pineapple and papaya juice, if you like."

What was I expecting? A Shamanic Chardonnay?

He pours two tall, frosty glasses, then asks, "Would you like to say a prayer before we eat?"

"I'd love for you to do it," I say, flustered.

Kaimana bows his head and then looks toward the sky. "Thank you, Spirit, for this generous offering. May all living beings have something good to eat and drink. Amen."

"Amen."

We sit down to a lovely meal of olives, sweet Hawaiian bread, a huge salad laced with Maui onions, all kinds of fresh veggies from his garden, with an opulent savory cashew cream for dipping. I notice he eats the onions without worrying, so I do, too. Over mangoes, dark chocolate, and macadamia nut pie I tell him about my crazy childhood, my super snotty prep school, and my years in medical school. I talk in great detail about Jess and my work.

At one point he stares at my wedding ring.

"Oh...well, I'm obviously not very married these days."

"There is no need to tell me unless you want to."

"I want to tell you, but at this point I'm not sure what to say."

We are quiet for a moment.

I feel so present with Kaimana, and so lost with David. "What about you?"

"I was engaged for a very short time, many years ago. She died in a car crash. We had hoped to have children, but it seems that was not to be in this lifetime."

There's a long, heavy pause. What I want to say is, okay, so why is there no woman in your life now? Every female in town must have tried to get your attention. You must have been hiding. Why? But instead I go in another direction. "So, let me in on your secret. What does Kaimana mean?"

"Well, it literally means 'a diamond from the ocean' or "ocean spirit.' My teacher, Akahi, named me Kaimana when I completed my apprenticeship with him. I am quite certain he still thinks of me as a diamond in the rough. I believe everyone would benefit from being given a spiritual name...a name to honor his or her soul. Don't you agree?"

"I've never thought about it. I can hardly remember my own name. I can't imagine what mine would be." Maybe it's She Who Stays Too Long in a Fucked-Up Marriage.

"Allow me," he says respectfully. "Yours is Makalapua. 'She who blossoms.'" He picks up his knife and gently taps my head. "From now on you shall be known as Makalapua. Ho, it is done!"

"Ho, it is done," I repeat, utterly delighted.

And then he anoints me with that smile of his. "This moment deserves something special."

Kaimana leaves, then returns with a tall, dark blue bottle and two martini shaped glasses. "Let us toast your new name with a cocktail of pink lotus blossom." He winks at me as he pours his potion into the glasses. "This is my special creation, to be imbibed on special occasions such as this. I steep the lotus flower in spring water with a touch of brandy. I hope you enjoy it... Makalapua."

It is indeed pink! And delicious. I am the newly appointed Makalapua, sitting by the Pacific with an Adonis, sipping a pink lotus!

A loud squeal interrupts the moment. It appears a certain small pig is about to go on a rampage.

"What's with Kanoa?" I ask.

"He is hungry. Frantically so, apparently. My apologies, Kanoa. I am afraid it is past your dinner time."

"Is this 'little piggy' a medicine animal for you?"

"He is one of my medicine animals, but he is my friend and companion as well. He is also an ambassador for his kind. I sometimes take him to town and invite islanders and tourists to visit with him. He enjoys the attention, and I like to give people an opportunity to see that pigs are much more than food. I am sorry to say that my neighbors not only eat pigs, they slaughter them in a very brutal way. I wish to help them understand that these beings deserve a better life. They deserve our respect."

He scratches Kanoa's nose. "He is definitely my great friend, though. Isn't that right, little one?"

"You don't eat meat at all?"

"No. I have been a vegetarian since I was a little boy. But it is much more than that. I have always felt close to animals, and from the time I was a child I just naturally trusted them. I see no reason to treat them with anything other than kindness and respect."

"I find the whole thing so confusing. I feel like even if I stop eating meat, I still wear leather and silk. I try to buy products made by companies that don't experiment on animals, but then I find out they lie a lot, or they contract out the testing to other companies. I don't see how anyone can totally honor animals in all the little choices we have to make every day. There's just very little out there to substitute for animal products. The worst thing to me is using them for medical research—and as a doctor I have to deal with that all the time. It's devastating. So it seems like no matter what I do, I betray the animals one way or another."

"Be patient with yourself, Kate. You already make many choices that reflect your compassion. If you feel drawn to move further down that road, then do so. The animals will thank you, I promise!" He smiles, and reaches across the table to touch the tips of my fingers. "It is very difficult, it is true, to live in our world without harming animals. What is important is that we try to do more, to choose more consciously as the years go by. There was a time when I killed one deer every year, with great respect for the enormity of his offering to me. I ate his flesh, used his bones for instruments and tools, his hide for clothing and for drums, and other items for my medicine...I did it all with reverence.

"But since Kanoa became my companion, he has taught me a new way of being in relationship with another being. I still use the leather and instruments offered to me by animals in the past, but I have chosen not to take another life in that way.

"I believe that when you are ready to choose alternatives to your leather and silk, Kate, you, too, will find other options available to you. Just be open to the many beings who speak to you, who come to you as teachers, and allow yourself to make small steps on their behalf. Each step will take you closer to living in concert with the gentleness in your heart. You can do no more than that."

alongside my Hawaiian friends and members of my mother's family. I drank in their stories, and they took me in as one of their own.

"It was during one of those visits that I was introduced to Akahi. He became the father I never had. He nurtured my spirit, and saw that I could follow in his lineage. He initiated me in his ancestors' healing traditions, showed me how to use the earth to heal people. Having him as a mentor lifted me out of my dismal relationship with my father. Meeting Akahi saved my life.

"By the time I was eleven, even when I was back home in India I was making remedies and salves out of flowers. During the day, while my father was working and my mother rested—she was sick a lot, I believe due to her despair—while she napped I would talk my nanny, Reshma, into taking me into the worst slums so I could give out my remedies. She was from a lower caste, and enjoyed those little excursions, a bit of rebellion on her part. Eventually we got caught. If my mother had not intervened, my father would have killed me. It was the beginning of a very difficult period in my life."

"I'm sorry you had to go through that."

"Do not be sorry. All of these experiences put me on my right path. My father had no mentor, no one to champion him. All he had was his wealth and his self-hating ego. He was empty inside, consumed by his fears. Drinking took him into a very different dimension. Akahi helped me to see that my father was seeking his spiritual nature through the alcohol. He also taught me that I must learn to rise up out of the ashes of my suffering. When he took me on as his student he gave me this phoenix." He tenderly shows me the carved bird hanging from a black cord around his neck. "It represents my life's path through this world."

"How so?"

"I am destined to experience many small deaths and rebirths in this lifetime. It is even written in what you call 'sun signs' in your Western astrology. You see, according to that system I was born under the sign of Scorpio, a sign whose attributes also include suffering and renewal. Each time we let go of our suffering we evolve into another form...just like the phoenix. And so, I keep my phoenix, my evolved self, close to me always," he says, fingering the little statue. "It reminds me that I have wings, and that I have the power to rise out of the darkest of circumstances. I also have a rendering of the phoenix on my back."

I know. I am mesmerized by your beautiful back.

He smiles that utterly disarming smile again. "But I know I am talking too much, Kate. It has been a very long time since I have been around someone who makes me feel so comfortable talking about myself. I have told very few people these stories. And yet you listen so patiently...I hope you do not listen only to be polite."

"I'm very happy sitting here with you, listening to your stories," I tell him. "And I'm honored that you want to tell them to me. I want to know them, Kaimana. Really."

He stares at the table for a moment, then looks at me intensely. "Kate. What I have told you is sacred to me."

"I understand. I will hold it in a very safe place inside me."

He excuses himself and returns with a carafe of water and two glasses. He very carefully fills the glasses, then sips in silence.

I want to know more. And I want to give him space to tell me as much as he wants to. "May I ask...how long did you stay with your father?"

Kaimana nervously sweeps some bread crumbs across the koa wood table. Finally he breathes, shakes the tension from his shoulders, and speaks. "Too long. As I grew older, the beatings intensified. One night he assaulted my mother. I burst into their bedroom and pulled him off of her. Her face was bloody, and yet she begged me to leave. My father came after me and, this time, I was not able to contain my feelings. I hit him! Numerous times in the face and in the chest, I hit him. Rage overtook me. When I finally retreated he fell over against the cabinet. He was barely breathing. I did not know whether he had passed out from the liquor or because of my attack."

Across from the lanai, the hibiscus are closing their buds in the evening light. Kaimana seems miles away, back in that bedroom watching the tragic event unfold. He just sits there staring at his clasped hands.

I break the silence. "You saved your mother."

He says nothing, so I wait.

Finally he clears his throat and returns. "My mother had hidden away a lot of money for me. While my father lay on the floor, she screamed for me to leave. She forced me out of the bedroom and dragged me down into the basement, where she gave me the deed to this land, an inheritance from her mother. I remember her words as though she were speaking them to me now. She told me, 'Leave now, my darling son. Leave now or he will kill you or me or himself.' The desperation in her eyes was all I could see. I departed that night."

"How old were you?"

"Twenty."

"That must have been so hard to do."

"The first few years, I missed my mother very much. I tried to convince her to join me here, but she refused. I think she believed that it would be the end of my father if she left. But my connection to my family here...not just my mother's family, but also the land, the turtles, the palm trees, the dragonflies, and more recently Kanoa...they all have helped me to gather my life. Through my studies with Akahi I learned how to connect with the Universe as well, and to direct healing energy. He passed down to me most of the instruments I use in my work. I feel his blessings and prayers in every sound they emit."

"When was the last time you spoke to your mother?"

"My mother made her transition last year."

"And your father?"

"I am told he lives alone in our big house in Delhi."

I see the deep sadness in those magnificent soft eyes, and feel a wave of compassion. Time to change the subject and get this big-hearted being talking about something that brings him comfort. "Does Akahi live near here?"

"Up island. I go there once a month to sit with him in silence. Sometimes I work with the people living in a tent camp close by—a place they call Lani Lanakila. It is the place where Ilima was raped. As I have told you, it is very challenging there. It is just a makeshift village. The residents are very poor, and there is a severe problem with drugs and alcohol. So much hopelessness. They live outside the system, but I set up a small clinic there, and there are a few people in the village who do their best to care for anyone in need. I am going there tomorrow."

Kanoa meanders in and I give his ears a scratch. "I see why you love him so. He's got quite a face," I say, cradling his head in my hands.

A sudden cool wind rises from the ocean, and I help Kaimana clear the table so we can go inside.

While he does the dishes—I am not allowed to help—I look around at the Hawaiian pictures and sculptures he has lovingly placed around the spacious sitting area at the center of the house. I want to know the people of these islands. I want to hear their stories, understand their history, their mythology, their traditions...their struggles and their triumphs.

I make my way back to the kitchen and stand at the doorway, watching this beautiful man feed some scraps of salad and fruit to his buddy.

"Kaimana, I want to go to the tent city you talk about. I want to experience the true Hawaiian culture and its people.

Kaimana looks down at the floor as if he is trying to find the right response. When he speaks, his voice is very serious. "Lani Lanakila is not representative of Hawaiian culture—it is a place of outcasts, the downtrodden. Because of that, it would be a challenging visit, Kate. There are very few haoles there."

"Howl-ees? What are howl-ees?"

"Ha-o-le. Haole, or haoles. White people. The residents of this encampment are very suspicious of haoles. They have learned not to trust."

"That doesn't worry me. I want to go. I want to feel that I'm helping the people here in some way. Everyone comes and takes from Hawaii. I want to give something back. May I go with you tomorrow?"

He walks over to me and smiles again...at last. "It will be wonderful to have you there with me, Kate."

The intimacy of our conversation has worn down our resistance and we are entranced in each other's eyes. I feel my boundaries melting into a pool of butter. He brushes a strand of hair from my cheek, which promptly sizzles.

Very softly, he says, "I have been alone for a very long time and at peace here. I have been very content to keep it that way. Now somewhere inside I feel myself shifting."

"Me, too, in a very different way. I'm shifting too."

This evening has been a lot for both of us, so we lightly embrace and leave it at that.

As I walk away I glance back and see that he is checking out my ass. Thank you, Jesus.

25

∪H-OH

The rain beats in a staccato rhythm on the roof and the darkened skylights. There's way too much thinking, thinking, thinking going on to let any sleep in. But what good is thinking when my body aches with this longing? I have a zillion reasons not to go any further with Kaimana, but none of them hold. I feel utterly electric and out of control. I'm scared that I am making more out of these feelings than he is. But I don't want any of this to stop. I feel more alive than I have in a very, very long time.

Finally it's daybreak...thank God...and with just a few hours' sleep my brain surrenders at last and goes quiet. I'm not thinking at all, just noticing my flesh, my heartbeat, my eyelashes against my cheek when I blink. It appears I am no longer trapped in the chaos of my mind, but am a full-on resident of one aging but still-juicy body, and I'm totally aware of its perimeters. I trace the edges of my naked flesh with enlivened hands. I feel good to the touch. What existed in me just days ago as a pale, arid desert is now vibrating in forest green and oceanic blue.

I look into the mirror while brushing my teeth and see myself with different eyes. These are not the judgmental eyes of my mother. There is someone new emerging, a genuinely self-accepting Kate. I like who I see. I find her easy to look at and a bit risqué. Where is all this coming from?

I laugh to myself, delighted to be laughing again.

26

HEAVENLY VICTORY AND THE WHEEL OF LIFE STOPS AT CRISISVILLE

When I arrive, Kaimana is outside packing the jeep. I walk over and he opens his arms to me and I walk in.

The back seat of the vehicle is loaded with food, salves, elixirs, jugs of water, and instruments. We climb in, and Kaimana hands me a beautiful little purple velvet medicine bag.

"I made this for you," he says.

We open the strings together. Inside are three small gifts.

He picks up a small, cream-colored carving and explains, "This statue is Quan Yin."

"Like the one near your front door?"

"That is correct. Keep her close to you. She comes to protect your feminine strength, your compassion."

Next he retrieves an iridescent pink stone from the pouch. "This crystal is kunzite from Lemuria. I found it on the beach. It is a stone with mystical powers. It opens an invisible gateway between time and space."

I put the piece of crystal against my cheek to feel its smoothness. The stone feels feminine and friendly.

The last item in the bottom of the bag is a small mountain lion. No explanation required.

"I love this," I say, grasping it in my hot little hand, and look up into the warmth of Kaimana's eyes. "Thank you. I will treasure these."

His face turns serious. "It is important that you wear this medicine bag while we are in the tent city. We are entering an impoverished area where there is often a shortage of food and bad sanitation. There will not be many white people, and probably no white mainlanders. It is not enough that you have good intentions or that you wish to help. These people have lost everything—their land, their work, their families. When they see you, many of them will be reminded of these things. It is essential that your energy remain strong, and that you feel protected at all times. Hold on to your medicine and stay connected to the power of the other worlds."

I kiss the beautiful little bag and tie the cotton string through a belt loop on my jeans. Immediately I feel a surge of energy shoot up my spine—it must be my imagination. But no, there it is...it's real, alright.

Kaimana puts the jeep in gear and we head west out of the cove, making our way up into the hills. After several miles of nothing but the lush Hawaiian landscape, we pass a tiny village, and then another, and another. Here are the Hawaiians I have been searching for! And their churches, schools, neighborhood grocery stores, and basketball courts. They mow lawns and wash their cars in the morning sun. We pass a poster announcing Sunday's Pancake Breakfast sponsored by the local fire department. At last I have escaped the tourists and found the real Mauians.

The road takes us over a ridge and then descends into a dense and dripping rainforest. The jeep swerves around boulders and through splashes of water gurgling down to the river, but we bounce along with it. Finally we enter a clearing with an eerie view of Lani Lanakila. As Kaimana drives along the outskirts of the village, I peer through a patchwork of barbed-wire fencing that screams for all visitors to stay out. Beyond is a gathering of wood and tin huts separated by sheets and giant palm leaves. The ground is littered with pieces of corroded automobiles and other hand-me-downs from a society in which everything is disposable. For a moment I feel I cannot breathe. I can't tell if what I feel is fear or deep despair.

Kaimana slows the jeep, pulls over to the side of the road, and explains, "This village has been here about ten years. It was built over sacred ground where many battles were fought. It is possible you already feel that. The residents are from many different backgrounds. Many were homeless, some are mentally ill, others are renegades, gypsies, outcasts. Some have broken away from the sovereignty movement. Are you familiar with the movement?"

"I've read a few articles about it. I read a story about one of these camps, and about the way the people in these encampments take care of each other. I remember that they live off the land, according to the values of Hawaiian tradition. They seem committed to keeping their native culture alive. I was impressed with what I read."

"The camps you allude to are those settled by members of the true sovereignty movement. The people there are almost exclusively native Hawaiians. There are people from all walks of life—business people, students, blue-collar workers, multimillionaire landowners. What they all have in common is that they are Hawaiians who are focused on reestablishing their own government. As you say, they are deeply committed to sustaining their own culture, their traditional way of life.

"This encampment, here, is quite different. The residents here are of many different ancestries. As I have said, many of them are outcasts...people who wish to escape the legal system and their own painful histories. They come from all over, looking for safety, food, a place to sleep. They come with nothing, and often they are addicted to alcohol or drugs. Many are gravely ill. Their anger and despair is raw...their anger is rooted in their fears. And many are full of judgment—they blame outsiders for what they themselves have created."

Kaimana sighs deeply and looks into my eyes. "Kate," he says quietly, "you will meet many people here who are in great emotional pain. You will meet children who have been abused and abandoned. It is good that you bring your compassion, your loving heart. But at the same time you must stay as detached as possible, so your heart does not get broken." He puts his hand over mine, and squeezes it for a long moment. Then he turns his eyes back to the road, puts the jeep in gear, and silently navigates the vehicle along the muddy path.

We park and gather up our supplies, and make our way along the rusted fencing. A hand-painted sign on the barbed-wired gate says, "Lani Lanakila," which Kaimana translates as "Heavenly Victory." There are many other signs, but he tells me only that most of them are not as benevolent. Welcome to Tent City, Dr. Blondie!

We walk through the crowds of people, and I see that Kaimana was right—there are no white faces among them. Everyone appears to be from somewhere in the Pacific islands. It's quite a parade. We pass what I guess is a Maori man whose face is almost completely tattooed with thick black symbols. He greets Kaimana but ignores me. An anorexic-looking island girl passes with her eyes to the ground. A gang of native boys, apparently high on drugs, lounge on a cluster of rocks and tree stumps. One of them gestures at me and says something in Hawaiian that sounds derisive, and the others laugh and slap him on the back, knocking themselves out with their pseudo self-importance. This is my welcoming party. I am clearly a pariah saved only by the presence of their shamanic savior. Now I know what my African-American pal means when she tells me, "You have no idea what it's like to be the only black person in a room." I get it now, Michelle. Right now I am the only paleface for miles.

Kaimana holds my hand in a vice-grip. I glance at him every few seconds to reassure myself. Where is the phoenix when we need him? Where is my mountain lion? Right here, right here. I clutch my little pouch. Suddenly I wish I could somehow become invisible.

We wend our way along a particularly circuitous path that leads to a rather large but dilapidated shack. There's a line of folks standing outside waiting to be treated. Word has spread that the shaman has arrived.

Kaimana leads the way as we go inside and put our bags and packages on an unstable counter. Outside the clouds are breaking up, and a few determined rays of morning sunlight make their way through streaked grey windows. The light illuminates the dirt-smudged sink and the rust on the folding chairs, and filters down to the dirt floor. Kaimana opens an old blanket and spreads it on the floor next to the wall, then carefully arranges his instruments on it. I look at the chairs covered in dust and grab a grey, mildew-smelling cloth and quickly wipe them off.

Kaimana pulls back a torn Japanese screen and wheels a long, narrow table in my direction. He pulls out a light pink sheet from one of his knapsacks. "Can you help me with this, Kate?"

I help him lay the pretty sheet down over the surface. There's one more table in the corner. We drag it out and Kaimana covers it with various bottles of elixirs and creams, and a simple white candle in a glass jar. From a leather sack he unwraps his special rattle, shakes it several times, and lays it next to a vase of orchids he has sweetly remembered to bring. He asks me to fill the little white vase with water.

Oy, the water! Nothing but sludge spews out of the faucet. I let it run, and after a minute it looks almost clear.

It's stuffy in here, so I open a window at the back of the room, hoping to encourage a little ventilation. But instead of fresh air there's a stench that about knocks me over. "Aagh! What is that smell?" I ask, afraid of the answer. I slam the window shut.

Kaimana looks up and shakes his head. "Don't ask. Do your very best to forget it.

No, that's not gonna work. I ask again.

Kaimana shakes his head again.

I give him a look.

"Okay," he says half-heartedly. "It's the smell of black dog."

"What?"

"Some of the natives boil the flesh of a dog and prepare it as a kind of delicacy. They call it 'black dog.' Sometimes the animal rots before they actually eat it. Under Hawaiian law, slaughtering dogs for food is a felony that carries strict penalties, even imprisonment. But many do not pay attention."

I am horrified. My mouth hangs open in disbelief.

"Now you really must do your best to let go of it." And then softly touching my arm, he adds, "Please."

Only a shaman could perform miracles in this hellhole. Only a shape shifter could transcend the grizzly vibrations in this abandoned ruin. What is a haole woman doctor doing here anyway? Here, where someone's best friend has become a gruesome dinner? I can imagine the scuttlebutt passing through the crowd about me out there in the campgrounds. I bet it ain't pretty. I mention this to Kaimana, who tells me to curtail my negative thinking and tune in to Quan Yin. It's amazing how fast my fears can take over.

I close my eyes, hold on to my medicine bag, and try to see myself in the body of a goddess transmitting love and compassion, nothing else. No matter what I am greeted with, I am going to stay calm and do my best to extend kindness to the people we came to help. Kaimana prays silently for a few moments, then begins to chant. As his rich voice floats through the air, the room is transformed...it actually starts to feel warm and safe in here.

Kaimana opens the door and I see that the line of patients has tripled. Families stream in one after another, babies and children of all ages, parents, grandparents, and elders who appear older than the island itself. Many of the people seem to be suffering from some kind of flu. Kaimana works tirelessly, lifting off layers of hopelessness and despair that have clogged their stomach cavities. One old man releases so much pent-up emotion he erupts in a fit of coughing, spewing yellow mucus all over Kaimana and me.

"Very good!" Kaimana says, congratulating him.

Really?

I try to contribute what I can...keep the candle lit, and sporadically add the vibration of the brass bowl to calm the atmosphere. Each adult gets a few drops of one or another kind of tincture in fresh water, and every child is rewarded with Kaimana's hands releasing warmth and comfort into their shoulders and spines. There are many well-deserved hugs for Kaimana, and nods to me. I'll take what I can get.

There is one hug that puts a knot in my stomach. It happens between Kaimana and a beautiful, sensual young woman—younger than me, unfortunately—who arrives late in the morning. She is wrapped in an emerald silk sarong and wears a gardenia in her long dark hair. No makeup, no jewelry...no sags. She has not come because she is ill or needs his assistance. She has come to say hello. I watch their interplay with nervous eyes. I start to feel like I'm intruding, so I step outside...but keep half an eye on things through the open door. Even from thirty feet away I can see that this woman loves and admires Kaimana...and something more. I can tell he holds affection for her as well, because they hold each other's hands throughout their conversation. Even though it is all innocent enough it leaves me feeling a bit off balance. When she departs he kisses her cheek so sweetly that I am ashamed of my uptight ego. I blow it off as best I can, but it registers as a note of fear in some quadrant of my vulnerable heart.

WE BREAK FOR LUNCH, and Kaimana tells me we will visit the orphans next. We gather up our gear and meander down another muddy path past shacks made from palm trees, sheets, and pieces of junk. There's obviously no working sanitation system, and a stream of excrement runs down the side of the pathway. A small pack of dogs, who appear to be distant cousins of African dingos, trot past us hunting for food. Roosters and chickens scurry around; here and there a cat appears. I hear pigs and goats in the distance.

I can't believe the size of some of these humans. They're gigantic—and thick. And it's not just the men. I wouldn't mess with any of these women, either. They're message is definitely, "Don't fuck with me, Mama," and I don't. I walk as I imagine Quan Yin would, light-footed and lovingly detached. I don't make eye contact but look straight ahead with a friendly smile on my face.

We approach a larger building, and from behind the walls I hear heart-tearing sounds of little ones crying out for attention. It's beyond unbelievable. There's a sign over the entrance that reads, "Lima Makuahine." Kaimana tells me it means "mama's arms." Let's hope.

Kaimana opens the creaking door and ushers me inside. It takes a moment for my eyes to adjust. Very little light makes its way through the filthy, cracked windows…the air is heavy, oppressive.

And the children…there must be at least twenty-five of them, all different ages, and five or so women holding babies. I work hard at staying non-judgmental and unafraid, trying not to be appalled at the number of abandoned kids. I keep telling myself that everyone here is working through something important. I hold on to my medicine pouch.

I walk over to the far wall where there are maybe a dozen handmade wooden cribs, really more like mangers. I slowly pass by each one and see the next generation of Hawaii gurgling, screaming, clenching their fists, coughing, and smiling. There are no toys to be found, no butterfly mobiles, no Babar books or Dr. Seuss. Sometimes there are two or three infants jammed together in a crib.

This is the sort of thing I imagine befalls another country...not the United States, the land of plenty. I wonder why the state of Hawaii doesn't intervene with funding. Then I get it that this is the downside of being independent of the state. These are a proud people who choose to live beyond what's best and worst about the United States government.

I see chaotic shelves of diapers that are crumpled up but clean...sort of. There is one changing table and a couple of half-empty bottles of disinfectant. There are no cleaning cloths to be found, just a few rolls of thin paper towels.

Kaimana stands in the center of the room holding a set of chimes. He raises the instrument high and strikes each chime one by one. To my amazement the frequencies calm the room, and the raucous din begins to quiet. Babies stand up and peer between the wooden slats. Toddlers quit pounding their sticks on the dirt floor and gaze in fascination at Kaimana.

I open several windows, but there aren't any screens and there certainly isn't bug spray anywhere, so I have no choice but to close them. I make my way back down the row of cribs, this time making eye contact, touching little hands. One frail looking infant reaches up to me, so I pick her up and hold her deep into my chest, the way my sweet

Jess does it. I feel my own tears coming, so I turn away from everyone and take a moment.

I invoke Quan Yin again, gather myself, and watch Kaimana work his magic. His powerful frame becomes the picture of gentleness as he moves from one child to another, rubbing salves into little backs and dropping tinctures in hungry mouths. Still carrying the baby, I walk up behind him and I ask how I can help.

"Just love them as much as you can, just as you are doing," he tells me. "This is what heals them." Then he turns and blows deep into the belly of a sick child...just like he did with the baby seal.

And so for the next few hours I hold these love-starved beauties as close to my soul as I am able. I sing little lullabies and they smile. "You're so pretty!" I tell them as they suck on my fingers. "You're such a sweet, strong boy," I say, picking dried-on food off dirty tee shirts with my fingernails. "You're so loved! Yes you are! Yes you are!"

One of the young women is holding a preemie so tiny it's amazing he's alive. I ask her to tell me the babies' names.

"No names, just numbers," she tells me, and points to the scribbles on the side of the cribs.

My heart sinks. I am dumbfounded. I pick up Number 19 and hold his little torso against my chest. "Let's see," I tell him, looking into his deep set eyes and broad grin. "I believe your name is 'Full of Joy.' How do you do, Full of Joy?"

He pumps his fists in the air and gurgles.

"And you?" I say holding Number 13, whose face is covered with an aubergine birthmark. "I believe you are 'Makes the Day More Beautiful.'"

Giggle, giggle.

I continue down the line doling out identities like teething biscuits, and the ritual seems to be quite popular. Not to mention empowering.

"Oh, Number 24," I say, smelling a very dirty diaper, "you must be 'Poops in His Pants.'" This does not go over well, and I have unleashed a flood of tears and wails from this little brother. I clean him up and try to make amends, saying, "Okay, now that you are spic and span I pronounce you 'Makes the Sun Rise.' How's that?"

Again with the crying! And now others are joining in the chorus.

Wow, this next one better be good! "Well, then, how about 'Brings Smiles Wherever He Goes'?"

Eureka, I have found it! He wiggles his toes and flashes a one-toothed grin into my worried face.

I continue to walk the aisles, introducing myself and bestowing names. She Shines Like the Sun. She Overcomes Her Fears. He Carries Wisdom Within. Twilight Wind Rider. Heart of a Flower. Love Warrior. Full of Grace. Spirit of the Rain. I'm having the time of my life, and I can see by their ebullient, lit-up little mugs that they are too! I could happily spend my life in this nursery wiping bottoms and holding little heartbeats next to mine.

I feed a group of toddlers some kind of pablum, and they wolf it down. There are only a half dozen dishes and spoons, but we make do. I'm elated and full of energy as I become the earth mother of this rainforest nursery. I do the dishes, wash some diapers, and lay down some fresh cloths as sheets. I can't seem to stop singing.

Kaimana motions that it's time to pack up and go. As we say our good-byes, most everyone speaks some version of Pacific Island-ese, but a few manage some pigeon English. I hear, "See you bumbai," "Tanks 'eh," and, "You au-right." Many stand at the gate as we pull out. One of the women from the orphanage waves good-bye, holding 'Her Courage Shines Through' in her ample islander arms. I am floating on a wave of serotonin.

A MILE AND A HALF down the road, Kaimana pulls the jeep to the side of the road in front of a small cottage.

"This is the home of Akahi," he tells me.

I can hardly contain myself, but try to maintain a respectful calm. "What an honor it will be to meet him," I manage.

"I understand. Please wait here a moment." He walks up the narrow stone walkway, knocks on the door, and goes inside.

A few moments later he returns, and touches my hand softly as he says, "I'm sorry, Kate. Akahi is not able to entertain guests this afternoon. He asked me to tell you he hopes to meet you another day."

"I'm so sorry he's not well. Is there anything we can do to help?"

"That is very kind of you, Kate. Akahi is not ill. He is a very old man, and much of the time he chooses to be alone."

Kaimana starts up the jeep, but just then a frail-looking gentleman appears at the front of the cottage.

"Wait," I say, and open the car door. Slowly I walk up to Akahi...and bow.

His face looks tired, but the eyes...well...his eyes are brimming with magic and mischief. He smiles, and that is enough.

THE RAIN BEGINS AGAIN, and Kaimana and I ride in silence, full of the sounds and smells and heartache and joy of the day.

The trip back is long, and we are both tired. Back at Kaimana's house we embrace again, but this time we linger. The warmth from our united bodies is overpowering. My mouth is next to his neck, and it would take such a small move to press my lips into his beautiful skin. I feel his breath against my ear, his strong heartbeat against my flesh. "Stay with me," it murmurs with each beat. I want to kiss his heart. I want him to kiss my eyes.

"Mahalo, for this day," I whisper, not wanting to leave his embrace.

"Mahalo for your love and kindness."

We move our bodies away from one another, but something does not separate...we have connected too deeply. We stand in the silence a moment longer, but when he doesn't say the words I feel, I slowly head toward the gate.

"I will not be seeing clients tomorrow, so you will have a day off," he says.

Even so, I have a sense that he wants me to come around anyway. Why won't he say something personal? Why won't he take the risk when I know it will be the most amazing healing either one of us could ever experience?

It took a lot for me to get to where I am now, to be ready to say yes to myself—let alone to believe he could ever feel as I do. But I know now that I am not in this passion and longing alone. I know it.

PART TWO

"LOVERS DON'T FINALLY MEET SOMEWHERE.
THEY'RE IN EACH OTHER ALL ALONG."

—RUMI

27

THE KISS THAT MADE PELE PUCKER

I've been tossing all night. It's daybreak, and uncontrollable desire is coursing through my blood and bones. I simply cannot contain it anymore. What I feel must be expressed, no matter what his response is.

I wrap the silk sarong around me, shivering as it brushes against my naked skin, and make my way down the path. The air is soft and warm and smells like honey. Or is that the fragrance my body emits when it's dreaming of love?

I knock on the door...no answer. I think he is still asleep, so I boldly turn the handle and walk back to his room. He's so peaceful lying there within the sheets. I am overcome with tenderness, caring. I don't remember a time when I was so completely overtaken by emotions like this. The intensity dissolves my fears…and I touch his face. He opens his eyes, half asleep at first, but then he smiles warmly. I open the covers and climb in next to him. He doesn't move. I pull him closer and begin to kiss him on his neck and cheeks.

"No, I cannot," he whispers, shaking his head. "It would not be right. "

But I don't believe his voice. I look up at him, and for the first time his eyes are uncertain…he's not good at lying.

I take another risk. "I have thought about it a lot, and in my heart I know it's right."

"I cannot be your teacher and your lover."

"Why not? You said we both have a lot to learn. Why can't we rewrite the rules and be everything to each other?"

I kiss his eyes while he remains still. I know he's trying to make this right. I kiss his lips but he remains inanimate. Then I stop, because I can be confident this way for only so long, and he's staring at me with such torment in his eyes that I'm starting to doubt my intuition.

When he speaks, it's the voice of a much younger man. "I honestly do not know…."

Finally!

"I want you, Kate. But I do not want to hurt you. I am frightened."

"I'm afraid, too. But I'm more afraid of not letting myself feel the love I have for you."

Kaimana turns away, and I feel the breath sucked out of my lungs. Then suddenly he turns back and sweeps me up in his arms.

And so it begins...a kiss so long and deep I lose all contact with the known world. It is a kiss that has everything, softness and sting, movement and serenity, wetness and a touch of fear. This kiss tangos us into the outer spheres.

Kaimana's hands ask me to let him in further and I do. Everything is opening in me like a teenage girl who has just been pinned. Or like a pink blossom...like Makalapua. My cheeks are flushed and he eats them like apples. My neck is a coiling white cobra hissing feverishly, "Come closer...closer!" I am a woman I read about in a story I dreamed of writing but couldn't find the words. She is fierce and yielding, attuned to the flow of life, not needing to prove anything, just following her intuition. I am aware that something in Kaimana wants to free me, and I want nothing less, because in that freeing I know I will come into my wildness. As the sun rises from the east, reaching high in the sky toward its destination on the far horizon, we roll over each other again and again, two untethered creatures floating high above the bed...two bodies, two souls, in one ever changing, never ending kiss.

This kiss reaches beyond touch or feeling. It is as if we have been kissing for lifetimes, under the Pacific, through the rainforests, over the deserts, in the Himalayas, on top of glaciers, in a distant marketplace. We are meeting beyond time and space into the void of eternity. No, beyond eternity. This one kiss would awaken Athena and undo Cleopatra. Kick Madonna in the ass and make Rhianna quiver. It would reach through death and seduce Liz Taylor into coming back again. It could birth a child, stop all wars, rekindle gratitude, take a moment's rest and begin hungrily, wholeheartedly, all over again. This kiss, our kiss, would nourish the world.

28

LOVE LOVES ME

We both need air after such entwining! I walk to the backyard and Kaimana goes to prepare some food. He brings me a veritable banquet on one small tray, and we eat papayas and smile a lot. Again I am pulled into his amber eyes. I feel captivated and unnerved. I attempt to gather myself by collecting the dishes to take inside. One by one he removes them from my arms and sets them down on the table. He takes my hand.

"This is the time the turtles will come near the shore. Would you like to meet them?"

"I would."

The sun is descending to the ocean in a dusky blue. We see many turtles in the distance, out at the end of the reef.

"Can we get closer?"

My lover—yes, the word tastes delicious in my mouth—takes my hand and we wade in, slowly finding our way over the polished stones and shells on the ocean floor. There are great flourishes of yellow tang, blue parrot fish, and angel fish. They swirl around us and kiss our legs.

Kaimana points toward the incoming waves. "Look, here comes one of the turtles to greet us."

We wade in up to our shoulders and wait, just long enough for me to be astonished at my lack of fear in the deep water. My medicine man's medicine never ceases to amaze me. My bravery is soon rewarded when a mother turtle and her baby paddle over to us. They bob in the waves and stare and bob and stare.

I just seem to cry all the time now, just a few long tears, nothing dramatic. Soon the turtles swim away and we wade back to shallower water, our clothes clinging to us. The air is cooler now. The palm trees are swaying in the gentle wind. Everything feels erotic against my skin.

Kaimana rests his forehead against mine, his hands gently on my cheeks. "I have dreamed of making love to you for so many nights. Have you had a dream like this, too?"

"In technicolor," I whisper.

He kisses me softly on my forehead. I feel small and delicate next to his masculine stature. My blood surges in my veins as he lowers his mouth deep into mine. In an instant we are in a dance like two dragonflies merging, struggling in the water with the weight of our clothes...until we surrender. He unties the knot of my silk sarong and opens it easily. Praise be to the genius of easy-off apparel!

Kaimana places his hot hands on my hips and pulls me into him. I unbutton his jeans and attempt to pull them down. They weigh a ton. We start laughing from the seeming futility of it all, but finally we are naked. We just stand and hold each other. My racing heart begins to settle down as I notice a feeling I have not felt with a man in a very long time...or maybe ever. I feel safe.

We lie down in the glistening surf, and for a while we just kiss. I feel his gratitude for me and I return it wholeheartedly. He kisses my breasts and traces the veins of my neck with his inquisitive fingers. I arch my back and let him consume me.

We move slowly into each other, seeking to discover our different desires in plain sight. I travel through his eyes down to a silent lake where I am so at peace that even my breath becomes still. I don't need to breathe because he is breathing me. I close my eyes and we are connected to another source, and it pours through us in waves of ecstasy and bliss. When I open them again the sky is so close I can touch it. Actually, there is no separation. I am the sky.

After what seems like hours and hours—maybe more like days—we rest. There is so much to learn, so many different destinations to sail to, and we are on course toward all of them.

And then later we are on his bed swimming in each other again, diving into the infinite wetness of our love.

"Makalapua, Makalapua," he chants into my vibrating body. "I don't know where I leave off and you begin."

Yes, darling Kaimana. Yes.

29

THE PAPAYA AND I
ARE ONE

I wake up after daybreak, alone in his large, warm bed with sheets the color of the earth. His body is not there, but I outline the place where it has been with my hand, and then slide over and feel the place where his warmth still clings to the sheets. I get so turned on I embarrass myself. Get up, woman! Put on some clothes! Comb your fingers through your unruly hair! Get that stuff out of your eyes! Find him.

There is a mug of mocha java waiting for me on the marble counter. From the window draped with bougainvillea and white geraniums I can see Kaimana sitting cross-legged on the beach, in the shade of a gigantic palm tree. He's probably meditating. I know not to intrude, so I sip my turbo brew and take him in from afar. His elegance is leveling. Kanoa lays at his side and the teal waves shatter against the cliffs, much bigger than yesterday.

Kaimana picks up on me and waves for me to join him. I walk out into the morning sun, and it dawns on me that there could be a downside to being with someone so psychic. The no-privacy thing versus the secretive psyche. I start to sit down next to him, but he takes hold of my arm to stop me, uncrosses his legs, and motions me to sit in the newly opened space in front of him. I love the proximity, and rest my back against his smooth, warm chest. We close our eyes and breathe into the wind.

"Every thought blows by like a leaf in the wind. You do not care," he tells me, and before too long I don't. Now, with my mind that's a miracle.

We stay like this until the sun is mid-heaven. It feels good to build spiritual bridges to each other.

He breaks the long silence. "There are many ways to meditate. Would you like me to teach you? I would enjoy that very much."

"Yes. Teach me everything you know," I say, turning to kiss his luscious mouth. "God knows I need it. If I go home feeling peaceful, then I can impart that same quiet serenity to my patients. What a gift that would be." A new feeling washes over me. Sadness.

"Stay here," he says, then gets up and walks across the beach to a cluster of flowering bushes and fruit trees.

At first I think he is asking me to stay and not go back to the mainland, and the sadness blows away. I am thrilled—but then I realize I'm projecting once again.

He returns with a couple of papayas. "We will do a papaya meditation."

"We will?"

"This is a meditation about being in the present and feeling oneness with all of life." He looks at me to see if I'm really getting it.

"I get it! I get it!"

"This is a teaching from Thich Nhat Hanh. He is a Vietnamese monk, and a great teacher and poet."

First he tells me to hold the papaya in my hands, in silence, and look deeply into its color and shape, its textures. I take in everything about it. I sniff it. I notice the flecks of oranges and greens that converge in one spot. I quiet down.

"Now take a moment and think about the history of this papaya."

I spend some time ruminating.

"Close your eyes and feel the hands of the one who picked the papaya. Feel the energy of his hands on the papaya as he plucks it from the tree."

I picture those hands. I also picture Kaimana's hands peeling this soft-skinned fruit and feeding it to me in his big ass bed. Calm down, Katherine.

"Every part of our world is in that papaya tree...the clouds, the rain, the sun, the bark of the tree...."

You, me, bee, tree. I feel the juicy universe and breathe into the fragrance.

"Now close your eyes and feel your hands on the papaya," he says. "How does it feel?"

"I feel humbled by the universe inside this papaya. And grateful."

"Very good, Kate. Now taste the fruit...really taste it. Savor it."

I take a bite of the fruit and feel the soft flesh filling every corner of my mouth. I am aware of what a different experience this is, the connection I feel to the papaya and to every being in turn connected to it, and how it all works together. Then I place the fruit against my heart so it will hold all the love that I am feeling. "My heart and the papaya are one," I whisper.

"Together, we are caretakers of the earth," he adds.

So beautiful.

We relax deeper into the silence, my head resting against Kaimana's chest. Kanoa's head rests against my hip. I look at his light eyelashes and velvet snout. The little pink dude knows relaxation inside and out.

30

YOB YUM-YUM

I have practically moved in, and everything is drifting along like we've been together for centuries. If there could be snapshots of us they would look like this: Here we are lying naked in the backyard taking in the sun; there we are naked snorkeling out by the black rocks; in this one we're naked bathing outside under the open-air shower perched under the thick leafy foliage. Everything—ferns, palms, Norfolk pine trees—are green down to their core and proud of it! And in case I have not expressed myself clearly enough, we are as free as animals...bare, unconcealed, innocent in our skins.

I stand washing my hair and the rest of me in coconut and pikaki flower essences that Kaimana blended with a little olive oil, every inch of me drenched in this incredible fragrance—again. This morning I was lathered and kissed into making love all over again. Just ten minutes ago I was astride Kaimana—again—who was sitting on the ledge of a lava rock. We were face to face. So much emotion passed between us that I began to howl.

Ah-ha! So this is where the word "haole" comes from!

That position, he told me, is called Yob Yum, and oh, it is yummy! I put my head back and let a gentle waterfall from the overhead rocks tumble onto my face. I climaxed again and again. There were sounds coming out of me I didn't recognize. I became a siren floating in an ocean of ecstasy, a young female pup in her first heat, a sex slave who has broken free to be with her true love. I recognized, too, my teenage self, Kathy, who was so angry and heartbroken when we met in my shamanic journey. I felt her rising up in me participating with joy and unbridled candor.

I relive the ecstasy of it all as the shower water gently washes the lather down my back, my ass, my thighs. I turn and watch Kaimana ringing out his long, thick hair. I find his comb and take over. His hair is black and glossy in the sunlight, and I let the cool strands fall on my arms and hands. Later I will make many braids and weave in a feather.

Again I feel I am in the presence of an ancient warrior. I don't know why I feel this, but I do. Maybe it's the books I've been reading, lying in his arms in our mid-day naptime. I find these stories of reincarnation, shape shifting, practical magic, sacred civilizations, and other unfamiliar notions strangely compelling. There's no doubt about it, I am under a powerful spell.

"Do you think a place like Lemuria really existed?" I ask. "That a civilization existed...or actually thrived, where women ruled benevolently, where there was no competition or wars, and where everyone was treated equally?"

Kaimana turns around and wraps a long strand of his wet hair around my neck, pulling me closer. "This cove is the gateway to Lemuria," he says with conviction. "Most people are afraid to believe it. They cannot imagine that a land so loving can exist. I feel it is part of my mission to show them that this is not only possible, it is right here. This is Lemuria. It is so simple. All you have to do is be kind and loving. That is all that matters."

I kiss his beautiful eyes.

IT'S AFTER MIDNIGHT. I feel I can be and do anything and he will accept me. I watch him sleep, then raise his hand to my lips, secretly hoping he will wake up and we can begin making love all over again.

He picks up on my vibes and opens his eyes. "Tell me what is on your mind, my darling."

"Well...maybe it would be better if I used the Hawaiian words...if only I knew them."

"Is that right?" Kaimana grins. "Why not show me what you would like to know."

"Great souls think alike," I tell him, letting my finger travel slowly from his mouth, past his chin, down the middle of his chest and across the center of his flat belly.

"You awaken my entire kino," he breathes, "from the top of my head to the soles of my feet." With a feather-light touch he traces the outline of my mouth with his thumb, and whispers, "Waha."

I close my eyes and repeat, "Waha." I don't remember my mouth ever feeling this delicious.

"May I kiss your perfect lehelehe?"

"Oui, monsieur," I whisper back, and I'm delighted when he kisses my lips like they are fragile petals from one of his precious hibiscus flowers.

"May I have your tongue? Your alelo?" he teases, licking his abundant lips.

"Uh-huh." Ohhhhhhhh. I move his hands down to my breasts.

"Your pu`uwaiu are so full and beautiful."

"They await your teeth, kind sir." I am swooning now. And bitten. "And, prithee, what is the word for heart?" I ask, turning toward his chest.

"Pu'uwai."

"Pu'uwai, you have made me feel alive," I tell his heart, kissing it deeply.

I feel Kaimana's heartbeat quickening, his body restless. He rises up and over me, and I melt into the pillows as his mouth travels down.

He licks my right hip, then the left. "Such gorgeous papakole. So curvy. So raucous."

"Mahalo," I quiver.

He's headed toward my dangerous ass. "Lemu," he whispers between licks. "Lemu...."

My body wants to buck like a wild mare. I turn to him and kiss his chest, his strong belly, his powerful thighs, and then look up and meet his eyes. "And this?" I ask as I disappear between his legs, rest my face in the warm flesh of his thighs, and slide his cock into my mouth.

"Ule!!!" He yells out. "Ule!"

"Ah, yes...ule," I say between strokes.

"Oh, now you are asking for it," he asserts in a hungry voice. Amid ferocious moans his long body coils and uncoils until his waha finds its way down between my legs. "Now I am going to devour your peo, centimeter," slurp! "by centimeter."

We both enter a place that's wild and deep, beyond words in any language. Then his eyes find mine again, and I inhale a deep breath of him and abandon myself completely as he enters me.

The rest shall be censored.

IT'S THE MIDDLE OF THE NIGHT and Kaimana is sound asleep. I know I should get some rest, too, but I can't.

Instead I take a turn for the worse. In the dark I give in to my insatiable curiosity, and untie his medicine bag and take out his little treasures. It's not that different from what I pictured—except for the wedding band. Here is the other shoe dropping, and my lustful bliss turns to icy dread. Soon I will find out that he is secretly married, that he has been lying to control and manipulate me. I will wake up tomorrow with his wife at the door with their tiny infant son.

The other, wiser, newly emerged side of me counters. "No, Katherine, you're wrong. Not this time! Not this man!"

Kaimana turns over and I quickly cinch up his medicine bag. Dammit, Katherine. What is the matter with you!

I go to the kitchen to get some water out of the refrigerator, and spot that coconut cream pie that he and I created earlier this evening. I cut myself a hefty wedge. Guilty eating...I've done it my whole life. As I work the silky lusciousness around in my mouth I start to fantasize about other ways it could be put to good use. Me and the slab head for the bedroom.

Slowly I apply dabs of cashew cream and coconut custard on Kaimana's neck and collarbone. I take a nibble. Kaimana sleeps on. I take a long lick and then I cannot stop. I layer the pie on his nipples and down his muscular arms. His body shakes and I realize he is laughing in his sleep. Or is he? I look up and he smears a handful of coconut goo on my nose, down my chin, through my sternum and all the way down to my hips. His tongue cleans up my sternum area and starts the long journey down. I am in hog heaven!

Sorry, Kanoa.

31

WHAT'S IN
YOUR MEDICINE BAG?

"I've got something to tell you that's bothering me," I admit, looking away from his intense eyes. They are almost yellow in the morning light.

He takes my face in his loving hands.

"Can it really be that bad?"

"It's bad. I know how important your medicine pouch is to you—how private it is." Sigh. Grovel. "My curiosity got the best of me and I uncinched it and looked inside."

"Oh, my Lord, is that what you are upset about?"

"Well, I touched those sacred pieces that mean so much to you. I didn't respect your space."

"Actually, I was thinking of showing you my medicine anyway."

Oh, I know your medicine intimately, darling one. "Really. You don't feel like I betrayed your trust?"

"Katie, you are very tough on yourself. I trust that you were curious about who you have been revealing yourself to so fearlessly. In your own way you were taking care of yourself."

Kaimana gets out of bed and his beautiful nakedness crosses in front of my hungry eyes. He sits down next to me, medicine bag in hand. "The pouch itself is made from deerskin given to me by my teacher, as I have told you. It was given to him from his teacher.

"This pink stone is kunzite, just like yours. It comes from Lemuria. I found it on the ocean floor about two hundred feet out. When I hold it in my hand it helps me remember to love without judgment, unconditionally, as we did in the old days when this land was known as the Lemurian Triangle."

Next he takes out the object of my biggest fears. "This ring is my mother's wedding band. She gave it to me when I left, so that I could keep her close to me."

I feel a wave of relief. I start to tell him of my stupid insecurity, but decide to keep silent.

"The last part of my medicine is in this tiny silver vial. I blended several essences that the ancient warriors depended on to dispel death. They bring me safety when I am faced with danger."

One by one he places the items back in the pouch. "So...the stone helps me to stay connected to my true home. The ring reminds me that I have been well loved. The medicine vial carries my survival." He turns to me. "I await something of yours."

"That's so lovely, Kaimana. I'm beginning to feel the importance of ritual and ceremony now, the power of the ancient ways. But what can I give you that holds that kind of meaning?"

"Well, let's see," he says, running his finger over my mouth. "Why don't you place a kiss from your life-giving lips against the pouch, and add your love and blessings to its contents?"

"Really?" I say lifting the light satchel.

"That way I can carry your love and strength with me for protection." Then he adds with a smile, "...and forever feel you kissing me."

I breathe deeply, bring the pouch to my lips, and with a very, very long kiss I pour my heart and soul into that bag.

WE SIT ON THE BEACH in silence, watching the layers of mauve and turquoise that paint the horizon grow deeper with the setting sun. We've made love a gazillion times, and we're both exhausted and completely, utterly at peace. My cells are in the process of integrating the endless ocean of love I've been swimming in with what I know to be true in the world. I think of Lani Lanakila, and the suffering and loss that has touched those people so deeply. Even so, it took so little kindness to make their faces light up with joy. I imagine making medicine bags for all the little ones. I envision their little necks encircled with little pouches that carry shells and beads and healing stones. In the middle of my fantasy Kaimana enters the scene. With their smiles and bright-eyed attention it becomes obvious that he is their true medicine bag.

"You know, my darling," I tell him, rubbing his formidable bronze shoulders, "those kids in the tent city have so little to inspire them. They are *so* lucky to have you. I wish kids everywhere could learn from you. Couldn't we just clone you?"

"How do you know that I cannot be in many places at once?" he says, grinning mischievously. "Soon, if you wish, we will invoke your magical shape-shifting power, too. That is, if you are interested."

A shape-shifting gynecologist. I fantasize traveling incognito around the world....

Why not? I already feel the magic moving though me.

32

THE TRICK IS STAYING
IN THE PRESENT MOMENT

I've finally made it back to Barb's. It's tough leaving the King of Kissers. This little house and everything in it have changed for me. I feel so full of love and gratitude that I'm walking around the place thanking the peeling paint, the dirty old rugs, the ceiling fan covered with dust. I no longer see them as negatives, just part of the gift of this whole experience. There was a time when I would have been utterly cynical about this sort of idyllic romanticism. But today I am overjoyed.

For the first time in three days I check in with my service. There is some disheartening news about Beth Wheeler, who I've been working with for ten years. She's been cancer-free for four years, but now the tumors have returned with a vengeance. I don't know what the next steps will be. I don't know what to tell her beyond what her oncologist has already said. What I really want to tell her is that she needs to see this shaman I know....

A new development: My Jess called to tell me she's been feeling sick with some kind of horrifying bronchial thing, and it has her feeling way too depressed. She's booked a flight home, may even be staying for good, and can't decide if she's more disappointed or relieved. I am thrilled. Nothing would make me happier than to have her work with me in my practice again like she did before she left. The Jamison girls were the best OB-GYN M.D.-R.N. team in San Francisco. What a joy that was, and a huge weight off my back. My patients eat her up like she's the center of a piece of chocolate volcano cake....they can't get enough of her rich, warm sweetness. Me neither.

But as I entertain the scenario of having Jess back in the picture, I have a hard time focusing on San Francisco. The notion of where my home really is seems to be shifting every day. At this point I'm not at all sure what I want, how much I have to give, or where I want to give it.

Max meets me in the bathroom and hangs out while I soak in some fragrant oils that Kaimana has gifted me.

"It's just you and me tonight, kiddo. My medicine man wanted me to stay, but I thought I should come back and be with you, you handsome thing, you...."

Max skitters up the side of the wall and then down onto the rim of the tub. I squirm a little. I like the guy, and all, but do I really want him to go rafting on my naked shoulder?

"Whoa, that's good right there, buddy," I tell him.

He complies. I feel he is a bit disheartened. Up close I realize he also looks a little under the weather. Man, I can really project my stuff, can't I?

Sleeping alone sucks. Not having Kaimana's body next to me is a shock to my nervous system. I've become used to so much touch and ecstasy that I've turned into a kind of heathen brat. It's only been two weeks since I first approached him on the beach, but it feels like eons, and already I can't imagine being without him. That's why I chose to come home to my little cottage—I needed to know that I could. Fine. I did it. Now I have to figure out how to go back to San Francisco and face the end of my marriage.

I flash on the last time I had sex with David, and cringe. Not that I wasn't sexually turned on. Hard as it is to imagine it now, my brain remembers that in some odd way I was. But even then I knew I was part of something that was no longer right. It's like what my inner teenager said...it's the prostitute thing, big time. My rationale used to be that if I didn't spread my legs and like it, he would leave. What's different now is that I don't give a damn.

And let us not forget the hundreds of patients who are into me like white on rice. And whose fault is that, pray tell, oh wise woman of the Western world?

Never mind. I have two weeks left in paradise, and I am going to let myself be as happy and fulfilled as I deserve to be. Then I will face the music.

33

LET ME TELL YOU, THIS IS NOTHING LIKE PACIFIC GENERAL

Kaimana and I sit under one of his flowering trees eating fresh taro chips and guacamole. The lemonade I made from fresh picked lemons is very tart.

"Man, this is desperately in need of some honey. I'll get some from the house."

I stand up, but Kaimana gently stops me.

"Hold still," he directs. "Do not move."

I feel the sear of the bite before he can get the animal off of me. He flicks away a small, purple-blue centipede, who skitters into the rocks.

"Is that what I think it is?" I say, holding my face.

"She is a poisonous centipede. We must tend to the bite right away. Come."

He picks me up in his arms and walks quickly to the healing room, then lays me out on the divan. He pulls out a small knife.

"I have to do this. The pain will be over quickly. You trust me?"

"Do it!" I half yell because the pain is already unbearable.

He makes a small incision then places his mouth on my cheek and sucks the poison out, then quickly spits it onto the floor. Then he takes a deep breath and places his mouth against my cheek again, but this time he blows deeply into the wound.

My cheek has a heartbeat all its own. I'm not that good with pain, but I fake it.

Kaimana rubs his hands together and blows into them. "We must heal this now or there will be a scar."

I nod for him to go ahead.

He points one hand up above his head and closes his eyes to pray. Moments later he places his thumb and index finger on both sides of the wound to close it. With his other hand he spits on his finger and layers the spit over the open wound several times, like he is suturing it shut. Then he holds my face between both hands while he chants.

"Now you must rest," he tells me. Silently he exits the room and closes the door behind him.

I still have the willies from seeing that centipede. And watching Kaimana suck poison out of my face seriously made me want to puke. Other than that I feel fine. In fact, I'm feeling so good I fall asleep. When I wake up I run my finger down my cheek and feel absolutely nothing. I get up and look in the bathroom mirror where I find the same face as always.

It occurs to me that I have now been kissed not only by a phoenix and a scorpio, but by a centipede as well. That's some serious island medicine.

34

MAX MEETS HIS
MAKER

D ays go by, and I return once again to my second
home, ready to give Max a sum-up. I search
everywhere but can't find him. Usually he shows
up in plain sight as soon as I come through the door. I
laugh out loud when I feel myself panicking. I pick up my
pace and a flashlight and look under the bed and chest of
drawers, behind the refrigerator, inside the kitchen
cabinets. Finally I remember how often I have found him
in the shower.

"Max," I call out, "where are you?"

I pull back the shower curtain and find him lying on
his back with a little puddle of orange liquid next to his

neck. I bend down and gently nudge him with my finger. He moves slightly.

"Max! Max...what can I do?"

His antenna moves a bit and then collapses.

"Oh no," I sigh helplessly. "I don't know what I'm supposed to do."

I gently pick up his seemingly weightless body and balance it in the palm of my left hand. I cup my right hand over his fragile frame and picture healing light descending into his body. I can't think of any words to say that seem appropriate, so I keep my mouth shut. It feels like there's hardly any energy in his body.

Through tears, I manage to get out, "Thank you so much for staying with me."

Finally I realize the truth and say it. "I love you."

For a moment he raises his legs and scrambles as if he is running away from death, but minutes later the universe claims him. I'm flabbergasted. I sit down on the bathroom floor and stare at his vacant body. What I found so abhorrent when I first arrived now seems like a work of art. Close up he is beautiful shades of browns, gold, and rust. His head and his spike-haired legs look delicate, pulled toward his belly like he's going back into the womb.

I remember seeing an empty little gift box on the bedroom floor. I wrap Max in Kleenex.... "Wait, what am I doing? You wouldn't want this! You'd want to feel the moist red earth of Hawaii absorbing your body."

I dig a deep hole under the black rocks by the edge of the beach and place a circle of shells around the spot where he lies so I can come and talk to him, let him know how things are going...so I can thank him again and again for the comfort and solace he brought to a lonely gynecologist, and how her heart calmed down because of it.

35

HULA HEAVEN, OTHER LIVES, AND EDIBLE PARTS

J ust one more week before it's time for me to leave. Leave. I want to run from any such notion. Kaimana has put the word out that he won't be seeing patients for a few days, so he and I will be able to spend more time together.

We reinvent the art of savoring every moment. We eat well, go for a drive, sleep for long stretches, make love in every position known to humanity, and probably to nonhuman animals too! In between I am given a mani and pedi with an all-natural nail file that is really a shell. My soles are treated to a massage of kukui nut and coconut oils. And for three days in a row I luxuriate in baths that have gardenias floating on the surface. Kaimana has sensed my loss over Max and is filling me with life.

Tonight he is treating me to his rendition of a hula dance and "talk story" of Hawaii. We have scattered candles on window sills, on tables, and on the floor of the healing room. The sun has retreated, and the sky is ablaze with pink and purple cloud striations that cast their veil through the open windows.

Kaimana cues me, and I turn on the traditional Hawaiian music. I quickly seat myself on a pillow on the floor. He appears wearing what seems to be a ceremonial loin cloth, a minimal covering that, when he turns gracefully, shows off his gorgeous lemu. Oh, baby.... The lei around his neck is lush green, set off perfectly against the glistening skin of his perspiring neck and cheeks.

I don't know how else to say it...this man becomes whatever he loves. With closed eyes and arms outstretched he embodies the emotions of the islands. I don't need to know what is happening because he becomes the passion and the beauty. That's all I care about. I am drinking in a moving prayer and the maker is my sleek love. Each of his flowing movements teaches me once more that we are at one with the earth, the animals, each other. My mind has only one response: I want to live like this.

After, we gnosh on chilled pineapple and papaya under Jupiter and Venus, who sit like star-crossed lovers in the night sky. I have found out how much I like juicy, slippery food, like papayas...and how much I love feeding them into his sensual lips. We're definitely into each other's mouths big time. Kissing with Kaimana is as powerful as making love. The story-dance of our lips and tongues has become a hula and we are inventing our own tradition, tapping into a history that lies deep in our cells. Loving him has opened me to new belief systems, and I suddenly find myself curious about past lives.

"What do you feel, have we been together before?" I ask, slipping another slice of juicy papaya between his lips.

Kaimana smiles. "Only about a million times."

"Tell me what we've been to each other," I say, fascinated.

"Well," he says, lifting me onto his lap into that glorious yob yum position, "when we sit this way something in me goes back to a time when we were lovers in India. I feel that we spent every possible moment together, but we were not allowed to marry. Your father would not allow it because I was of a much lower caste. We were exquisite lovers, but our pain was great. We lost each other in the end."

I place my hand over my breasts and sternum. "As you say that, I can feel it here in my body."

He kisses my chest.

I feel a deep undercurrent of worry running through me. "Were there others like that, I mean lifetimes where we couldn't be together?"

"Close your eyes and hold on to me, and allow our energies to merge, then see what memories come to you."

"What if I'm just imagining it?"

"You will know the difference."

I realize I'm a little scared entering these waters, like it's against my religion or something. But heck, I don't follow a religion. For a moment I worry I'm getting too far out and won't be able to return to my other life. What exactly is making me panic?

"I don't know how to do this," I tell Kaimana a bit defensively.

"Yes, you do. You are only afraid of how powerful you are. I am right here with you, and I want you to be all that you are by allowing your vastness to lead you. So...close your eyes. Put a movie screen in front of you and see what comes to you. Do not force it. Just breathe and allow the wise woman that you are to track your soul's history with me. Let the screen reveal it. And if nothing comes, so be it."

I look deeply into Kaimana's eyes, half scared of what I will find, and the other half overjoyed with the space he has given me to find the bigger parts of myself.

I close my eyes and a screen appears over to the left. Before I know it I am sitting on a horse next to him, looking out on a red-earth canyon. We are both young men, Native American, I believe. Yes, that feels right. The energy between us is wonderful. We are great friends, and it is our responsibility to look out for the others. I tell Kaimana what I see.

"That feels correct to me. Go on, Kate. Find out more about yourself...and me."

The screen goes dark, and then a new picture evolves. It begins with an endless orange sky. "Now I see us here in Hawaii," I tell him. "We are little."

Kaimana interrupts. "But I am the girl...."

"Yes, that's right, and I'm the boy. I'm a boy, we're swimming in the ocean, just playing and laughing...we're so happy!"

"Are we brother and sister?"

I breathe into myself and see what I get. "Yes. Yes, we are. We swim far out past the reef. I'm getting scared. You hold my hand and pull me along, but I sense danger. There are sharks out here. I'm scared!"

"Do not be scared. The sharks are not paying attention to us. Just send them peaceful energy. Stay calm."

In my vision I feel their massive grey bodies glide past me. I feel one swim toward me, then he comes even closer, eye to eye. I am terrified, but I try to calm my energy, and he takes off. Kaimana and I stay out there playing with the turtles.

I open my eyes. "It feels like we were right here in Seal Cove, doesn't it?"

"That feels right," he agrees. "We were here a very long time ago."

"Wow, do you think I'm really seeing our past lives? Maybe I'm just making it all up. Or maybe that's why I've always been drawn to the Hawaiian culture. But you know, about that caste thing...I can't imagine being higher than you. Maybe sexier...."

Kaimana rolls over and pulls me under him. "I am certainly glad we are not siblings in this life."

I agree. "Or two male warriors."

"Well...we could be homosexual lovers," he murmurs with a smile, between kisses. Then he stops and pretends to give me a serious look. "Or we could simply be two devoted companions who have great respect for one another."

"That's true. But, my darling heterosexual lover-man, I'm pretty crazy about what we right have now."

His eyes light up with the light of all the stars shining on all those many lifetimes.

Incredible kissing will now go on for many hours.

And examining of body parts. For the umpteenth time I revel in how amazing it is that my lover devotes himself to massaging my sexual organs...that he admires and raves about my magnificent vagina, and that he points out the various areas of my body like he's on the greatest adventure of his life. Oh, the pleasure of having been seen in bold daylight after hiding in foggy San Francisco for thirty years! I learn that my skin is abundant with chi and the color and scent of honey, that my legs are powerful like a Lemurian goddess, and that they are long so they can encircle his willing waist. My nipples? Well, he tells me they are innocent, yet so very tantalizing he licks them this way and that. My belly inspires love sonnets. And my hips...to my utter amazement he toasts them for the way they curve like the arc of the crescent moon outside our open window. Every inch of me comes alive to his glorious whispers and to the realization that this form called Kate has made a shaman cry out for more!

Every once in a while amid the revelry, scenes play out in a part of my psyche still stuck in another place. I try not to go there, but there is a young married Kate who can't quite take in this abundance of love. My mind conjures a memory of a wishful me in bed with David, the air thick with that awful feeling of being judged...I had decked myself out in a beautiful new nightgown from a French lingerie shop, and was sitting next to him as he read the sports section of the *New York Times*. I felt pretty, and I wanted him to acknowledge me. He peered out from behind the papers with his bifocals hanging low on his nose.

"That nightie would look pretty in another color, darling. Take it back and see if it comes in black. Black is sexy, and it hides our little mistakes."

I was hurt and furious and crushed, too unconscious to realize David is incapable of loving me just for who I am.

The movie plays on. I remember how I gradually left him in my mind—not walking-out-the-door leaving, but the emotional abandonment kind of leaving. How I would make nasty asides to myself, like, "Oh look, he's got a pimple on his back. Gross!" Or, "It seems like his arms aren't as firm as they used to be. He's really getting flabby as he ages." It was my way of creating little doors so I could leave him temporarily, so I might feel okay about myself and safe around him. But of course I didn't. I did feel shocked at the fear and resentment that lurked inside my heart, and that there was such a nasty bitch hanging around trying to protect me. Why didn't I just say, "It doesn't feel good when you talk to me that way"? Why couldn't I tell him how much he hurt me? Why didn't I try harder and be more courageous?

Be still, Kate. You have tried everything you could think of to try. There was that year of individual therapy, for each of us. And joint therapy, when he could make it home in time, which was maybe five times. Alternative therapies—one with a very intuitive psychic who called him on an affair he was attending to after each session. Then there were the trips to Esalen for couples' "releasing," and the Golden Door Spa. But even when he was lying naked on his belly with a towel over his ass, he could only hold still for short periods of time before he started flirting with the massage therapist. Right in front of me. Just like he did with that blonde bartender at the Four Seasons. Of course, we made plenty of attempts to connect across our gorgeous dining room table...those mostly ended in sighs and futility. And then there was his suggestion that we try an open marriage. That one made me laugh...for days. In my book he'd been living as if it was an open marriage since our second date.

Kate! Stop living in illusion and get on with it. You're just reliving all of this because it takes you out of the moment. You're really worried about leaving *this* man. Just don't start analyzing this. *Please!*

With that bit of badinage I am back on the Balinese bed with this...this...this Eye Full, this spectacular, spiritual sexpot who is plying me with every erotic enticement he can come up with. Again, I let go and am totally inebriated in this bottomless ocean of love.

36

I AM A DOCILE DOLPHIN ENTERING DEEP, DANGEROUS WATERS

As I lie in bed licking the last globs of banana cream pie from my fingers, I notice one of my nipples peeking out of my sarong. "Hello there," I tell this sweet pink face. I never noticed before that my nipples are getting lighter—like baby flesh color—as I get older. Maybe Kaimana has kissed all the color out of them.

Speaking of magic, Kaimana comes down the hallway carrying all kinds of ocean diving paraphernalia. "Come, woman, get up! We are about to enter another realm. You will be filled with ecstasy. *Come!*"

"We're going snorkeling now? It's dark out!" I tell him, my voice choppy with terror.

"It is as smooth as glass out there. We will be able to see everything. Get up! This is unlike anything you have ever experienced before. You might meet a unicorn fish, or a goatfish, or a raccoon butterfly fish! You might even come face to face with a Picasso fish! Just imagine, Kate, how amazing that would be. Come on! I have everything we need—flashlights, fins, face masks. Get up, it is time to get going!"

"But there are all kinds of dangerous fish out there, too. You said yourself there are sharks and eels and sea snakes...."

"I should not have told you that. I frightened you. Do you really think I would lead you into a dangerous situation?" He continues arranging the equipment in two neat configurations, one for him and one for me. "Let me explain what we will do."

And he does. And I feel like I'm going to vomit up that lovely pie. It isn't that I don't trust him. But it's nighttime, for Christ's sake! What if Jaws is out there waiting to munch on one of my baby pink nipples or my well-taken-care-of ass? What if I lose Kaimana and get sucked under by a current and get pulled far away from shore and don't have the energy to swim back? What if I swim into a nest of moray eels and they decide they don't like me much, which I can guarantee they won't. What if my foot gets stuck in seaweed and I can't see the murky bottom enough to extricate myself. What if I die?

I guess my face is taking on a pallor of anticipated doom, because Kaimana stops what he's doing and comes to the rescue. He sits beside me on the bed and takes both of my hands in his. "What are you afraid of, Kate? I will be right there with you."

"I'm afraid I will die, that's what I'm afraid of!"

"I will do everything I know to keep you safe. Everything. I promise. But if something happens and you die, then I will die right there along with you. How does that sound?"

"Hokey. It sounds hokey. Why would you do that? You've got your whole life to live."

"I am not afraid of death. If that is what is to be, I welcome it."

"But I've only just found you. I don't want to lose you."

"What makes you think you will lose me? Besides, most likely there is far more freedom to express love on the other side than here—and in ways we have never even imagined...if that is remotely possible," he adds with that delicious smile of his.

Suddenly it occurs to me that for a woman who has been around death as much as I have, I have given it very little serious thought.

He leans over and kisses me.

"Okay then," he says, surrendering to my neurosis. "You stay here. I will be back very soon. See me having the time of my life. I am just going in up to here." He puts his hand up to his chin.

"Is that all?" I grit my teeth. "Well, hell. Hold on." I'm not sure if it's because I don't want to disappoint him or he's managed to make the whole thing sound more enticing than terrifying. Probably both. Anyway, there's no way I'm sticking around for another piece of pie. "I'm coming with you."

THE MOON IS LYING FLAT on the surface of the ocean and the air is perfectly still. My nervous feet fidget in the wet cool sand as we sit putting on our gear. I can't help but wish I had a waterproof Quan Yin I could wear next to my panicky heart.

I hate wearing a facemask! It feels so tight and claustrophobic, but in order to see under water it's mandatory. I'm getting scared again. Before we put the snorkels in our mouths, I say my final words. "Don't let go of me, okay?"

"I promised you, remember?"

On go the masks and Kaimana takes my hand. We wade into warm water. The air is balmy, the moon is glistening on the surface of the gentlest ocean I have ever seen…it's a lake out here. The truth is I'm actually pretty excited.

The water covers my shoulders. Kaimana points his flashlight down under the water and motions to me that it's time to put our heads under, so I take a deep breath to ground myself and put my face in the water and kick my feet out behind me. The water feels cool against my skull. We float just beneath the surface, letting the occasional tiny wave pull us a little further out.

I feel like I have entered a movie set of an ocean adventure film. Schools of parrotfish pass by my shoulders. Blue tang, yellow tang, and something with an orange face skitters up. Turtles head toward us, peer into our masks, then pedal away. I scream, totally enraptured. We are still in shallow water, drifting gracefully with the soft waves the way anemone float in the currents along the deeper ocean floors.

Dark shadowy movements pull my attention to the left as a dozen or so massive manta rays swim toward us and surround us. These are formidable creatures—their wingspans are at least eighteen feet wide. I squeeze Kaimana's hand. I know mantas are supposed to be a bunch of pussycats, but I could use some serious reassurance.

Kaimana puts his flashlight near his mask so I can see him smiling back at me as if to say, "I know! They are magnificent, are they not?"

I nod as I pray. I can't help it...it feels like they stay with us too long, like perhaps they are interested in a little somethin' somethin'...and then miraculously they turn and flee like black sports cars racing down the final stretch. And then, as if not to be outdone, a gigantic octopus undulates past me. Whoa.

The next wave of excitement moves through. We head out into deeper water, and schools of tiny silver creatures flash by with gigantic groupers bringing up the rear. Great whooshes of energy surge, announcing, "Look at me! Look over here, look here!"

Suddenly Kaimana pulls back hard on my hand telling me we must stop. My heart lurches—if he's stopping, he must have spotted some kind of serious danger. I break the surface and spit out the snorkel, and we both tread water, bobbing in the surf. Twenty feet away looms a huge tiger shark, his eyes shining in the moonlight. That is one big motherfucker. I remember Kaimana's words: *Send positive energy.* I close my eyes and think of the serenity of the bamboo forest. I become bamboo. Finally the shark has had enough of us and turns away.

He glides through the water, but while I can still make out his shadowy shape, something changes. It looks like he's wrestling with something. Oh my God, it's my worst fear—the shark has a seal in his grip and death is in front of me whether I want to deal with it or not! And this time it comes with particular violence. The space around me swirls with blood.

"Kaimana, *I want out now!!*" My voice pierces what is now an eerie silence, and I tug urgently on Kaimana's hand. We turn toward the shore and swim a bit, then feel the ocean floor and walk the rest of the way in.

"Come here," he says, opening his wet arms to me, and I do. "You are safe now. Breathe...."

But I don't feel safe. I feel terrified, invaded, betrayed. Finally we let go of each other and I go in the house to get warm.

Kaimana's way of dealing with it is by practicing chi gong in the backyard next to a sleeping pig. I take a shower because I feel blood on me even though there's nothing there. It seeped into my consciousness and I'm trying to wash it out of my brain via my hair. As hard as I try, I don't understand the scheme of things, why God or whatever created it this way. It makes me angry.

Kaimana knocks on the door and asks to come in. I open it without saying anything.

He sees my distress and rubs my shoulders softly with a towel. "I am so sorry I took you out there. I believed that it would be magical for us. Please forgive me."

"It's not your fault. It's nature's fault.

Long silence. "Seeing the world that way must be very painful for you."

"I don't know how else to see it," I answer, a little startled that I sound as crabby as I feel. "It's the way it is. There's always a perpetrator and there's always a victim."

"If you truly believe that, it will always cause you suffering. I prefer to think that there are no victims. A shark must be a shark, and a seal must be a seal. At an unconscious level, each of us volunteers to experience the life we have chosen, so we can learn our lessons and evolve."

"What does that mean? You think that seal volunteered to be skewered like that?"

"I think there is a lot we do not understand. Perhaps that seal felt honored to be eaten by such a regal animal. Maybe it is part of her karmic destiny to feed another being and then to be rewarded by coming back in another form. I think unconsciously we create all kinds of situations—those that bring joy and those that bring pain. These are not events that are brought upon us by someone or something else. We are not victims. In truth...yes, Kate, I do believe that we volunteer for these challenges."

"Are you telling me that my patients create their own cancer? That women who are raped create that atrocity?" I feel my voice rising to an unattractive pitch. "I can't believe you believe that New Age bullshit."

"It is my belief that we reincarnate to receive the lessons we need, so that we can grow and move on. I know that what you witnessed tonight was horrifying for you, but I am not going to lie about my beliefs to make it okay for you.

"I believe that in our evolutionary process we have been everything—every species, every gender, and every kind of temperament. How else would we learn compassion and forgiveness if we have not walked in different shoes? The problem is that most people do not clean themselves of old emotions. Or they believe that they are unworthy and should be punished, so they unconsciously create negative situations so they can suffer and feel redeemed. Oftentimes they subconsciously volunteer for suffering in order to learn the lessons that suffering can teach, or to resolve what they think was bad karma that they created. I feel that what I went through in my childhood was an expression of what I needed to experience. Of course I did not know that at the time, so I was able to get the lessons my soul needed. I have done a great deal of past-life work, and I have seen lifetimes that I found difficult to accept. But I can tell you this, Kate. I have been the tiger shark and the monk seal, and both experiences are equally important in this journey of ours."

Again I go silent. Pieces of some grand puzzle are moving around inside of me and now I don't know where they fit. It's like someone put my life in a salad bowl and then tossed my beliefs, ideas, philosophies, dreams, fears, and wishes up in the air and now they are cascading all over the floor.

I have nothing positive or hopeful to say. "This doesn't sit well with me. I'm sorry. I think I need to go home."

"Please do not leave like this. I know we can figure out how you can have your beliefs and I can have mine."

"I just need some time alone. I need to figure out my life. I'm going home in less than a week and I'm not who I was. You get to stay here in the life you've always had."

All at once Kaimana's face shifts into sadness. "You do not think my life has changed? You are an integral part of my life now. I do not want you to go, but I stay quiet because I do not want to confuse you even more. Katie," he says in the gentlest voice, "I love you."

The words I have lusted for feel now like fifty-pound weights anchoring my feet to the floor when all I want to do is run. Tears burn beneath my eyelids, and I don't dare let them start to fall. "I have to go. I'll come back tomorrow."

I grab my purse and turn to say something, but I cannot. I close the iron gate, not knowing if I will return.

37

LI'L OL'
CONTROL FREAK ME

'm a basket case—no, a mental case. I pace and pace, with no Max to vent to. Thank God it's time for me to return to San Francisco. I have had my big Hawaiian adventure and it has gotten a little too out-there for me. I need to call the airline right now and get my ticket.

What was I thinking, letting myself fall in love with a medicine man who espouses this uncaring, detached, metaphysical mumbo jumbo? It's true he is a great healer. I saw it, and I get it that that stuff does exist. He knows how to release disease from people. He knows how to make healing remedies. He is an amazing person—but he's just too far out for me. How can he possibly fit into my world? What could I possibly be to him in his world?

First of all, I am nearly ten years older, I dye my hair, my body is sagging and soon he will lose interest. I've seen the statistics a hundred times. Secondly, I have a home in San Francisco that I love, and a dog named Bella who misses me even though she's staying with her favorite sitter and probably hasn't given me one thought. Thirdly, my Jess is coming home and I need to be there for her. Fourthly, I believe in western medicine—after all, my whole life has been about being a medical doctor, and I have derived great joy and meaning from that. Fifthly, I enjoy blaming someone else besides myself for my shitty relationship! Sixthly this relationship is too good to be true, it is destined to fall apart and I won't be able to bear that after being with this kind of love for years and years....

And this incredible bond would go on for years and years because this is true love, isn't it, Katherine? This is you in all your full-blown fear, trying to figure out if you trust that someone has your back, could celebrate your deep femininity, desires to know you, feel you, help you create a life that is "vast," as he would put it.

Yes, this is it. I don't know if I'm strong enough to let this in, even if I did create it....

I call and make a reservation to leave on the eleven a.m. flight. My stomach is churning. If I pace any more I am going to wear a path in Barb's decrepit floor. I take out Lady Val from her medicine cabinet and hold a yellow 5-milligram tab in my hand. I put it on my tongue and then spit it out. I finally sit down and close my eyes. Kaimana's face looms before me, such a loving mirror to look into. I pretend to meditate, but my thoughts are ruthless bastards that pull me in all directions. I wish I could lie down in those lavender fields and bliss out. I wish I could hold that baby monk seal in my arms. I wish I could have the courage to let my life unfold without trying to control everything. I cancel the flight.

38

I MEET MORE OF
MY SELF

The sky is tumultuous, shifting into morning light. I run out to the black rocks where I know I will find him communing with something far sweeter than me. He stands and opens his arms and I see that he has been crying. We embrace into a state of instant forgiveness. And then we go inside and resume our deep, connected love. The combination of our earlier clash and my imminent departure back to the mainland has fueled a fire that burns between us all day and long into the night.

WE HAVE SO LITTLE TIME LEFT, so we pour ourselves into each other and a few of his grateful patients. It doesn't matter whether it's just the two of us or we're seeing patients, no matter what is happening it feels like we are making love.

Our work with patients is different now. He has taught me to stand in front of him while he channels universal healing energy into my body. All I do is close my eyes and place my hands on the patient...and let go. The way he channels is quite enterprising. Yesterday he placed his mouth against the base of my spine and gently blew the healing light into my body. The feeling was inexpressible. On the one hand it was healing, on the other it was full-on erotic. Today he asks me to place my mouth on the stomach of a patient who has what I would diagnose as colitis. So of course I do as he asks, and then he places his mouth on my spine and blows a powerful energy frequency into me. I feel orgasmic, but I control my body and transfer the light coming through my mouth into the patient. Kaimana's lips exude a surging warmth that heats up my spine and sends my hormones soaring! I feel as though my adrenals are waking up, and I find it hard not to swoon and sway. I wonder who is being healed the most—our patient, Kaimana, or me. The patients' responses are stunning. They all seem to be amazed by the depth of healing they experience. If my colleagues could see me now!

With each session, any lingering skepticism I have dissolves a little more. I don't just see the power of these unorthodox methods, I feel their authenticity. I'm beginning to understand how Kaimana and I could work together, merging some of my tradition with some of his. But I will have to speak about illness in a different way— an impermanent way—and lose terms like "stage four," "terminal," and the like, words that are so final that when they enter your belief system they can cause you to die. What a different way to think about healing. It's absolutely thrilling!

After our work each day, Kaimana shows me different ways to let go of any energy I might have taken on that isn't mine. He shows me how to "release the day into the earth," as he calls it, how to picture my cells clearing themselves and returning to a state of harmony, how to check for orphan souls caught in my aura who need to be healed and sent home. There is a richness to these ancient rituals that I mysteriously understand, and at the same time I know I'm entering a new realm of understanding about who I am and my place in the world. There's a vastness inside that I never imagined there could be, and a peacefulness. Most of all I'm discovering a well of compassion and strength I never dreamed I was capable of. I feel blessed and healed in a way that's far beyond the miracles I see in Kaimana's patients. The healer is healing herself, and the miracles are everywhere.

39

MY INTUITION, MY HEARTACHE

Kaimana and I walk hand in hand on the beach, part of an unspoken ritual that's evolved as a way to complete the days we spend with patients. Out past the rocks, he lets go of my hand and shows me how to do what he calls "walking meditation." We move ever so slowly, placing one foot in front of the other, heel to instep to toe. At his encouragement I clear my mind and immerse myself in the present moment. I'm aware of every sensation inside and out...the soles of my feet against the warm sand...the first twinge of hunger in my belly...the breeze against my cheek...the birds hovering above the waves. In this silent state of pure awareness Kaimana and I walk, and after merging and channeling energy all day I'm in a serene and still space inside.

Suddenly I feel a wave of concern about not checking my cell phone messages for a couple of days. I don't even carry my phone with me anymore. My intuition tells me to go back to Barb's and check in. I surprise myself and tell Kaimana I'm actually going to remove myself from his presence for a short while.

He gives me a concerned smile and squeezes my hand. "I hope that whoever is calling you is not in grave danger, Kate. It is good, though, that you receive the call with such clarity."

He's right. A few weeks ago I would have shrugged the feeling off as paranoia. Nice to have someone listening when my intuition speaks.

Within minutes I'm back at the cottage and on the phone, listening to the message I've dreaded for almost twenty years

"Katherine, it's Jerry, David's racing pal. I'm so sorry I have to make this call. David's been in a crash, and they're flying him in from Monaco straight to San Francisco Pacific. He'll be in the I.C.U. there, should arrive in about an hour or so. He shattered his left hip, screwed up his neck, and fucked up his collarbone. Oh, and he broke his right wrist, too. But I think he's going to make it. That David is one lucky son of a bitch. Please call me back and let me know you got this message. I can give you the details when you call."

I sit down on the bed and stare at the floor. Everything is swirling and shifting again. For a moment I can't remember where I am, or maybe I just don't want to. I know I must go home out of duty and be an advocate and good wife because that is who I am. But I also know my heart and newly awakened soul will remain here with Kaimana.

My God, how to face this. After all, I'm the one who sent David away, didn't want him here for my own selfish reasons—reasons that just might break my heart now.

40

WE WILL NEVER
BE SEPARATE AGAIN

I make my reservation for the next morning and pack my suitcase. As I empty the drawer in the nightstand I find the pearl necklace David gave me a few years ago to win some points after one of his flings. I took it off when I arrived here and haven't touched it since. It feels tight around my neck now...but that's impossible.

I take one last look around, and thank the spirit of the house for bringing this new life to me, and ask that it hold a special place for me so that someday I can return. I lock the door behind me, pack up the car, and walk to Kaimana's gate. He stands there waiting...of course he's tuned in to the crisis.

"I have to go," I tell him.

"I know."

We walk into the house.

I tell him what has happened and he rubs my shoulder as I sob, saying, "I don't want to go. I don't want to leave you. I'm not ready."

I kiss him and pull his body into mine. He pauses, and fingers the pearl necklace around my neck. Without asking he puts his warm face against my neck and bites into the pearls. The necklace falls to the floor, pearls scattering in every direction. It's an act of unbridled sovereignty that ignites a lust in my body so raw I roar with longing. From nowhere, my mountain lion approaches and bounds into my trembling body. I am ferocious, hungry for Kaimana's love. Amber-eyed, ample-fanged, pink-tongued, my body leaps into his and we make love again and again with total abandon. Throughout the house, statues sway under our volcanic influence: Ganesh's ears flap uncontrollably, Buddha's head detaches and rolls to the foot of the bed. Guadalupe murmurs, "Ay, yi yi yi!" Bells chime voluntarily, and outside in the dark Pacific, humpbacks breach and beat their fins against the waves, signaling wildly to approaching females. We all intermingle in a chorus of transcendent fervor.

When we finally rest, the sun is a blaze of fire emerging over the horizon.

"I love you so deeply," Kaimana whispers, lifting my bangs away from my damp forehead. "I know you know this, but I want to keep telling you so you will never forget. I am yours. Nothing can stop that. Nothing! Our life together will be waiting for you, no matter how long it takes. I see you coming back to me, and I will live with that vision until you return."

I feel a terrible desperation overtaking me. "I want something of yours to take with me. I need to have you close to me."

Kaimana goes into his bureau drawer and pulls out the blue feather he sometimes braids into his hair. He cuts off a piece and gives it to me to put in my medicine bag.

"If you are ever in danger, call my name and I will come."

I'm not sure what he's saying, but I nod. "Me too," I add.

Kaimana smiles, knowing I don't see it yet.

WE STAND HOLDING EACH OTHER in the shadow of the great palms beside the black rocks, out by the darkest part of the ocean. Kanoa squeals and nudges his snout in between us. Tears stream down my face, and I feel the old fears setting in.

Kaimana pulls my watch out of his pocket and holds it out to me. "Do not forget this."

I look at the face and the hands that have stopped moving. I throw the relic of my schedule-driven life into the water. And then my wedding band. The watch floats for a moment, but the ring sinks like a dead weight.

"I will wait for you," Kaimana whispers softly, "and we will make a life. I know this in my heart."

We dip into a basket of plumeria blossoms and scatter them on the surface of the Pacific. We speak out loud our prayers and gratitude. Watch or no watch, I must go. As I walk away, Kaimana stands at the gate, smiling, being strong for us both.

I PULL OFF THE ROAD several times as I drive toward the Kahului Airport. Everything in me wants to stay; only the past drives me toward the future.

On the airplane I look down on Maui, trying to figure out where Seal Cove is. I feel panicked because I don't know where Kaimana is. It dawns on me then that I don't have his phone number, no email, not even a street address.

"I don't even know your last name!" I say out loud.

Just call my name, he promised, *and I will come immediately.*

But how? What if I lose trust in all that I've learned, and it turns out I'm no good at using my intuition? What if David can never walk again and I am stuck there taking care of him? What if I never kiss your beautiful mouth again? I close my eyes and speak softly to my endangered heart.

I would have had to go home anyway to finish with David. I am strong enough to do this now. I know where my destiny is. I will be back as soon as he is healed.

And for a hot Maui moment I actually believe it.

PART THREE

"NO KEIA LA, NO KEIA PO, A MAU LOA"

FROM THIS DAY, FROM THIS NIGHT,
FOREVERMORE

—TRADITIONAL HAWAIIAN BLESSING

41

SO KAIMANA, I CREATED THIS CHAPTER OF MY LIFE BECAUSE...

Nothing feels the same to me as I scan the freeways eighteen thousand feet below, and I can feel my stress level rise as the plane descends into SFO. We are on approach over Silicon Valley, where left-brain, major bucks, young blonde mothers are being rude in SUVs as they chat on their newest iPhones, while twenty-something millionaires are getting sloppy in their track mansions, and a general sense of entitlement rules the day. The landing gear hasn't even touched the tarmac, and already my bitchy inner sister has raised her judgmental head.

There's a gnawing sense of dread in my gut as the cab pulls up in front of my Pacific Heights address, where I will drop off my luggage, change clothes, and drive to the hospital to sit at the side of a man who is in a lot of agony. It occurs to me that this might be the first time he has had to feel torturous pain. After all, this is the guy who has confided in me on several occasions that he doesn't *feel* pain, he *gives* it.

Uh, time to get that compassion rolling, Nurse Ratched....

All the usual sounds of the city seem amplified. Jackhammers and horns irritate the hell out of my nervous system, now more accustomed to silence and solitude. Brakes screech, car doors slam, and a hair-raising car alarm wails fifty feet from my front door. I can't wait to get inside and shut the door behind me.

This can't be my home. It must belong to someone much tighter than me, someone who has never been in love. This air is stuck and cold and *everything* is black, white, and grey. I can hardly breathe because there's no flow, no space to take a deep breath. Orchids greet me in the foyer—dusty silk ones! Leather couches, leather armchairs, big brass lamps, paintings and sculptures we accrued on our travels—I can't remember to where—clutter our family room. I feel like I am walking through a wealthy bachelor's penthouse. Now that I think of it... David, wealthy...bachelor? Perhaps I am seeing the future.

Sepia-toned photographs of David and me, the happy couple, line the hallways. Here we are at a Giant's game, wearing matching caps, holding up our giant franks. Here I am holding baby Jess, husband in absentia. Look, here are the Jamisons at the opera, at the French Laundry, and many, many shots of David winning award after award after award.

I drop my bags in the bedroom on the rug we bought in Morocco. What year was that? What lifetime? I grow dizzy looking into our clothing closet, which is roughly the size of Montana. I try to choose something simple to change into, but then I feel Kaimana's touch on my sweater and I cannot take it off. I lift the sweater up and rub it all over my face...my tears.

Things will be livable when Jess comes home, and I can pick up Bella tomorrow. That's it, that's how I will get through it. Tell me I'm going to survive. I open my medicine bag and stroke Kaimana's feather.

INSIDE THE HOSPITAL, many of my colleagues welcome me back and ask how I feel about being home. I want to tell them how I now know for the first time what it is to be at home, and about a modern day sorcerer whose arms held me in a sanctuary of peace...my real home. I do my best to respond in ways that would make sense to them, and smile so much my jaw hurts.

A perky young nurse directs me to a private room that David has just been moved to. I have no flowers or teddy bear, only a ton of apprehension and bucket load of concern about what kind of patient a Type A personality will make. The astringent smell of the hospital corridors seems oddly foreign, and I realize I'd forgotten the way my shoes make that irritating squeaking sound on the high-glossed floors. I wave to several nurses who work with me in OB-GYN.

I needn't have worried about my lack of flowers. The room is well-stocked with red roses, yellow mums, and purple gladiolas. As I walk toward the bed I am absolutely delighted to find that I'm not even tempted to read the cards.

Okay, I take back all of it. This creature in the hospital bed is no perfectionist waiting in judgment. This is a beat-up, broken body with a splintered ego. Here lies a needy eight-year-old boy looking through the eyes of a fifty-eight-year-old man. I sit beside him on the bed and take hold of his good hand. He opens his eyes and seems overjoyed to see me.

"So happy you're here," he manages to say, grasping my hand and bending his head forward like he's going to kiss it. Of course this hurts his collarbone and elicits heavy moaning and sighing. And a compelling need for more drugs.

"Tell the nurse I need more morphine, honey, will ya?"

Within minutes he is half-dozing, a reckless smile on his swollen face.

"Poor baby, this is not your idea of a good time, is it?" I manage.

He mumbles something incoherent and then checks out. I wipe the hair away from his eyes and feel Kaimana's warm hand tenderly brushing my bangs aside. For a few moments I am lost in that warmth. I let David sleep, and take the elevator down to the award-winning cafeteria that offers meatloaf and macaroni and cheese. And grey corn. There is the prospect of being treated to watery split pea soup—with ham, of course. I think not. I feel Kaimana's exquisite fingers feeding me his freshly made banana bread. I let the crumbs accumulate on my lips because I know he will lick them away.

I stare at my cup of coffee and eat a double espresso chocolate chip cookie. It's going to be a long night.

I try to sleep a bit next to David, but my mind is filled with details and worries. I would love to do a walking meditation down the hallway...the way Kaimana and I did by the ocean, in that deep state of peace. But the nurses would want to know just what exactly I'm doing. That's a very good question. As a matter of fact I have no idea what I am doing. Wait...yes, I do. I am trying to find my way back to my other life...my new life, the one where I actually get to show up as the real me. But from here it feels way too easy to fall into old habits, and every small step I take feels awkward. Maybe I should show the nurses my pink stone from Lemuria, my Quan Yin, and my rarified blue feather? Again, I think not.

Even in his sleep, I can tell that David is processing the impact of the crash, because he's apparently starring in a dramatic nightmare that features him rolling over and over in his racing car. Just before daybreak his pain level soars, and he takes another huge dose of painkillers from the I.V. Before he zonks out again he props himself up as best he can and blurts out, "You're not going to leave me, are you, Katherine?"

"No, I'm not going to leave you," I assure him, but his eyelids are quivering and he's already racing off to the next track. And then, looking away, I whisper softly, "...now."

THREE DAYS INTO HIS RECOVERY I feel strangely peaceful about his condition. I know he will make it through this and be on the track again. That's the way he does his life, challenge by challenge.

I must say he's been quite attentive. Maybe it's his confinement, or maybe he's picking up on the shift in me. He's certainly asking lots of questions about my trip. I feel protective about the experience, but give him bits of jaw-dropping data like my deep connection to Max, snorkeling with manna rays, and my healing session with a Hawaiian shaman.

"So," he says with a smirk on his face.

"So what?"

"So do you still have migraines?"

I pause for a moment and reflect back on the last few weeks. I had actually forgotten that I ever had a migraine. "Not a one."

"Wow, maybe I should go to Maui and find this guy. Maybe he could fix me up quicker."

Yeah, that'd be swell! "He's pretty busy working with this community of people up north. I went with him to see if there was some way I could help. The place is fascinating."

"How so?"

I elaborate on the conditions people are living under, and my idea of starting a foundation that would fund a major cleanup, plumbing, and a new building for the children. I propose that we do a fundraiser with his business associates and some of my wealthier clients. My idea sails high and then crashes into a sea of boredom. He snoozes on.

42

WHAT WOULD HAPPEN IF EVERYONE ENVISIONED A PEACEFUL, LIGHT-FILLED HIGHWAY?

David's been out of the hospital for forty-eight hours, and as usual our three-story house is shaking from the nerve-jarring vibration emanating from one of three obscenely huge flat-screen televisions positioned throughout the house. Today it's the sound of speeding cars tearing around Le Mans or wherever, but if it's not the revving of engines it's the sound of Rafa smacking an ace onto the far court, or cheers for the Lakers, or the droning voice of whoever is the commentator at the ninth tee. Every day is a veritable playoff or championship here at 2626 Octavia Street.

I am in my study lying on the floor next to Bella, my shepherd mix, and looking earnestly into her one blue eye. "Did you miss me? I missed you."

Bella rolls over onto her feet and leaves the room. I miss Max and Kanoa and that coconut cream pie between my legs. I miss the late afternoon swims in the nude and greeting Kaimana's patients with a compassionate curiosity. I miss the feeling of the waves against my face, black sand under my lemu, and the ease and grace that was my life. That *is* my life!

It occurs to me that my life would be a helluva lot easier if I was like other heroines who feel their romantic adventures slipping away once they return home and just accept it. Not in this lifetime. Amid running to the dry cleaners and making sure David's pajamas are perfectly ironed, supporting his body as he gets out of his chair and heads to the john, ordering special gourmet "soft" foods from the deli so he feels taken care of while he's healing, counseling anxious patients over the phone and praying that one of them will go into labor so I can flee my home base, walking ungrateful Bella and picking up her entitled turds...as I perform these and a thousand more duties, I am incessantly focused on Kaimana's gold-green eyes and scheming my return.

I savor a moment of private silence in my car in front of the terminal at SFO, waiting for my darling daughter's wonderful smile to come through the arrivals door. I want to tell her everything but I don't want to overwhelm her.

After all, she has been dealing with her own illness and, like me, she's leaving a whole other reality behind. Maybe she'll want to be left alone after all she has encountered.

"Mom!" she yells, waving her *very thin* arm, pulling two large suitcases toward the car.

I jump out and throw my arms around her. She buries her face in my neck. The agitated parking cop yells at me to move it. It takes everything in me not to invoke my mountain lion and send her to teach him a thing or two with her big paws and flailing tail. It takes both me and Jess to lift her baggage without adding yet another broken hip to the list of family ailments. We're on Highway 101 when she lights up a Virginia Slims and blows it in my direction.

"Excuse me, am I supposed to like that? Roll down the window. Now!"

"I'm sorry, Mom. I just feel so nervous and weird about coming back to the States. I already miss my other home."

I understand, my darling.

"I feel nervous about Daddy. Is he going to be okay? I mean, the same?"

"Well, let's see. He lies on his back placing orders for breakfast, lunch, and dinner, and once in a while he gets real friendly when he needs a strong body to support him on his way to use the john. The rest of the time he is mentally competing with every sports champion on

DirecTV. Oh, and he does yell into the phone when he talks to one of his underlings at MetroMax. Does that sound the same?"

"You don't sound like you like him much."

"I like him. He's just a lot of person—as you know."

"I was kind of hoping you two would get closer because of his accident. Weren't you scared?"

Oh, my dear Jess, you really have no clue what has happened between your dad and me, so you're still wishing…. I am so sorry I have let you down. "I'm doing my best, Jess."

"I'm not judging you, Mom. I just want your life to be easier. Lighter."

Well, that ain't gonna happen as long as I'm here. But let me tell you about my life in Maui. How I have come to discover the real me, the one who can actually trust that she is loveable. The one who knows she is more than what your father will ever see in me. Allow me to describe to you the depth of my love for this man, Kaimana, how I've learned to appreciate a simpler life. And do I have some tales to tell you about shamanic healing! Wait till— Stop, Kate! Jess is not your confidante. Don't put all of this on your kid.

The responsible mother speaks. "I know, darling. It is what it is. It isn't going to change."

A bright purple car squeals in front of me, obviously angry that I'm not moving fast enough. My mouth begins to form a nasty response, but the new me stops and sends light in his direction.

Jess notices a change in my energy. "What are you doing, Mom?"

"I'm sending good energy to that guy."

My daughter can't believe my mouth is uttering such nonsense. "To that asshole?!"

"It's something I learned while I was in Maui. I learned to detach a bit and be less reactive to the rest of the world. I guess it's called patience. As you know, sweerie, that has never been my strong suit."

"You're sounding a little New Age-ie, and I know you've always hated that saccharine stuff."

"Well, I've changed a lot. I've actually become more open to many spiritual ideas that I was closed to before."

"Why? What happened?

My stomach is telling me to cool it. "Lots of wonderful things. I don't think I know how to talk about them yet. It's not that I don't want to share them with you. I'm just not ready."

We drive in silence.

When we're almost home, Jess clears her throat and takes a deep breath. "Mom, I've thought a lot about going back into practice with you, like you mentioned while you were in Hawaii. I've decided I love the idea. When can we start?"

"Let's talk about it a little later," I tell her, my gut tightening. The truth is I don't want to lie to Jess just so she doesn't worry. But the other truth is that just mouthing words that suggest I might not return to paradise could start a crying jag that would flood Highway 101 and sweep several thousand cars into San Francisco Bay.

43

IT'S ALL
IN YOUR INTENTION

I turn on the shower as hot as I can stand it, trying to jar myself into facing just one more day in my first week of work on the wrong side of the Pacific. I'm in a rush to get an early start because I have a lot of patients today, appointments scheduled all day long. The hot water streams down my back, and...something happens. I stop my busy brain for a moment and cup the water in my hands, the way I held the papaya with Kaimana in Maui a month ago. Suddenly I realize how precious water is, and how we must protect it. I feel a prayer rise up inside me, a prayer to all the bodies of water on the earth...I thank them for feeding us, nurturing us, cleaning our clothes, creating sanitation, irrigation—all of it.

As I towel myself dry I'm aware the day is already very different from what it was ten minutes ago.

OKAY, MAYBE I HAVE gone a little over the top. I arrive home late in the evening to find David lying back in his zero-gravity chair, hidden amid a veritable jungle of cymbidium, phalaenopsis, and miniature palms, all delivered this afternoon.

He is not delighted. "This place looks like a fucking florist shop. What's going on?!"

"Just bringing in a little color, darling. A little softness," I tell him, clearing away the pile of dirty dishes beside his chair.

I chuckle to myself...if he only knew, I've done the same thing at my office, although there I've created a living bamboo divider. I think it makes for a great healing space. Besides, it gives me and Jess a little privacy in our respective work spaces.

I do wonder if my patients totally get it. When Suzanne Martin showed up for her checkup this afternoon she pushed back the palm leaves and asked, "Is this a new hobby? I didn't know you were into horticulture." It really did make a difference, though. She's never been so relaxed for her exam...or maybe it's just that her doctor is different.

I realized I'd overdone the whole flower thing when the boatload of exotics I ordered from the islands arrived at the office. They were gorgeous...anthurium, protea, ginger...can't even remember what all I'd picked out. And why not? Hawaii's economy needs it. But there just wasn't any more room in my office. No matter. I sent them up to the hospital, put them in the nurses' station and divvied them up among patients on the maternity ward.

Yes, David, there certainly is a whole new level of lushness and color blooming in my world.

SATURDAY MORNING the UPS packages I've been tracking arrive. Amazon.com is very pleased with me. I'm pretty sure I've ordered every meditation, Tibetan bowl, and Australian didgeridoo CD ever recorded, along with every variation on the sound of ocean waves.

One of the boxes is a set of tapes that promise to teach me to speak Hawaiian in thirty days. So after David settles in for his noontime nap, I put on my headphones and get into it. Right away I feel like I'm getting the hang of the pronunciation and the rhythm of the language. Looks like I picked the right tapes, too, because I quickly learn some key phrases—the really important ones, like, "Aloha way ia oe." I love you. Of course. And "No keia la, no keia po, a mau loa." From this day, from this night, forevermore. I fantasize repeating these words at our wedding ceremony. I breathe.

I can't seem to find the translation for "Hey, handsome, where's the whipped cream?"

Apparently David is thinking about food, too, and his pleas for dinner bring me crashing back to earth. I'm determined to stay in island mode, though, so I morph into a Pacific Islander chef and invent an elegant salad laced with slivered macadamia nuts, shaved ginger and coconut, organic tomatoes imported from upcountry Kula, golden beets, sweet cilantro—all drizzled with premium aged olive oil and pineapple vinegar. I pair it with a huge bowl of chilled black beans tossed with coriander and coconut rice. Culinary heaven.

"I never knew you were into salads like this," David remarks quizzically as I surround him with my tropical cornucopia.

"I enjoy creating these lush, life-giving extravaganzas," I explain, letting a small stream of dressing run down my chin just a little. When that doesn't do much I start eating with my fingers.

"Jesus! You *have* gone native."

If you only knew.

"I want a steak, Katherine. Just a simple chateaubriand. What's the problem?"

"I guess I finally got tired of feeling guilty about eating animals. So we're trying something different."

"You, the champion pork cheek stuffer? You, who devours rack of lamb like there's no tomorrow. Who are you kidding?"

My God, who was that woman? Okay, I know. She was David's denial-packed, prostituting wife who passed away in Maui. "I want to get a kick out of eating again without the guilt, so I'm experimenting. Please bear with me, darling. I'm going to get really good at this."

David grumbles and mutters something about me being totally out of control. Wait until he goes to the shower and finds a bottle of awapuhi oil and plumeria shampoo to use on his short C.E.O. "do." Oh, and an Ocean Essence Body Bar to cleanse away all of our sins. I don't care what he thinks. From now on I'm going to surround myself with things that heal me.

AFTER DINNER I HEAD to my study to practice walking meditation in the graceful presence of my absolute favorite new acquisitions. Thanks to the miraculous internet, the space is now home to a five-foot-tall, mahogany statue of Quan Yin that I have imported from Thailand, and a thirty-inch golden Ganesh who has the most whimsical ears and trunk. Together we will remove any obstacles from my life and everyone else's!

I bow to my new friends and ask for their help. "Good evening Quan Yin. Namaste, Ganesh. Help me to let go of all my negativity, my unkind words, thoughts, and actions. Please release all illness and negative energies from me, and from this space."

I envision Kaimana's graceful, tattooed back in front of me, Kanoa snoozing peacefully at his side. My beautiful shaman's voice drifts into my consciousness.

"Slow down, Kate," he tells me tenderly. "Honor your intention."

I silently renew my resolve to clean up my mess, my marriage, and return to him and our little cove.

I turn toward the new hand-woven Navajo rug in the center of the floor, and imagine that the earth is at its center. I walk slowly around the perimeter, sending love all over the globe.

I can't believe how much this new practice does for me. What a difference from my old philosophy, which was basically that the world is going to hell and there's nothing I can do about it. As I walk, I revisit what Kaimana has taught me...to connect with the Creator's light and let it fill my cells, then send it down through my feet. I envision that sacred light reaching out to all the living beings of the world so they may feel safe and peaceful wherever they are. I feel inspired. I feel empowered. I feel that I am a force for good. Mahalo, Kaimana.

I continue to walk and my awareness goes even deeper, and I see everything...no, I *experience* everything as a meditation. Every moment is an opportunity to focus on the good in everything. "Please, Universe," I pray, "help us to be and live with the consciousness of oneness, sharing our loving energy like the water—flowing, pure, and abundant, always giving back to the earth."

I feel so connected to the Universe! I'm in great shape!

I finish my prayers and head back upstairs. I see that David has fallen asleep on his massive chair in front of the TV, and say a silent thank you to Quan Yin. I slip into my bedroom, close the door, and turn on a CD of didgeridoo played over the sound of the ocean. I lie on the bed blissed out, envisioning the turquoise waves washing over me and you-know-who.

I hear David's footsteps coming down the hallway. Mercifully he walks past the door and heads to the bathroom.

On his way back to his TV he grumbles, "That goddamn noise—I don't know if it's agitating or mind-numbing, but you sure as hell better turn it off before I come to bed."

I'm completely unfazed, content to allow him to rest in his own personal state of resistance. I gotta tell you, the vibration of the didgeridoo—even the digital version—is anything but mind-numbing, and it certainly isn't agitating. It is powerful, though—so powerful it will blast your soul wide open.

My soul and I drift happily, openly into sleep.

44

MY HIDDEN HEALER EMERGES

The rich batter oozes over a layer of pineapple, and I put the finishing touches on the upside-down cake I'm creating for our Sunday brunch. I hear David's voice wooing me from the living room, and my brain instinctively starts thinking about a place to hide. Why am I such a child about this? I want to run away from home.

From the comfort of his zero-gravity chair, David calls, "Hey, cutie. Come here, will you?"

I put the cake in the oven and open the refrigerator, hoping he'll get distracted by whatever is happening on the TV. No such luck.

"Darling, I really need a haircut. And a nice steam and a shave, while we're at it. Come on, cutie, do it for me like you used to. Would ya, could ya? C'mon, it'll be fun."

Uh, no! It would be a torturous, shady moment in what I'm trying to transform into a different kind of life. My whole body fills with dread.

This whole business of living two lives—or between two lives—is making my head spin. I have to admit David has been much nicer lately. Maybe he just feels grateful for all I've been doing for him. Or maybe he's not the prick I imagined him to be. But, whatever, when he reaches to take my hand or actually sits back and listens to what I am saying, my stomach knots up. I try to keep it as neutral as possible. Carrying pans of urine, helping him up out of a chair and supporting him, holding his vulnerable hand— these things are doable. But anything more intimate than that, and I start to choke.

Like right now. "Jess," I yell, "Come help Daddy while I run a few errands."

Thankfully her sweet face emerges at the kitchen door. "What's up, Mom?"

"Your dad needs a hand, sweetie. Help him out for me, will you? And keep an eye on the cake in the oven. I'll be back before it's done."

A wave of relief washes away the guilt. It feels much clearer this way. I just don't want to put out any energy to David that feels intimate and connected. I also want Jess and David to bond more, and here's a great opportunity. If I don't start backing off as his wife, how will I ever eke my way out of here?

I do my brief disappearing act, and linger in the car when I return home. I take a long, deep breath and hold on to one more moment with Kaimana's delicious presence all to myself. Suddenly I feel his hands slowly touch down on my shoulders. They are warm and full of caring, and a lush, soft rain of energy travels down my arms, into my chest, flooding into my heart. I put my head back and close my eyes. "I love you," I whisper. "Keep it coming." Before my heart beats again, the vibration switches from loving to sensual, and his lush breath moves down through my belly and across my pelvis and hips. My breathing eclipses my heartbeat and I hold on tight to the steering wheel, because at any minute I could launch into the luminous San Francisco skyline.

"Mom!" Jess is tapping on the car window. "Are you okay?"

I roll down the window, my whole body trembling from being jarred back to this world. "Yes, Jess. I'm fine." It's impossible not to sound breathless.

"What are you doing out here?" She sounds genuinely worried. "Aren't you coming inside?"

I want to scream, No! or at least, Wait till I take a shower and get some clothes on! But I retrieve myself as best I can and demurely open the door.

Still waving away Jess' worried looks, I reenter the Hawaiian garden that has replaced the arid desert that David and I used to call home.

It occurs to me that I might use my heightened state to do some good. Perhaps that would assuage some of my guilt for not reaching out to my husband in the ways a wife would. Then it occurs to me that in my soul I am another man's wife. Whatever—if I can bring some healing energy into the mix, it has to be a good thing.

"David," I ask, "would you like me to do some energy healing on you? I could try a little something I learned from that shaman on my trip."

David's face registers confusion, then surprise, then fear. But he's an adventurer at heart, so in the end he gives in to his curiosity. Sort of. "Well...sure."

I push the controls until his special chair goes all the way back, and have him close his eyes. I feel the connection with the essence of Quan Yin and call to her to fill me with her light. Then I place my hands on his semi-healed hips and picture the source of life pouring through me.

"What are you doing?" David asks in a relaxed voice. "It feels like there's heat coming into my body from your hands."

"I'm just bringing through some healing energy that I'm tapping into from the Source."

"The source of what?"

"The source of energy that creates all living things."

"You mean God?"

"Sure. God. Or Buddha. Or Allah. Or Quan Yin. Jesus or the trees or the oceans. The stars...whatever you feel connected to."

David is quiet. There's not much to say because there is obviously something happening, and I'm sure he's thinking to himself, Who cares where it comes from, this feels great. I decide I'm going to do a lot of this with him so he can get up and get back into his life—and so I can move on.

"If you're open to it, we can work like this every day," I tell him. I try to be open hearted and giving—but not too much.

"Bring it on! I want to get back on that track!"

Amen, brother.

45

COMING OUT OF
MY CLOSET

E very time I venture into my personal Wardrobe City I feel like screaming. It's the size of ten normal closet spaces merged into one humongous Disney World for an upper-class yuppie. I must have twenty-five cashmere sweaters, all folded perfectly, some still attached to their sales tags. Suits! Think every shade of the rainbow, think silk, gabardine, tweed, and stripe. Here they are, the princes and princesses of the realm...Donna, Calvin, Dolce, and Stella. Shoes? More than seventy pairs reside here, some never having made contact with the pavement. To the left dwell David's racing uniforms, helmets, and boots, his tuxes and C.E.O.-wear. Belts, suspenders, ties, cufflinks, and trousers are jammed into a labyrinth of shelves and over-stuffed drawers. Not a sarong to be found.

Our housekeeper, Concepción, has committed to help me thin out this extravaganza, and I hear her footsteps coming down the hall. Actually I wish I could just give her most everything, but I don't want her to feel that I'm handing castoffs to the help. I hate that! Talk about rankism. It's really very touchy. I'll try to be subtle.

"You ready now, Mrs.?"

"Scary in here, isn't it?"

"Many pretty things."

"Many pretty things that don't fit me any longer. Know anybody who might want a new suit or sweater? How about shoes?"

"Why you no want them, so pretty!"

"I have too many." Besides, now I believe in bare feet. "Can you help me out?"

"Mrs., give me whatever you want. I find a home for them."

"Really? Don't you like any for yourself?"

"Not for me, for others."

"Okay," I say, loading up boxes and bags, arranging a Dior gown on a hanger. "What about these fur coats? Do you know someone who might want them?"

"I will take them! So beautiful!'

So dead. I can't believe how unconscious I've been about what the rightful owners of these skins went through, all in service to my vanity. The side corner looks like a burial ground for foxes. "Please take my mother's fox coat, and that old mink."

"Yes, Mrs."

We are really making headway. I only need three suitcases when I leave: one filled with clothes, one filled with books and music, and the third packed with instruments to surprise Kaimana.

"Concepción, why do you wear Guadalupe around your neck?"

"She protect me and my family."

I go to my secret drawer where I have hidden my medicine bag and take out the little statue of Quan Yin. I show Concepción.

"So beautiful. Guadalupe's sister."

"Yes," I say. I'm amazed that Concepción knows Quan Yin, and overjoyed that someone else understands. "Yes!"

She takes both of my hands in hers. "You need this," she says softly, looking deep into my eyes. "She bring you courage to face many things. I feel your sadness, Mrs. She bring you balance."

"She already has. She teaches me how to pray."

"Oh, it's good, Mrs. You softer now. I like." Concepción kisses my hand and holds it next to her cheek.

I will miss her.

"What's going on?" Jess asks, wading through the clothes on the floor.

"Just giving away a few things."

"A few things? This is the bulk of your wardrobe."

"Well, I would've given them to you, honey, but since you are size triple zero...."

She watches as Concepción carries a few more armloads of clothes out of the room. "Mom, could we talk? I'm feeling concerned about you."

"There's nothing to be concerned about."

"I know you! You're definitely going through something, and you're shutting me out."

Concepción calls out, "Goodbye, Mrs."

Now I'm officially cornered. "Come on, Jess. Have a seat."

We walk to the big bed and sit down. No worries about David hearing our conversation, because he is busy blowing out his eardrums in the living room.

"So, what's going on?"

"Listen, Jess...I had a very big experience when I was in Hawaii, on Maui. I met a man, a shaman, and we spent a lot of time together. His name is Kaimana. He's a very special person, very loving and devoted to his work. I saw him heal people with his hands, with sound, and with all kinds of remedies and salves that he creates. I did a lot of personal work with him, and resolved all kinds of issues I've been carrying around inside for a very long time. I believe this is the most important thing that has happened in my life, besides having you."

"What about Dad? You don't seem to be including him on your 'most important' list." Jess' blue eyes look intensely into mine. I can see that she's searching for information that will help her feel secure about our marriage. I have none to give her.

"Come on, Jess. You know it's been uncomfortable between your dad and me forever. The only reason I have stayed for so long is because I was afraid to leave. I was afraid to hurt him—that's assuming, of course, that he could ever be hurt."

"Why do you demonize him like that? You've had good years. I know. I was there."

"There were some good years, but mostly because I designed a lifestyle that allowed him to do and be whatever he wanted."

"He gave you a lot of independence and freedom, too. I thought you liked that."

"I did and I do. There just wasn't enough connection. Once I really connected with Kaimana, and felt the incredible bond that can happen between two people...it just became clear to me what I *don't* have with your father."

"For Christ's sake, Mother. What are you telling me?"

"Hon, please, stop raising your voice. There's nothing to be afraid of. I want you to be happy for me. I have found happiness and love and meaning in my life. How many women can say that?"

"So—I can't believe you're saying what I think you're saying. You're in love with this Hawaiian guy?"

"Yes, Jess. I am. Very much."

"But what about Dad? Are you just going to dump him?"

"Well...I hope to handle it a little more respectfully than that. But honey, your dad and I are over. As soon as he's back on his feet, I plan to return to Maui."

"What about your practice, your patients? Why did you even want me to come home?"

"It's complicated, Jess. You know I've been asking you to come home for a long time, and at the same time I've been very supportive of your work in Africa. Even after I move to Maui I'll set it up so I come back here to work in the office every few months. I care deeply for my patients, you know that. But I'm in the midst of learning new ways of healing that far surpass what I've been prescribing for all these years. I'm tired of the old protocols. I have seen genuinely miraculous healing occur right before my eyes. I can't turn back now. I'm going to immerse myself in that consciousness."

"Maybe you're just blindly in love and about to destroy your life. Maybe he's good in the sack and Dad isn't so great any more. Mom, you've been married for a very long time. Doesn't that *mean* anything?"

"Jess, please don't. I'm grateful for the good years, and the things we created that are lasting. But I have been living a lie for too many years, because I was too scared to leave. I'm not scared any longer. It's time for me to leave."

"This sounds like a mid-life crisis to me. How old is this guy? Are you going to live in an ashram or a thatched roof hut and subsist on macadamia nuts?"

"I don't know exactly how old he is. He owns a beautiful home and he's a marvelous, interesting person. He's magical and lives an easy-going life filled with purpose. It's all new to me and exciting. You will like him. Really, darling, he's an amazing person. It makes me very happy just to walk beside him."

"If you've changed so much, why don't you just leave Dad and live on your own? Why do you have to go to this other guy right away? This doesn't feel like growth to me. It feels like replacing one situation with another so you don't have to deal with your own insecurities. Think about it, Mom, what if Michelle or one of your other friends came to you and told you the same story? Or one of your patients? What would you say to them? I think you'd ask them to take some time just for themselves after a long relationship. Or maybe you'd ask them what they were running from."

Silence. So, Mom, what are you running from? Are you ever going to stop and figure that out?

Jess stands up and takes a step toward the door. "I can see this conversation is going nowhere."

"That's not true. I just let you in on my life. If you can drop your judgment and let just one part of you be happy for me, I'd be grateful."

"You know what, Mother? I liked you more when you were an unhappy wife—Daddy's 'victim'!" She tosses angry air-quotes into the air, then turns abruptly and walks out.

What did I expect? She loves David and forgives his shortcomings. She doesn't see his narcissism—she calls it selfishness, but that is very different. My heart feels torn, and I can only hope she'll find a way to see what I see—not just about David, but about a different way of being in the world. I wish I had said that to her. I should have explained to her that moving to Maui is about coming into a new self, a new way of being. It's not only about being in love, it's about learning to be a different kind of healer, about developing a spiritual practice...it's about so many things....

Breathe, Kate. All that matters is that I stay clear and not fold. I still need to tell David, sooner rather than later, and that terrifies me. There's so much to figure out, and I don't mean who gets the horrible yellow lamps and who gets custody of Bella. In fact, I can't imagine taking much with me. It all feels so impersonal now, designed to present an image of sophistication and class. Just one happy family. Really? Twenty-five years of living in the same space, decorating and redecorating in an effort to make him happy, creating a formal space for David's corporate meetings and a casual space so he could come and go easily...holidays blessed with my daughter and a myriad of mixed emotions, all awash in his ongoing absence. The power of denial is undeniable.

As I fold up more clothes to be donated to a homeless shelter, I hear a whisper of that old inner schism again. There is a ring of truth in my daughter's tirade, particularly in her suggestion that perhaps I should have time alone before I commit to another relationship. The problem is I am already committed. Now, being alone feels like backtracking.

Careful, Kate. Don't unravel.

46

IT'S NOT WHAT YOU THINK,
IT'S WHAT YOU FEEL

Wednesday night is group night for my cancer patients and their families. We sit in a circle in a small room and talk about the non-medical aspects of treatment. Mostly it gives them a chance to air their concerns, talk about how they're dealing with the whole thing emotionally. I've decided it's a good place to introduce some of the concepts Kaimana talked to me about on Maui, like the whole issue of "victims" versus "volunteers."

"So I had a very interesting experience when I was in Maui that I would like to share with all of you. Is that okay with everybody?"

Of course nobody objects. They seem relieved to be talking about something besides cancer.

"I visited a healer, there, who uses energy and sound to do his healing work. He refers to himself as a shaman, and he's studied with teachers who use ancient techniques to release disease and imbalance. I had the opportunity to watch him work with a number of patients, and I was utterly amazed at what he could accomplish. Most of his work involves connecting with what he calls the Source—what you might call God. He transmits the energy of that Source into his patients' bodies. When I watched him work, I could actually see the whole process unfold, and the transformation in the patients was nothing short of astounding. I could hardly believe my eyes."

I pause and scan the room. There's a lot of resistance going around.

"I know you've heard a lot of stories about different kinds of healers, and believe me, I have, too. I pretty much assumed most of them were more or less snake oil salesmen, more interested in making money and selling woo-woo products than in actually healing anyone.

"But I can tell you, this healer—Kaimana is his name—he's the real thing. I actually saw him release chronic inflammation, and even stage-four throat cancer. The hardest one for me to accept was the most amazing one. I saw him work with an eight-year-old boy diagnosed with schizophrenia and bipolar disease. From Kaimana's perspective, the boy's body had been taken over by the soul of another young man who had died—but whose soul was deeply troubled, and was 'stuck,' you might say, in the physical world. I actually witnessed this healer release that soul's energy from the boy's body, and help it pass over to the other side."

One member of the group gasps, another whispers, "Wow." Most of them exchange looks somewhere between skeptical, amazed, and perturbed.

"Yes, I know. It's pretty hard to believe. I'd be very skeptical if I hadn't seen it myself. The most convincing part of it was the transformation in the young boy. Before it was all over, I watched this medicine man work with the child energetically, and within a few minutes he became a very balanced kid again. The whole thing was remarkable."

Twelve pairs of eyes are riveted, just waiting for whatever's coming next.

"The most compelling thing I learned from Kaimana was something that was actually very difficult for me to accept at first. He believes that we create everything in our world by the kinds of thoughts we have and by the choices we make subconsciously, or even on a deep spiritual level. He teaches that we are not victims of anything or anyone. He believes we have spiritual lessons that we enter this lifetime to learn, and before we are born we set these rather challenging courses for ourselves in order to achieve self-mastery. I had a hard time with this when he first started explaining it. In fact—I kind of yelled at him."

Everyone laughs. Thank goodness. The tension was getting a little thick in here.

"I'm not kidding! I said to him, 'You mean people who have cancer created it for their own betterment?' Well, it was more like I accused him. I couldn't believe that was really what he was suggesting. But he said that was exactly right.

"It took me quite a while to get past my resistance to the idea. But then when I saw the difference in people who held the same belief, that they created their sickness so they could heal it, I became fascinated. Because, guess what—when those people were able to understand the deeper lessons behind their illnesses, their physical bodies healed."

I scan the room again. This time I can't tell what the heck they're thinking. I try to ignore the knot of fear that starts to gather in my stomach. Go for it, Kate—the best way to find out what's going on is to ask. "I'm wondering what you feel as I'm talking about all this."

Winnie Tomlinson, a young woman who lost her mother to uterine cancer a year ago, and who just started chemo for breast cancer, stands up and walks toward the door. She turns to me, shakes her head with disbelief, walks through the door and closes it soundly.

Everyone squirms.

"I want to believe it," Tina Barnes, a breast cancer survivor says quietly. "But I guess I'm scared to adopt that way of thinking. Because the thing is...what if you put your heart and soul into healing yourself and you die anyway? That would be really depressing."

"More depressing than feeling like you're stuck with no options?" I ask. "You're already putting your heart and soul into it, aren't you?"

"I kind of like what you're saying," Bill Stratton tells me and the group, shifting forward in his chair. "My wife does acupuncture and listens to hypnotherapy tapes. They give suggestions to her subconscious, telling her she's healing, that her immune system is attacking the tumors, things like that. She says they really make her feel better...stronger. I know she's a lot less depressed when she listens to those tapes every day. And the acupuncture even makes her headaches go away. I don't think there's any harm in that."

Thank you, Mr. Stratton. "You're right, Bill. There's certainly no harm in any of that.

"You see, everyone...it's just an entirely different way of looking at illness. Kaimana wouldn't even let me diagnose any of the 'imbalances,' as he would call them, because he says once you name them you give them a presence in your life, and then they want to move in. I think that's a cool concept, too. What do you all think?"

Johanna Steiner sits forward, too, but with a more aggressive posture. "I wish he was here so I could ask him why I would want my baby to die. How would that serve me?" Her voice is quiet, but I can see that she's so angry she seems close to tears.

"I know, Johanna, this kind of thinking challenges all of the ways we deal with traumas and crises in our lives. It asks us to step into our power and work with the Creator to heal ourselves, to forgive ourselves, but also to see how much we can expand and survive in times of crisis. Sometimes I think we're addicted to suffering. We see it all around us and think it's incumbent upon us to keep the bad news going. This other way of seeing the world asks each of us to look deep into ourselves to see how our illnesses and challenges have served us, or how they've strengthened us in some way."

It's more than Johanna can stand. "Forgive myself?? Addicted to suffering?? You think I should feel guilty because my baby died? I'm sorry, Dr. Jamison. I just can't believe you're selling this shit. Just who do you think you are to tell me that?" She picks up her coat and purse, and can't get out of the room fast enough.

I'm seriously questioning whether the group was the right place to introduce this stuff. It's very quiet, hardly anyone meets my eyes as they file out. I know that some will not return. One patient does hang around though, Sandra Boynton, a twenty-something redhead who has been fighting breast cancer for a year.

"Your shaman sounds very interesting, Dr. Jamison. I've been reading about other practitioners of the healing arts, and I can't help wondering how I would do with their modalities. I'm tired of the kinds of treatments I've been getting...it just feels so futile. I'm tired of feeling sick. I think," she pauses, and then says triumphantly, "No, I *know* I'd like to get in touch with your friend and ask him some questions. Could you give me his phone number?"

"I think it's wonderful that you're exploring other ideas, Sandra. But Kaimana—the healer—doesn't have a phone."

"Okay, then his email."

"Nope," I say quietly, hoping his distrust of technology won't turn her off. "He's not big on technology. He's very into human contact."

"A purist, huh? Well, I guess that makes sense. Actually, if I didn't have to make so many doctor appointments I'd throw my iPhone over the Golden Gate...."

"I often feel that way, too! So, I guess if you want to get in touch with Kaimana you'll have to hop a jet to Maui."

"Now that would be a terrible thing, wouldn't it?" she says breaking into a smile. "What torture!"

"Yes, it's horrible. Think of it: palm trees blowing in the warm wind with blossoms blowing by, spreading their light perfume around you. Gnoshing on fresh pineapple and papayas. Dawdling for hours in turquoise surf!"

"Appalling! Here, twist my arm!" And with that Sandra exposes a thinning arm that has seen too many I.V.s.

I grasp that arm gently and contort my face like I am going to make her pay. It doesn't happen often, but when I do get a chance to giggle with my patients it sure feels good! "One other thing," I tell her, letting go of her wrist. "He lives off the beaten track in a place called Seal Cove, and he doesn't have his name or any other information outside his door. I'll have to draw you a map."

"Great. I'll call it my miracle map! Sounds like quite an adventure." She looks down at the floor for a moment, and when she looks up again her expression is very serious. "You know, Dr. Jamison...I'm going to go online tomorrow and make a plane reservation. I'll get the directions from you at next week's meeting. I am going to Hawaii to see your medicine man."

"Well, Sandra...it just might be two of us!"

Again more giggles and smiles. And I get a big hug! Before she leaves she turns and puts on some fresh lipstick, getting ready to face the night.

A wave of peace and hope washes over me. If one person can be open enough to want to seek out what Kaimana does, then I know many others can. It may take time, but I will continue to look for opportunities to mention how he works. I'll just keep testing the waters.

As I drive home I expand on the idea, and let myself run with a fantasy of accompanying patients to Maui, and

Kaimana and I teaching them how to release their pain and suffering so they can bring more love and joy into their own lives and to the world in general. I know that this is the reality I want, and I know there are many others who will eagerly follow in my footsteps. Doctors, nurses, volunteers...I hold a vision of a simple clinic in Maui that offers conventional Western medicine as well as shamanic healing. I can see transformational work being accomplished by those who can get with the program. It's moments like this when I feel I am walking into my destiny.

47

THE COURAGE TO DWELL IN THE MIRACULOUS

I come home late from the hospital and find David walking down the stairs without his cane. This is a new milestone. Hallelujah! Soon he won't need me at all anymore. But there's that knot in my stomach—his recovery also means I'll soon have to lower the boom. No more hiding behind his injuries...for me or for him.

"Good for you!" I tell him triumphantly.

"Yeah, it won't be long before I'll be ready to take on the world!"

Shit! But I smile, nodding. I grab Bella's leash and take her out for a walk.

It's a lovely evening, except that it's pouring rain. I keep going until I think David might be dozing and dreaming of the next LeMans. When both Bella and I are thoroughly drenched, I do my best to get in the front door without making a sound. I spend a very long time in the upstairs bathroom toweling both of us off.

"Where is my darling wife?" I hear from the other end of the hallway. "I think you should come to bed with your sexy husband and see what happens."

My husband is very sexy—to himself. He's a good-looking man with a nice body, but when it comes to sex he's into it for himself, which never did work for me. I have no interest in going to the bedroom and fighting him off.

"I have a lot of work to do for tomorrow," I feign. "Good night, darling."

There's no response accept for the barrage of commercials from the television blaring through the house. Tonight I couldn't be more grateful for *Sports Roundup*.

This is a perfect time to do my walking meditation, so I head downstairs. Somewhere in the midst of my bliss state, Jess appears and watches me in silence. I hear her crying and give her my full attention.

"What's the matter? What's happened?" I ask, pausing with one foot behind the other.

"It's another crisis in the Village of Peace, and some of my patients there have been badly injured. There've been several more rapes in the last two days, not far from the encampment. It's devastating. I feel so full of rage, Mom— I want to shoot all those soldiers!"

I'm very quiet because I have no answer for her. "Darling," I finally whisper, "why don't you join me in my walking meditation? It's simple, and it's a great way to calm down and get rid of all of those terrible emotions that just hurt you in the end. It might be the one thing you can do in this moment to make a difference for the people who are hurting."

"Don't be ridiculous! How can I make a difference by walking around the living room?"

"This is one of those things you have to be open to, and let yourself experience it. What are your choices here? You can remain in hell, or you can transform your negative thoughts into peaceful ones."

"Is this what you learned from the shaman?"

"It is. He showed me many ways to find inner peace."

"He sounds too good to be true."

Again I do not answer, but instead I put on Tibetan bell and bowl music and light a few more candles.

"This seems ridiculous. But...I'll try it. What do I do?"

"First let's walk to let go of all of our fears and frustrations. Walk very slowly, putting one foot just in front of the other. Try to focus only on the movement, and the sensations of your feet against the floor. If you start thinking about other things, then just bring your attention back to your walking, and begin again. Okay?"

Jess looks bewildered, but agrees, and we begin to walk. Several times she stops, agitated by her awkwardness. But after a few minutes she calms down and settles into a steady rhythm.

When I finally settle back into my own silence, it comes to me that we can send love to the women who have been raped, right here, right now. What we have to do is see the light moving through us, send it out, and watch it entering their bodies. That intention will help them release the violence and heal.

Jess loves the idea. "Do you think it will work? I mean, how does it work?"

"It's a way of taking action and being powerful...directing the light of the Creator with our love and compassion.

"I'm willing to give it a shot."

We walk for a long time, the vibrant resonance of bell and bowl moving all around us. The big clock in the vestibule suddenly strikes midnight. Somehow the reverberations give me an even bigger idea.

"You know," I tell Jess, "the women at the encampment are so powerful, they live through everything. They're unstoppable. It's the soldiers who are really in trouble. While I was walking I thought of the soldiers being poisoned by those delusional drugs—their cultural superstitions, all the fear and crazy belief systems drummed into them. I think *they* need to be healed."

"Those bastards? They even rape babies, Mom! How can we possibly help them? They ought to be castrated and put in prison."

"Well, that's one way of looking at it. But what if we were to get really big and see them as lost souls? What if we send them the most powerful rays of light, filled with their mother's love? What if that powerful love broke through the cultural hypnosis they're under? I wonder if they could still rape and destroy, if the tenderness of their mother's love and their own forgotten innocence were running through their systems. I doubt it.

"Come on, Jess. I'm going to picture the faces of those soldiers who have been demonized, and I'm going to send a mother's love like a perfect arrow into their consciousness, into the area above their eyebrows, the third eye. I'm going to believe that using the force of universal love we can break through this insanity. Are you with me?"

"It sounds pretty farfetched. But I guess I'm willing to try. I have to tell you, though, Mom...I'm not at all convinced they deserve it."

As we walk I take the journey back there with her, and together we work on the soldiers. I talk Jess through a meditation in which we watch as the young men's cells fill with light and their nervous systems relax. One by one we see them putting their weapons down and taking off their military uniforms. We watch them falling into a deep sleep, remembering the love their mothers gave them. We see them waking up out of the drugs and deprivation and finding the strength to leave the armies and escape.

"Wow, that was a trip, Mom. I feel really good...I think I want to do this every day." Then she wraps her arms around me and adds, "I'm sorry I've been so hard on you lately. Turns out I'm loving the new you. Will you teach me more?"

"Everything. I'll teach you everything. I'm going back to Maui soon. Maybe you'll come too."

Jess smiles. "It's just oozing out of every cell of your body, Mom."

"What is?" I say, grinning ear to ear.

"Your voluptuous new life."

I walk Jess to her bedroom and we embrace. Tonight there are no boundaries left between us.

48

CUTTING LOOSE

I've come to welcome these moments when I'm on the edge of sleep, knowing I'm a breath away from feeling Kaimana's touch. He visits more and more frequently lately, especially when I'm asleep. As my brain begins to slip into that other realm, I wait for the smell of his skin and the pleasure of his body gliding onto mine. We embrace under waterfalls and let the water pound over us, make love in the dark on the floor of Haleakala volcano, beneath the Sagittarian and Aquarian stars. We roll in the rust red dirt, and play with humpback mothers and their babies in the harbor off the whaling town of Lahaina. My body is a vessel of pleasure, drifting in a sea of love.

Suddenly David is shaking my arm. "What the hell is going on?" he demands. His voice seems angry and confused at the same time. "What the hell kind of dream are you having?"

I'm flustered and half asleep, and I don't know what to say. Also, I am tired of lying.

This is the time, Kate. Tell him now. But I'm so scared. I cannot stand to hurt anyone. And I'm terrified of David's rage. I also smell alcohol on his breath.

Do it anyway. Be in your power all the way.

I sit up and turn to look at him. "David, I.... I had some very powerful experiences in Maui that I want to tell you about. But I'm afraid. I keep trying to find the right time, but I don't...I can't...I guess this is the time."

David turns on the light.

"Turn off the light."

He grumbles, but complies.

"This is hard enough to do as it is." I suddenly feel cold and pull the sheet up over my shoulders. "I'm not even sure how to talk about it, but I'll do the best I can." I am shivering with fear. "As you know, I went to see Kaimana because my migraines were so severe. We had several pretty far-out sessions together, where I got into a really deep state of relaxation and sorted out some of the angry feelings I've carried around since I was a kid. But I've been burying the anger all these years, and in those healing sessions I started to see how that was causing my headaches. As soon as I acknowledged the feelings and stopped running from them, the headaches went away. It was really amazing."

"Sounds like it. Is this Kaimana an attractive fellow?"

"Um...yes...he is. Anyway, I was fascinated with how he worked, and I wanted to learn more. So I started helping him work with patients in his home. I saw him work what I would consider miracles. It was thrilling. Slowly we became friends. I even learned to play some of his shamanic instruments."

"You what?"

"I played Tibetan bowls, used a Hawaiian rattle. I actually tried blowing through a didgeridoo from Australia."

It's very quiet.

"Cut to the chase, Kate."

"We traveled all around the island, to some really remote areas. I met many different kinds of people, and learned more about plants that heal...." My voice is wavering. Even I know I'm stalling.

"I said get to it already!"

"Well...then," I say looking away, the guilt sucking the breath out of me, "we got really close."

"You slept with him."

"Yes, but it was much more than that." Then I wait.

David gets up and goes to the bathroom. He returns looking relieved. "Well, my dear," he says nonchalantly, "it all sounds very exciting and sexy. Good for you! Actually, it helps me feel less guilty. So thanks."

I am dumbfounded. I let go of a sigh so deep I feel my soul turning over. "David, I'm so sorry to have to tell you this. But I have to say what's true for me now. The romantic part of my relationship with you is over for me. I am very much in love with Kaimana. I'm going to go to Maui and start a new life there. I want a divorce."

"Oh c'mon, Kate, don't be immature. We don't have to do all of that. Just go there on another vacation, fuck your brains out, and bring all that new sexual energy home to me."

"No, actually, it isn't going to be like that at all. This isn't anything I intend to share."

"Well, that's kind of selfish, isn't it?" He strokes my arm seductively.

I pull it away.

The clock ticks.

Then he shifts gears entirely. "Seriously, Kate. You can't really mean you're leaving me."

I never thought I'd hear David sound vulnerable, but there it is.

He keeps trying. "Is this about the other women again? If it is, I promise I'll stop all of that."

"This is not about you at all. This is about me."

"*I said*, I promise I'll stop all of the carousing. I'll stop racing, too. I know how much that upsets you. Tell me what to do, and I will do everything in my power to change for you."

"You don't need to change for me. You need to let go. I will always love you and be grateful for our good years together. But I can't be in this with you any longer. I want to be with someone else."

I am so not into soap operas, but this one just keeps on going no matter how unequivocal I try to be. David promises all kinds of reparations but I don't believe a word of it. I also sense an escalating note of aggression that I attribute to him being so accustomed to getting exactly what he wants...my fault, too, for not saying no often enough.

"Well, then," he says magnanimously, "I hope you will find what makes you happy. But let me say this. If you think for one moment you will be happy without all of the accoutrements that I have given you in this life, you are absolutely delusional. The idea of you living the simple life out there on some island, away from art galleries and opera, five-star restaurants, all of the things you love...."

"Those are the things *you* can't live without, not me. You have us confused."

The vulnerability is all gone now. He's all assertiveness, and then some. "It ain't gonna fly, Kate. You'll be back here in six months, bored as hell, wanting an adrenaline rush. You know you will, honey. Now, come over here."

David moves over in the bed and grabs me by the waist before I can get out. I try to be gentle fighting him off because of his newly healed body. But he climbs on top of me. He breathes stale brandy close to my lips.

"Stop it," I say too kindly.

He starts groping me, and I punch him hard on the shoulder. He winces, and backs off.

I make a move to get out of bed, but he grabs my arm and pulls me over to him. He presses his mouth to mine and I feel his erection pushing into my nightgown.

"Stop it, David!" I yell at him, and bite into his lip.

He pulls back for an instant, runs a finger over his lip, looks at the blood, then licks it off. And then he forcefully pulls me toward him again. Now I'm getting really scared. I try my best to fight him off, but I'm losing the battle.

In desperation I cry out, "*Kaimana!*"

In an instant the room is flooded with light. A blast of wind blows through, knocking books off the nightstand and sending papers flying through the air. A wedding picture falls off the fireplace mantle and crashes to the floor, spraying glass everywhere. The ceiling fan spins wildly and the door to our bathroom bangs open and closed. An image of a soaring phoenix rises up over the velvet curtain.

David is stupefied, and I am able to break free.

I grab my winter coat, fly down the stairs, and dash out into the evening rain. The cold night air fills my gasping lungs, as though I've been retrieved from nearly drowning. Now that I've escaped I don't know where to run. I dig into my coat pocket—thankfully I have my car keys.

I CAN BARELY SEE through the driving rain beyond the flapping windshield wipers, but I manage to make my way up and down the hills on the narrow streets of Pacific Heights. Nothing scares me now—my adrenaline is already pumping full blast. I haven't felt this wide awake in years, so I drive downtown toward Union Square. It's amazing how many people are out walking in this relentless rain. I keep going and enter the Tenderloin. Prostitutes in short shorts and leather jackets walk up to the car and check me out, their bright orange wigs sopping wet. It's too much for me, so I drive back toward the house. I pull over and put my head down on the steering wheel and weep. I cry for myself, for Jess, even for David. And then compassion flies out the window and I yell his name with an assortment of epithets...but then the tenderness returns, for all of us.

Finally the rain stops, and my erratic heartbeat settles down. Tears fall warm and steady down my cheeks.

"Kaimana, Kaimana, please free me from my fear. I feel your strength and love, right here, sitting next to me. I want so much to leave my marriage with integrity, in a peaceful way. But you see how it is! What can I do? I feel like just abandoning everything and coming to you...right now."

My breath is coming easier now. "Thank you, my love, for being there for me tonight...just like you promised." The tears come faster again, and the sobs come from deep down inside.

But wait...he is here. I feel Kaimana's warm arm encircle my shoulder. I lean back and close my eyes.

"You sense I'm coming, don't you? I know you do. And I feel your love and protection."

Soon, I will be there with him. Soon!

I feel there is something important he is trying to convey...there's something in his eyes. It's like he wants me to trust that we will be okay. I do trust, and I'm ready for our life to begin. His soft lips cover mine and I drink him in slowly.

I OPEN MY EYES, and for a second I'm startled to find I've been sleeping in the car. The sun is coming through the windshield and a car engine is starting up right behind me. I decide not to go back home, but go straight to the hospital instead. Thank goodness I keep a packed bag in the trunk of my car for overnight deliveries and emergencies. I can catch a shower in the physician's lounge before my first client.

49

IN A TIME OF CRISIS, BE STILL AND BREATHE

For the past week I've been designing my getaway. David and I cross paths in the house, but we have not spoken. He has started working again, and it's been wonderful to have the house to myself now and then. And I now sleep in the guest room. What a relief.

It is so hard not to be able to talk to Kaimana. But I figure I'll be out of here in another week or so. I've been taking inventory, finding out how much it will cost to send my things, composing a letter to my patients explaining how my practice will be changing. I feel like I am right on track.

I slip on a pair of sandals as I get ready to head to the Hayes Street Grill for lunch with Barb. Our friendship has totally changed since my sojourn in her house. A mutual love of Seal Cove will do that to a couple of soul-seeking women.

Before I leave the house, David stops me to ask when I'll be home, says he wants to talk later. He looks like a different man, clean shaven, dressed to be the star that he is. There's no denying he's a good-looking man, and yet I feel nothing but friendship. I pray that he's ready to look at our finances, and not hoping to discuss why we should stay together.

Barb is late, but I don't care. I don't seem to care about anything except staying positive and moving along in this adventure. Finally she arrives, looking really upset.

"Kate, there was an earthquake thirty minutes ago." She is breathless. "6.5, in the Hawaiian islands. I just heard it on the radio. It was centered near Maui. It's bad. Really bad. Terrible destruction everywhere. I don't know if my little cottage still exists."

She's trembling, so I take her hands and hold on tight.

"Can we call someone near Seal Cove?" I say, trying hard to stay grounded.

"There's no power anywhere."

The room is swirling, and I feel panic rising in my throat.

Kaimana, Kaimana, please be safe. I love you so.

Barb leaves quickly to try to find out more news, and I sit staring at the restaurant table unable to move. When I finally focus my thoughts I realize I have to get on the next plane and find him.

I STARE AT THE SECOND HAND on the clock above my office door. Absurdly, it moves in perfect rhythm with the hideous music playing in my ear while I sit on hold, waiting for the airline attendant to find out when I can get on a flight.

"We don't know yet when the planes will be allowed to land," she says calmly. "Only airplanes carrying supplies and rescue crews are being allowed in. Please check back with us tomorrow morning."

I put my head down on my desk. Moments later Jess' gentle hands rest on my shoulders.

"I just heard, Mom. What can I do?"

"Get me on an airplane," I say, tears streaming down my cheeks. "I have to get over there. Now."

"I think you should ask Dad. He can use the corporate jet—he can also call the appropriate parties to get clearance."

"That's assuming he will. I told him everything. He knows about Kaimana. He knows I'm leaving. That's why he's been so upset."

"You know, Mom, you demonize Dad way too much. Let's give him a chance to be a hero for a change. He owes you that."

I pick up the phone and dial David's cell. My hand is shaking, so Jess takes it and places it next to her heart.

"It's the haolie!" he says sarcastically.

"There's been an earthquake in the Hawaiian islands. It's caused a lot of devastation. I need to go there, but they won't let me fly in on a commercial jet. David, will you help me?"

My voice is jittery. I'm starting to sob, and Jess shakes her head for me to stop and get a hold of myself.

"I will of course help you, Kate. But I'm telling you, you won't be allowed into a disaster zone without clearance from the government. I think I know who to call. Come home and let's organize this the right way."

"Thank you, David. I—"

He hangs up.

"Mom," Jess tells me as she squeezes my hand, "I want to come. Please let me help you."

I agree.

BY THE TIME I ARRIVE HOME, David is in his office working the phone. He's already contacted the right people and pulled the right strings. He's arranged to bring in food and supplies, which opened up channels only he knew how to navigate. The bad news is it will take at least thirty-six hours or so to put all the pieces together. We'll take off at 8 a.m. day after tomorrow, and land at a small airport near Ka'anapali, where there will be military waiting to help. David—amazing.

"Start packing," he says. "Just a few things for me. I won't be staying more than a few days."

My stomach falls to the floor. "David, you don't need to come. You did the hard work already, and I love you for it."

"I want to make sure you get there safely and are hooked up with the right people. It could be very dangerous for two women in the more remote areas over there right now."

"We'll be fine. Remember, Jess came back out of a war zone in Africa. We can handle it. I'm sure the National Guard will be there."

"Just the same, I want to fly over and make sure everything is set up appropriately. So get going. I need to get the paperwork started."

What do I pack to enter an island that has been hit by a huge earthquake, and with ongoing aftershocks? Adrenaline races through me as I collect my clothes and a few other things. I remember my medicine bag and put it around my neck. The evening news is blaring from the living room. I hear that several of the big hotels on Maui have been leveled. The aftershocks are measuring in at around 3.5 to 5.0, and in some areas the waves are thirty feet high. I try not to cry...I just keep picturing Kaimana safe and protected. I see him flying high above Maui on the wings of his miraculous phoenix, but I know in my heart that he is doing everything he can to help freaked-out survivors get back into their bodies.

I make David turn off the TVs, because it only makes things worse. I visualize the people and animals of the tent city uninjured and moving forward, clearing away the debris, getting ready to build again. I think of those babies, and then I see the childlike face of Ilima, the frightened pregnant girl who asked for help. I close my eyes and pray that everyone is safe, and that those who have been injured are found. The wiser part of me remembers to pray that all of those who need to pass over have an easy transition, and that Kaimana will help make their journeys seamless.

Nearby, I picture Akahi, Kaimana's teacher, sweeping away debris and broken glass from one of the windows in his tiny abode. That sweeping is a meditation that spreads throughout the countryside and calms the Maui terrain. I feel helicopters setting down with many volunteers, tons of food, and fresh water. Above everything else, though, I feel the soul of Maui intact, healing in the morning sunlight.

AS WE TAKE OUR SEATS on the jet I see two men from CNN boarding the plane with cameras, and a woman with a recording device.

"What's going on?" I ask David, grabbing his arm. "You didn't tell me reporters were coming."

"They're journalists. When they heard about what I was doing—what *we* are doing—they wanted to come to document the story. It's part of the deal to be able to land and deliver supplies. We have to let them tell the story."

Now I get it. The Great White American, David Jamison, Saves the Day Again. But this time I say nothing. I will let him be the hero on the evening news. It's all part of the divine plan. Who am I to judge it?

A light breakfast is served, but I have no appetite. Finally the lights dim.

My Jess sits down beside me. "How are you doing, Mom?"

"Scared," I tell her, and she puts her arms around me.

"Why don't you just call him?" David asks impatiently.

"He doesn't have a phone."

"You're in love with a man who can't afford a phone?"

"He can afford lots of phones. He just doesn't want any. He doesn't own any technology. People come to him."

"I bet he wishes he had some now."

Let it go, Kate. Be still.

Silently I keep calling out, Kaimana, Kaimana! but he doesn't respond. I close my eyes as we speed toward the ailing island. I am focused like never before. I try to see him coming toward me again and again, surrounded in light...my safe, healthy, shamanic warrior. But as I catch a first glimpse of the islands off in the distance, my hands start to shake. I sense something has happened and I cannot calm down. The closer we get, the more I'm filled with dread. I try to divert my worry again and again but my mind obsesses on it. I attempt to connect with my guides on the other side, but nothing happens…it feels like there's no one there. I am a victim of my own earthquake and the ground inside me is shifting in panic mode.

50

DAYBREAK...HEARTBREAK

As we circle the tiny airport, the air is convulsing with cargo planes and chopper wings. We are entering a tropical inferno. Our contact with the control tower is spotty, so our pilot contacts the other aircraft directly in an effort to steer us in for a safe landing. We're told some of the smaller planes have opted for the lesser risks of landing in open fields rather than the chaos of the airport. We all agree this will be our best bet, too, and notify our contacts on the ground to meet us.

As we descend we begin to see the wreckage in horrific detail. Ancient lava rocks, black and forbidding, have been hurled down the mountainsides, into the resort areas and residential neighborhoods, all the way out to the coastline. Many of the beaches seem to have dropped off and been carried into the ocean. My beautiful turquoise Pacific roils brown and thick as Turkish coffee, waves smashing high and reckless against the aftershocks still rippling through the ocean floor. In the morning light there's a strange, sickly, pale tinge frothing over the surf.

"I wonder what the damage to the crater looks like." The detached curiosity in David's voice is unnerving. "I would think you boys would want to head over to Haleakala to cover that whole situation. The footage would be remarkable. Of course, who knows how far you can really travel into the crater. Who knows anything, really?" He seems almost ecstatic, like this is just another one of his bold adventures.

Finally, after hours of circling we land on a little private airstrip above Hana, about three hours from Kaimana's home. I duck out of the airplane and a gust of coarse, hot wind whips my hair into my eyes. The air is filled with sandy dirt that tastes like a mixture of sulphur and salt. My nostrils burn and my eyes fill with tears against the stinging specks of dust churning around us. It hurts to breathe.

Two national guardsmen meet us on the field. One of them takes me and Jess each by the arm, and guides us into a rugged military vehicle. David makes sure someone will escort us to Seal Cove. Of course I want to go to Kaimana's home first. Our driver, a young Hawaiian soldier named Marco, tells us that many of the roads are totally obstructed but, predictably, David heads off in a van toward the crater with the reporters. I have no idea when or if I'll see him again.

Jess slides into the front seat next to Marco. I am so grateful for this darling young man as he deftly maneuvers the jeep around the uprooted trees and the foliage strewn across the road at every turn. We pass one of the grandest hotels on the island, now with several walls reduced to rubble. Rows of people are lying on blankets and sheets outside on the front lawn. These are the wealthy tourists, people who might have been my San Francisco neighbors. There is obviously a shortage of ambulances, and I wonder if the hospital is still standing. My heart turns over as we pass closer and see Hawaiians sitting with the injured vacationers, holding their hands, mopping their foreheads, passing out food, and offering simple human comfort to the haoles.

As the jeep rumbles ahead and the scene disappears behind the hillside, I catch my breath, suddenly aware that as a doctor I should stop to help. But how do I choose who to help first? I shake my head...never mind. There's only one person I want to help now, and he's not at that hotel.

We head north toward the coast, past fields of sugar cane waving in the breeze, seemingly oblivious to the surrounding chaos. Boulders and landslides litter the roads, and we get out of the car often to clear the way. Marco is well equipped with shovels and picks. This is not easy work. I'm not complaining, but a pile of mud weighs more than I ever imagined. Aromas of jasmine and rotting bananas waft by as our wheels splatter mud on beleaguered flowers along the roadside. The sugar factory itself stands like an ancient dinosaur, still upright but exhaling black fumes into the morning sky. Small fires burn from the bottom floor of the old building and send flares out into the fields. Trucks pass by us, headed in the opposite direction, filled with dazed, brown-skinned families trying to make their way to...somewhere safe. I feel another wave of guilt about choosing to be a woman before a doctor. But, for now, there really isn't any other choice for me.

It's late in the afternoon by the time we pull into Seal Cove. Marco turns off the engine at the end of the driveway, and I tell him and Jess to wait in the jeep. When I turn the latch on the gate the whole thing falls over. My leg is cut, but I don't care. I'm more careful as I open the big, heavy door to Kaimana's house. Please, God, let him be okay.

"Kaimana!" I yell. "Where are you? Are you here?" There is no answer. I walk from room to disheveled room. I am surprised at how little structural damage there is. Of course there are items that have fallen from tables and shelves, but the Quan Yin sculpture near the front door and the one that graces Kaimana's meditation room are both undisturbed, as is Ganesh. In the healing room the couch and divan are covered in debris, but Kaimana's instruments are strangely intact, standing or sitting peacefully along the walls.

I walk in the bedroom and find the ceiling fan lying in the middle of the bed along with most of the ceiling. The little closet has also collapsed, and the tip of Kaimana's beautiful hula pareo pokes out from under piles of plaster and wood. I shake out the dust, fold it up, and place it under what used to be my pillow. The kitchen is covered in sand and silt, broken dishes, and jagged pieces of glass bottles and vases. There's a good-sized hole in the middle of the tiled floor, thankfully not large enough to hold a human.

I search everywhere and through each chaotic pile of strewn materials for some kind of clue, some evidence that he was here after the quake...alive...but I find nothing. Nothing!

A scent of lavender fills the air, the smell of his warm skin, and I feel like he is standing right next to me. "*Where are you?!* Please just one word...*something!*" Silence.

I feel like I'm going crazy, but I keep telling myself that he is safe, that he's escaped and made a fast exodus to the tent city. I'm frantic to find him, but I don't know what to do. I'm not sure it would be safe for Jess and me to go there, even with Marco.

I start to head back out to the jeep, and realize my leg hurts more than I want to acknowledge. The gash is gaping and blood is still dripping down my ankle. I grab my favorite shirt from the floor of his closet, turn it inside out and make a temporary bandage that I bind tight enough to stop the bleeding.

His orchids! I turn back and head out behind the house, frightened of what I may find when I enter the little garden shed. It has definitely taken a good shake. I open the door and see the space inundated with piles of pots and plants. Nothing stands in its original space. Kanoa has made a sort of nest for himself under one of the shelves that's still standing. He looks a bit banged up, but his breathing sounds clear and steady, and he seems to be sleeping peacefully. I reach out to touch him and he wakes with a start, looks up at me with terror in his eyes, and scrambles deeper into the corner.

"It's okay, Kanoa. You know me," I say quietly, but he is terrified and turns away, burying his head in the corner. I attempt to stroke him and reassure him, but he runs past me and hides under one of the gardening tables. I can see him shaking.

Suddenly I realize I'm as frightened as Kanoa. I crumble to the Maui earth and sprawl among the broken terra cotta and the purple and white flowers...and I weep. All of this beauty leveled in...what, one minute? Thirty seconds? Kaimana, why in the world did we create this?

"Kaimana!" I scream, pounding the dirt. "Please speak to me *now!* I can't bear any more pain. If you are alive, show me!" The sobbing takes over my body.

My leg begins to itch, so I unwind the cloth. I watch as the two-inch gash gathers together and begins to mend itself millimeter by millimeter, until there is no opening left. Until there is no bruise, no scar. I feel his weary energy wending its way through my blood and bones.

"Is it safe for me to come to you?" I call out.

In the ethers, distant yet clear, I hear "Too dangerous tonight. Tomorrow. Need your medicine."

"Yes, yes. I am your medicine," I whisper. In an instant my fears are gone, and I know what I need to do. "I imagine there are many who need help. We will come tomorrow. Don't worry."

Then I hear him begin to speak again, much more faintly this time, when Jess interrupts.

"That's some communication you two have."

Jess is standing over me. I guess her unconscious mind heard his voice, too.

"What about me, Mom? Can I be of assistance to the shaman and his medicine woman?"

I nod yes, and am flooded with gratitude and another wave of tears. Jess kneels down beside me and holds me in her arms. We don't speak. Finally I can breathe.

51

EVERY MOMENT
I AM GETTING CLOSER

The sky is getting dark, and there is nowhere safer than right here for now. I desperately want to go to Lani Lanakila, but I know we must wait. Marco has set himself up near the front of the house, standing guard. Bless that young man.

I sit cross-legged in the center of the healing room, surrounded by candlelight, and watch Jess move from one instrument to the next, touching each one with a reverent curiosity.

"What does Kaimana do with all of these?" she asks, shaking a rain stick. As it shares its incredible shower of sound, Jess' eyes open wide, and she looks up at me in amazement. Abruptly she puts it down. "Mom, is it okay that I touch these?"

I can hardly hear her words, but I try to focus. I recall how he cautioned me originally not to play with a shaman's tools. But this feels different, like he is somehow beckoning her to get to know him through his sacred instruments. "I think he would be happy to see you interested. When he does his work, he moves the vibration of the instrument in and around people who are ill, and it helps him bring them back into balance. The sound takes them into themselves so they can gain control over their negative emotions and their physical health."

But Jess isn't listening. She continues to circle the room, wiping the dust from shelves and instruments, trying out different drums, blowing badly into all sizes of flutes, shaking shells strung like dried red chilies, strumming a twelve-string guitar, ringing Tibetan bells and bowls, turning indigenous rattles over in the palms of her hands.

It's getting late. We share some of our food supplies with Marco. I have no appetite, but he and Jess dine on toasted almonds, canned garbanzo beans, dried fruit, and chocolate, and slug back water from Marco's army-issue jugs. Everyone agrees there won't be plumbing for a while, so we designate an area in back of the house for our bathroom breaks.

Jess and I have cleaned Kaimana's bed, and we climb in. The soldier sleeps at his post near the door.

Somewhere around midnight another aftershock rolls through, giving us all a good toss. I'm grateful that life in San Francisco has made me pretty good at riding out these temblors. So when a 3-point-something hits we aren't exactly grinning with glee, but we're not shaking in our boots, either. Jess and I will ourselves back to sleep, holding hands.

I'M UP AND MOVING long before the sun breaks through all the volcanic fog and earth dust. It feels like 4 a.m. What I would do for a cup of coffee.

I reach under the bed to retrieve my running shoes. When I shake the dust out, a yellow centipede wriggles out and skitters across the room. Reflexively my hand goes to my cheek, and I remember the intensity of the bite and how Kaimana healed it. Before the days of Kaimana and my Max, I would have been horrified at the sight of a skittering centipede. Now, in the midst of disheveled turmoil, I feel compassion for this tiny being struggling to find a new home.

Jess and I sit on the beach waiting for daylight. We hold hands as another aftershock rumbles through. A dark wave rolls in and out, exposing an army green underbelly. The waves continue to be formidable compared to what usually rides into this little cove, evidence that aftershocks are still creating chaos on the ocean floor.

I know I must walk to Barb's house and check it out for her, but I put it off as long as possible because I hate to be the bearer of bad news. I'd rather not know how bad it is, especially where Barb is concerned. She's not good with tragedies. Besides, I want to take advantage of this time alone with Jess to let her in on what may lie ahead today when we enter the tent city.

"Before the earthquake, things were tense up there, Jess, so I can only imagine what it'll be like now. You and me and Marco may be the only haoles, so stick around me and Kaimana, okay? I don't want you to get into a situation."

"Mom, I just came back from living with hundreds of Africans in a very dangerous 'sit-u-a-tion' that never got any better. I grew eyes in back of my head, and ears the size of that elephant statue in Kaimana's house."

"That's Ganesh, a Hindu god. He's believed to be a dissolver of obstacles. How great that you grew ears like his! Lucky girl!"

"I don't know about that. I just know I'm super sensitive to my surroundings. I've never been that trusting of men to begin with, so now that I survived those drugged-out insane African soldiers, I'm really awake. Hyper-vigilant. Sometimes I wonder if I'll ever actually calm down again."

"Well, this is really different, obviously. Once Hawaiians get to know you—and word travels fast—they welcome you with plenty of aloha spirit. Even some of the more hostile ones started to warm up to me in the short time I was here. But some of them really can be unfriendly at first. They're tired of being treated as second-class citizens on their own land, kind of like the Native Americans on the mainland. They don't want to be invisible, they want their power back. Anyway, I don't know what we're going to find this time, but I know we need to play our energy down. I think we need to be prepared for trouble."

"You mean opportunity," Jess says with a kind smile.

"Yeah. Much better. It's an opportunity to be as loving and compassionate as possible. I'll ask Kaimana if we can work with the children and the women. Okay with you?"

"Perfect. Let's get going. Should we bring along some blankets and pillows in case we spend the night?

"Good thinking, my wise girl. You go on back to the house and start packing. There's something I need to do before we go," I tell her.

Time to face the music—and the possible demise of Barb's house. Marco accompanies me down the long path between properties. He helps me climb over the collapsed fence, and clears away a pile of rocks. My heart turns over as we turn up the driveway. There's hardly anything left.

"I won't be long," I tell him, dreading the decisions I will have to make.

I walk through what used to be the rooms of Barb's sweet little house. There are no doors or walls or windows left, no structure or form to call a home. I try to let the energies of her house lead me. I find several shirts and dresses among the debris, and choose one of each to take to her. In the remains of her bedroom I pick through her jewelry box. How can I know what holds meaning for Barb? I grab the whole box. I pack photographs inside a coat, along with the clothes and jewelry box, and then I remember the stack of letters tied with a ribbon that I found when I first met Max. I duck under a fallen beam and find Barb's dresser, still more or less intact. I pull on the drawer handle, which promptly falls off. But then the whole front of the drawer falls off, too. I pull out the letters and stash those in an inside pocket of the coat.

Out in front of the house, the placid view of water entering the cove is the same. But now most of the sand has been washed away, so the water comes all the way up to the grass. The big waves after the first shock must have funneled straight into the tiny inlet. I get as close as I can to the area where only a couple of months ago I buried my cockroach confidante, but of course nothing is left. The waves have taken him deep into another home. It looks like he never existed. But I know better. The dude made it to Lemuria.

52

INTO THE CHAOS

Finally we're on our way to the tent city. As we drive out of Seal Cove, starving, stressed-out dogs circle warily around the car. Marco keeps moving, slowing the jeep just enough to avoid hitting them. We pass families on foot carrying the last of their belongings. An elder walks under a hot pink umbrella in an effort to deflect the approaching heat. A straggler here, a straggler there, a huge group of haoles trying to hitchhike out of the area and get off the island. There's no need for them to hurry, because Marco tells us the major airlines are still not able to fly in or out, so no mainlanders are going home today. It will be days, maybe weeks, before everything is working again.

We pass Kaimana's teacher's cottage, and I am gratified to see that it appears to be in decent shape. I ask Marco to stop. I start to get out of the jeep, but change my mind and tell him to drive on. Once again I'm stunned at how narrow my willingness to help has become. Until I can lay eyes on Kaimana, I don't seem to be much use to anyone. Part of me is terrified that I have somehow invented the communication from him, telling me that he's alive and needs my medicine. I put all of my trust in that communication—it's how I have survived emotionally for the last twelve hours. Soon enough I'll be forced to face reality, whatever that may be.

As we near Lani Lanakila we see increasing numbers of people from the tiny towns nearby, making their way toward the tent city. The fence around the enclave has fallen back against the tall grass. The old sign that once marked the entrance to the enclave is lying tattered in the grass, and has been replaced by a much larger billboard-sized painted plywood sign announcing a temporary shelter. All kinds of people are milling around, wandering in and among the scattered structures. What was once the closely guarded territory of a menagerie of homeless folks, gypsies, freedom-fighters, abandoned kids and the like, has now become a massive outpost for neighbors who have survived the quake but lost their homes.

We make our way into the commune and pass a makeshift commissary staffed by islanders passing out food, water, and other emergency supplies. Someone has scattered pink plumeria blossoms on the tables and sprinkled yellow hibiscus flowers among them, creating a moment of joy and innocence amid the chaos. I can hardly believe this is the same encampment I saw just a couple of months ago, where Black Dog was the Special of the Day.

Jess notices an area designated for injured and abandoned animals. She can't wait to see what's happening there, but I cannot bear to go. Sometimes for me the suffering of animals is even harder to take than that of humans. My brave daughter investigates, and she lets me know that a few of the local mothers and a nurse from the nearby clinic, now leveled, have set up a makeshift veterinary clinic. The animals are being fed and cared for just like everybody else. I shake my head in amazement.

Jess and I push through the hoards of people, and I lead her toward the little clinic where Kaimana and I saw so many people on my first visit. The scene is both the same and totally different—the line is ten times as long, and it winds like a boa constrictor around several shacks and makeshift tents. There is a real mishmash of homemade crutches and splints, freestyle walkers and wheelchairs. But what's even more startling is the assortment of people. Where before there were only native Hawaiians and a few castoffs from other islands, now there are people of every race, class, and skin tone. It's a veritable United Nations of Hawaii's assorted residents and tourists. Looks like those big scary natives really have opened their gates and their hearts.

We make our way to the front of the line and I push ahead through the door. I'm so excited—I can't be patient! But once inside, my heart sinks through the plywood floor. There is no Kaimana, just a young medical doctor and two nurses.

"Have you seen Kaimana?" I ask, trying to keep the apprehension out of my voice.

"I don't know anybody with that name," the nurse tells me, and turns back to her patient.

"He's been working here as a healing practitioner for a long time. He has long dark hair and is about six feet tall and...."

Both shake their heads. I grab Jess and walk to the barn where the children are. Inside, in a sea of young Hawaiians, I notice a young woman who was a patient when I was here with Kaimana. I ask if she has seen him, but she says he hasn't been there for a long time. I am terrified. I know now that I must find Akahi. He will know where Kaimana is.

And if he doesn't?

After shoving our way as politely as possible through the multitudes, we finally make it back to the military jeep and head back toward Akahi's home. I worry that he will not feel up to seeing me and not answer the door. I rehearse in my mind all possible events, just to keep me from going nuts. If Akahi does not answer I will pound on the door until he opens it. He will see my face and understand, then he will tell me Kaimana is safe and where to find him.

Please, Universe, let it be so.

53

SOME VOWS MUST BE BROKEN

We pull up to the cottage. Jess starts to follow me but I shake my head.

"Not this time, Jess. Wait here. I won't be long."

I jump out and work my way through piles of palm branches and scattered foliage. Akahi's house is absolutely untouched. It's remarkable that it somehow withstood the devastation surrounding it. Bells chime in the smoky wind as I step onto the creaky front porch. An awfully large spider weaves a new web by the entrance. I knock, but nothing happens. I knock again, and the door opens to Akahi's bright eyes and welcoming smile. He bows and I bow back, then he takes my hand in his shaky hand. He looks tired...tired and as ancient as the forest surrounding him.

"You do remember me, yes? Katherine?"

"You are Kaimana's friend. I believe he calls you Kate."

"Yes, that's right."

"He has told me many wonderful stories about you. Come." Akahi's voice is rickety and weak as he shuffles over to the worn, grey sofa. He is careful not to step on the hem of his faded black kimono robe. He motions for me to join him.

"Would you care for some tea?" he asks as he pads out toward the kitchen, calling back, "I have steeped a fresh pot of jasmine."

"Yes, thank you, Akahi. That's very kind of you." I sense I must take my time, be respectful, and try to hide my desperation.

The room is sparsely furnished. Besides this couch there's a wicker chair, and a table that holds a small pink orchid. I'm immediately drawn to an altar over against the far wall. I walk over and bend down to look at the photographs. There are pictures of a youthful Akahi with a beautiful Hawaiian woman who holds the hand of a little boy. There's a sign above them written in Japanese characters. Next to that is a picture of Kaimana and several other younger men, and a photo of one fierce-looking gentleman, probably Akahi's teacher or an elder in his lineage. I can't help myself—I reach over and touch Kaimana's framed face. I hold back anxious tears.

Akahi returns carrying a tray with tea and little cookies, passes a cup to me, then settles himself into the wicker chair. The essence of the green tea is so strong it's as if the cup is filled with freshly picked flowers.

"How are you feeling, Akahi? This was quite an event."

"You know," he says, looking up from his tea, "Kaimana and I, we watched the animals. We felt the change. It was odd. The nightingale who wakes me each morning disappeared, and the neighbor dogs howled too early. Then the breeze carried a heaviness. It whispered of the earth changes that my ancestors warned of a long, long time ago. Of course, no one can understand the true meaning until the changes come."

The sun pours in through the one small window in the room. As he passes me my cup of tea, his sleeve falls back and I notice the small tattoo of a phoenix above his delicate aged wrist. This is not the ferocious firebird I know, but a gentler version, subdued in its weathered patina. I wonder how many others have chosen this medicine animal, and if this is a symbol of their lineage. I wish I could ask, but I know I would be trespassing.

"This is a difficult time," he continues, "but we will survive. We have lived through many hard times before and we will survive many more. It is a good time to learn."

He starts to cough, gets up again, and pads across the room.

The coughing subsides and he comes back and sits down. "My child, I know why you are here, but I am afraid I cannot help you. I love Kaimana as I loved my own son." Akahi stops and looks over to the picture on the altar. "And I must protect him always." He turns back to me and looks deep into my eyes as he speaks. "Kaimana came to sit with me, as he often does, after working up the road at Lani Lanakila. That was several days ago. I have not seen him since. He was very weary. He works too much! But that has been his way from the beginning. He listens to the stories of too many. In a way, he takes on their burdens. Yet he knows that is the way to lose his power." Akahi leans toward me for emphasis. "Too much energy! He must learn to take time to restore himself. You must help him with that."

He pauses to take a bite of almond cookie and a tiny piece falls on to the floor. Akahi bends down and picks it up from his meticulously kept carpet. "Well...that afternoon we practiced our forgiveness meditation outside in the garden, as we often do. His eyes were heavy—not at all like the soul who is part man, part phoenix, who carries such light! Perhaps your absence played a part in his despair. Who can say? I went into my medicine cabinet," he stops and points to a small lacquered chest, "and prepared a special tonic for exhaustion. Kaimana graciously took it with him when he left. The earth shaking started the following day."

"Akahi, I have communicated with him numerous times but his voice is getting so distant and weak. I have looked everywhere for him," I say, feeling the earth quaking in me. "I need to find him right away. I'm so afraid I will be too late. Please help me."

His eyes rest on my trembling hand. "I cannot break a vow. But I can tell you, you have not looked everywhere."

I fight hard to keep my voice from shaking. "Akahi." I gaze at him, hoping he can see what my words can't begin to explain. "Kaimana is not only my teacher. He is my best friend. He is my love. My ally." I lean forward. "He's my life. Please tell me. Please!"

Akahi closes his eyes as if he's saying a silent prayer. I close mine, too, because they burn from hot, dusty tears. After a while he gets up and sits beside me. He takes my hand again.

After a long while, he speaks. "I have asked the Universe if it is for his highest good that I tell you." He pauses and takes a long, deep breath. "It has been whispered to me that in an arduous time such as this, you will need great energy to find him...that is, my dear, if he is still alive." Akahi lowers his head for a moment as if to catch his breath. "Kaimana confided that he trusts you, and that he has taken you to his sacred home in Hele Aku. This was his vision—to take a retreat." Akahi's voice becomes softer now. "That is...before the earthquake."

Akahi walks over to the altar, reaches under it, and pulls out a large leather-bound book. He delicately thumbs through many pages of yellowed paper and takes out a torn page. He passes it over to me, and I see that it is a map. The road to Hele Aku is clearly marked, and there's a diagram of the inner sanctum, the cavernous room where I sat with Kaimana and felt the stories of the ancestors come alive through my fingers as they explored the ancient walls. I feel adrenaline rising under my skin.

"Now listen closely," he says. "I have seen much destruction in Hele Aku. It will be very dangerous terrain for you to navigate alone."

"Oh, I would never go there alone," I tell him with a nervous smile. "I will have to have help. I don't know my way around there at all. It was dangerous before the earthquake—I can only imagine what the land is like now. The truth is, I was terrified when Kaimana took me there."

"No!" Akahi says sternly, shaking his head. "You must not take others with you to this holy place. It is a temple that very few of our people are privileged to know about, let alone enter. The ancestors are making an exception for you. In return for this kind gesture you must promise to protect our ancient traditions." He stares at me with such intensity that I know I must agree.

"Yes, of course," I tell him...and I'm totally unable to imagine how I could possibly find the courage or the strength to make my way into that terrifying place alone.

Akahi picks up on my fear. "Before you go, you must pray. And as you pray, attune yourself to your spirit." He pats his sternum. "It waits for you right here. Focus on the everlasting part of you that does not know fear. That is where you find your connection to the source of life. Do you see? It knows it will live forever. It is the magical part of you, my dear girl. Do you understand?"

I nod half-heartedly. I want to feel it, but my fearful everyday self rears its head.

"It is imperative that you be attuned to your spirit on this journey. Do not attempt to find Kaimana until your spirit is leading you...until every part of you remembers that the essence of who you are," he says, grasping my hands even tighter, "cannot die." Akahi's cough overtakes him for a moment and he turns away. He takes small sips of tea. "Once inside the caves you must act wisely—pay attention, listen to the earth, move with your soul."

He takes my hands in his again, more gently this time. "I feel your fear, Kate. You must relinquish it. Rest a moment while I bring you medicine to awaken your courage. It is a tincture drawn from the fruit of the Bodhi tree."

Akahi returns with a dark blue dropper bottle. "Tap it like this...." He gently thumps the bottom of the bottle. "Then put thirty drops of the tincture under your tongue. No more, no less. Until you are in his presence, see Kaimana reaching out to you. Call his name again and again." He presses the bottle into my hand.

Both our hands are shaking.

"Go now, Kate. I will continue to pray...for both of you."

"Thank you, Akahi. I will find him and bring him home. I promise!"

In my naiveté I move to hug Akahi, but he quickly bows, and I understand that this is not the correct thing to do. He looks concerned as he bows once more. Before I go I look deep into his ancient eyes, trying to convey my immeasurable gratitude. I feel him all around me as I make my way down the stone path.

ON THE WAY BACK to Seal Cove, heavy trucks pass by carrying soldiers, construction workers, strong looking individuals whom I desperately wish I could take with me into Hele Aku. If I announced that their medicine man was missing, all would eagerly volunteer. But I have made a sacred vow and I cannot break it. Even a haole knows that. But it's okay. As the jeep bounces along the road, Akahi's face does not leave me. It is as if he is imbuing me with courage.

By the time we reach Kaimana's house the sun is setting into the mountains, and it would be useless for me to try to find my way to him now. I will leave at daybreak.

For a brief moment I panic, terrified that it may already be too late. I do what Akahi instructed me to do and see Kaimana alive, reaching out to me, calling my name as I call his.

Moments later I feel his faint breath against my cheek.

Commanding myself to think positively, I walk out to the little building that holds his precious family of orchids and flowers. I sweep away the broken pots and scattered flowers, and gently water the ones that are left. "He loves you all so much," I tell them. "Soon he will come home."

I turn out my flashlight and envision Kaimana calling to me to come and see how beautiful the orchids are, blooming in the re-built, sun-filled room. That's it, Kate. Keep seeing him back here with you, happily doing what he loves.

Jess is asleep in our bed, but I am strangely awake. I wrap one of Kaimana's pareos around me and tie my medicine bag around my neck.

From the lanai I can see that the waves are calmer now, breaking gently over the rocks. I match my breathing to the rhythm of the waves and try to find a still place inside, to begin making the connection that will secure my journey to Kaimana. I know I must follow Akahi's wisdom or I will not find him. I close my eyes, hold on to the little velvet bag, and picture the Pacific moving through my cells, connecting me to the source of all life. I feel every cell in my body surging with oceanic power. I focus on that inner surf, and feel stronger with each breath.

But something in me still wavers. I look at the sky, then down into the earth. I feel confused as to where I should be connecting to invoke more confidence, to find a deeper, stronger belief that I will find Kaimana, that he and I both will be safe. I realize that it is my doubting self that is asking to connect, not the eternal part of me.

"I need to know more. Show me more!" I say, opening my arms to everything. "I am still afraid."

Somehow I feel myself shifting gears into an empty space that I cannot name. Within moments I feel a profoundly loving, protective energy that beams a purple ray across the sky into my still doubting heart. A peaceful wind blows the pareo against my arm. I open my eyes and watch as the roots of the young Bodhi tree, just beyond edge of the lanai, fill with light that shimmers up through the earth. Slowly, slowly Quan Yin's elegant form shimmers and spreads out through the bark, the branches, the leaves. The stones from her divine headdress send sparkles across the surface of the Pacific. Under the dark sky, the tree of her is a shining beacon of hope responding to my call.

I am beside myself. "Quan Yin! You are here! Help me to find the place inside me that knows I'm not alone. I beg you, please!"

I close my eyes and focus on her purple frequency as it fills my heart. And then a vibration so warm yet authoritative, so tender yet fierce, encircles me like a silken cocoon. I feel my nervous system slow down, my eyes soften, and her very being enters mine. As she weaves her energy into my higher self I feel a universe of love open inside me. I am no longer searching for proof. I am strength. I am courage. I am living within the consciousness of Quan Yin, who I believe has mirrored the eternal part of me.

Slowly the shimmering body of light dims until the tree goes totally dark. I open my medicine bag and hold the miniature statue of Quan Yin in my warm hand, and hear the words, "Do not be afraid. I will never leave you," blowing in the wind. My gratitude could fill one million oceans. I walk to the black rocks where I watched the spiritual warriors make their exodus, where Kaimana and I declared our vows before I left for the mainland. The wind slaps the waves below me, and I join with its power and balance myself, eager to take my stand.

"I'm coming," I say with quiet confidence. "I will be there in hours, wrapping my arms around you. Breathe me in, Kaimana. Live! Live!"

This time I do not wait to hear his voice. I sit as one with him, connected and whole, patiently waiting for dawn to break upon the ocean.

54

I WILL NEVER
LET YOU GO

"**M**om, please let me go with you. This is crazy." Jess has a hold of my arm and is trying to physically stop me from getting into Kaimana's jeep. "You could die out there alone!"

"Jess, stop it—*now*!" I pry her fingers off of my arm and look into her worried eyes. "I have to go now, darling. I'll be okay. Really. I know what I'm doing—you're going to have to trust me."

"But Mom, you can't—"

"Please don't be afraid. I want you to put your energy into seeing me coming back tonight with Kaimana."

She starts to protest again, so I use my stern mother's voice. "Enough now, Jess! I have to go."

I ease the jeep into gear, Jess' beautiful frightened face framed in the side mirror, and drive down the long path onto the cracked cement road. I am forced to drive slowly, circling the potholes and debris. There's not much daylight yet, and it smells like a rainstorm is coming in. Oh God, give me some leeway here.

I've loaded the jeep with everything I can imagine we might need. Kaimana's wetsuit and a pair of his jeans and shirt, my heavy "mainland" jacket and boots, a flashlight, canned food, chocolate bars and water bottles, my small emergency medical kit, his mother's handmade quilt, and towels are all stacked in the backseat. I have made my prayers, called on my guardians and ancestors, and have dropped Akahi's tincture under my tongue. I scan my brain for anything else I might do or bring to make this trip easier, but there's nothing. I'm half way down the road when I remember the worn-out map that Akahi has gifted me. I gratefully finger it in its safe place in my pocket.

I make my way up the winding roads and come to the first of many bridges. I get out of the car and walk slowly across, trying to determine whether it's stable. Between the shaking of the earth and the waves that came crashing in afterward, there's no telling how much damage these bridges have incurred. This one feels pretty solid under my feet. I think I can make it. I hold my breath as I drive across. On the other side I find three huge palm tree branches blocking the road. I lug them out of the way, and the exertion leaves me short of breath. A fine mist blows over my face, and I glance up at the purple clouds building in an already ominous sky. "Things are constantly changing, Kate," I say in the most confident voice I can muster. "It's going to be okay. Get going!"

The road is climbing higher again, and going deeper into the rainforest. I haven't seen a single other car since I left Seal Cove—it's pretty clear that I'm on my own out here. Second bridge, third bridge, and this time I feel the now fragile boards splintering beneath my wheels. I make it to the other side and exhale. The bridges and road and I are one, all participants in the journey to Kaimana. If we make it, we make it together. So far, so good.

Around a bend two soldiers stand blocking the next bridge. I stop, put on the brake, and walk over to where they're standing.

"No one gets through here," a young white kid tells me. "Too dangerous."

"I have to get through. My best friend is hurt. I have to get to him. I'm a doctor."

"Sorry, no one's allowed through. You'll have to try later when the crews have been able to assess the damage. I can't let you go through. Too dangerous."

"I see. I understand," I say nodding my head, pretending to acquiesce. I return to the car and back up a bit. This can't be it! I close my eyes, tell myself to detach from the answer, and ask the universe if disregarding their instructions and crossing the bridge is for my highest good. I open my eyes and see that the soldiers have walked away. I put the car in drive, press the accelerator to the floor, and within what seems like a split second I'm across the bridge. In the mirror I watch that same young man, hands on hips, shaking his head. I wonder if he will report me. As long as no one follows me I don't care. I drive as fast as I dare on the edge of a cliff down to the sea, until I put some distance between me and the soldier. Just another ten miles or so and a couple dozen hairpin turns along the rim of the ocean, and I will enter Hele Aku.

The air is colder now. I pull to the side of the road and zip up my jacket. The sky has cleared a bit, and a magnificent rainbow spreads across the grey sky ahead. This must be a good omen...I relax a little.

The road descends back to the shoreline, and runs right alongside the ocean. As the waves break, they spray icy water into the car window. I pull my jacket collar up and roll up the window. The angry surf has changed the landscape dramatically. I swerve around dead birds, scurrying mongooses, and a family of feral cats. Not one human face on this stretch of road. No soldiers. Nobody. Maybe it's the power of the ocean, but I'm feeling impassioned and positive like nothing can stop me from getting there now. One more stretch of rainforest to pass through and I am there.

"I'll be there very soon," I call out. "Can you hear me?" I hear his voice but can't make out his words.

I am minutes away and everything is changing. That rainbow I have been following seems to be melting, the different hues bleeding into each other and dissolving into the ocean. Soon all that is left is a black rainbow, devoid of any color at all. I shudder. What is this, some new kind of omen? I approach the sparse scattering of buildings at the edge of Hele Aku, and pull over. The wind begins to kick up and I feel as though a thick fog enters my brain. The landscape looks so different now, and I can't tell where the heiau is. I feel desperation rising up in my body...and then I remember Akahi's words. I hold on to my medicine bag and close my eyes.

"Quan Yin, please come to me now. I need your help!" Slowly a warm tenderness moves through me, down my arms, and into my hands. I feel her energy directing me, so I shift the jeep back into gear and go. The steering wheel moves on its own under my now warm hands. The ink-black surf crashes against the shards of rock, throwing an angry spray high into the air. Hoards of dead fish cover what beach is left.

My car continues to move slowly alongside the shoreline—and then everything in me says, Stop! The wind blows the palm trees so hard that they bend their heads close to the ground. I open the car door and am pummeled by a relentless wet, cold wind. The cave is just ahead.

I continue my mantra. Kaimana. Kaimana. Kaimana. I am almost there!

I pull on his wetsuit, rolling up the long sleeves and legs, and zip up my boots. I grab the medical kit, water, towel, and quilt, stuff it all into my backpack, and hoist it over my shoulder. I unfold the map and take another look. The paper is filled with hieroglyphic kinds of symbols and arrows guiding me through a very circuitous route. My finger traces the many turns and comes to the fork. Oh yeah, I remember the fork now. I fold up the map and hold it in my left hand, grab the flashlight with my right, and head toward the entrance to the cave.

Inside is nothing but blackness, and a rotten, salty smell in the air. I'm terrified of the darkness, dizzy with fear of what I will find there. I remind myself that I am divinely guided. Be strong. Deep breath.

With one movement my finger clicks the flashlight on and I realize I'm walking through a sea of crabs the size of my hand. I recoil from the sight, and drop the map into the water. As I watch it swirl away I feel screams jamming up in my throat. Hundreds of crabs scramble over my boots toward the darkness straight ahead. I push on. Water drips off the sides of the walls, and waves a foot deep rush in and out of the cave. Scorpions, geckos, and all kinds of birds float by. I can't make up my mind if I hope they're dead or alive. Keep moving.

As I go deeper into the cave it becomes clear I'm in a soup thick with the bodies and body parts of sea and coastal creatures of all kinds. I say a little prayer for all of their remains. An anemone floats by, and a slimy tangle of seaweed grabs hold of my clenched left hand. I just keep telling myself that I have nothing but love for these creatures. And then of course I am tested to the core when the decapitated head of a hammerhead shark bangs into my knee. My God, the eyes seem alive, and I swear they're staring straight into mine. "I'm sorry," I whisper as it turns over and rushes past me in a swift-moving current.

My legs feel like blocks of lead as I wade through the dark water, and I start to doubt that I can make it. The weight of what I carry is almost too much. From the corner of my eye I see something move on the ledge above me, and it stops me in my tracks. When I peer into the darkness I make out a faint silhouette and two golden eyes peering back into mine. Slowly the body emerges, filling in the shadow one glistening hair at a time. My girl, my mountain lion stands before me ready to pounce into my aching body, my weary soul.

"Come now!" I tell her.

She jumps effortlessly from the ledge and circles close around me, rubbing her body deeper and deeper into mine, entering every cell, infusing my bones, my blood, my gut, and my heart with stamina and courage. A ferocious confidence flows through my veins. I feel I am more her than me. Full of gratitude and grit I wade forward.

I turn another corner and sense his presence. "Kaimana! Kaimana!" I call out. "Where are you? Say something so I know where you are. I know I'm close. Say something!"

In the distance I hear a low moaning sound and my heart knows it is him. I am at the fork now, and a narrow beam of light streams in ahead through a crack in the wall, illuminating the cavern. The water rushes in the other direction here, and I feel stable land under my feet. As I enter the great room, the first picture stories appear to vibrate on the cave walls, just as they did before. Kaimana lies on his back near the empty fire circle in the center of the space. His eyes are closed. I crouch down and take his hand in mine. It's ice cold.

"Kaimana, can you hear me?" He doesn't move.

"Kaimana! Can you hear me!" I put my head against his chest and hear a faint heartbeat. I check his pulse and it is nearly non-existent. The skin on the inside of his wrist is flayed—it's a miracle his blood vessels are intact. I kiss his bruised face and neck and smell blood on the collar of his shirt. There are dried blood stains on the legs of his jeans, and as I gently turn him over on his side he cries out and falls over onto his chest. The back of his shirt is torn open, and now I see the wound. It looks as if something has stabbed his phoenix through the upper wing, in back of Kaimana's heart. The flesh is swollen, raging, and encircled in red, badly infected. Kaimana and the great bird are suppurating into death. His muddied medicine bag, also torn, lies on the ground. The silver vial that once held his death-dispelling tincture lies beside it, open and empty.

The tears are coming now. I know that he is walking between two worlds. I cover him with the quilt and open the medical kit. Just swabbing the puncture with alcohol and covering it with gauze will not save him. I remember how he sucked the poison from the centipede from my cheek and spit it out...how it sickened me to watch him do it. No time for that now. I cover the wound with my mouth and suck the infection up out of the hole. I spit out the yellow liquid again and again, fighting back the vomit rising in my throat. I feel dizzy, and for a moment I must stop and close my eyes to regain my balance, my courage. When I feel there is no more poison in the wound, I swab it out with alcohol and cover it in gauze. Then I take a couple swigs of water and spit out the remains. Kaimana still does not move. I feel hopeless.

"I don't know what to do, Kaimana. Help me."

My mind flashes to the first time I saw him on the beach, and how he saved the seal by placing his mouth against his chest and blowing energy into his body. I have seen him do this successfully again and again with his patients. I did it, too, but with Kaimana blowing energy into my spine. I was only a student assisting a master healer. That doesn't mean I can do it on my own.

And then I remember his words: Healing is not about the healer, it is about what moves through the healer. I feel the pictures on the wall sending new life and guidance in some sort of cryptic message. It doesn't matter that I cannot read it...I feel its intention. And I answer with a loud invocation. "Please help me! I need your guidance now!"

I close my eyes and envision the light of the creator and see it breaking through the black sky and walls of the cave, effortlessly moving into my body and filling me with healing energy. I place my lips against the bandage on Kaimana's back and begin to steadily blow the light into him, blowing deeply into the wound. I clear my mind of all words and thoughts, getting out of the way while the light moves through me into his body. Then I gently roll him onto his back, and place my mouth against his solar plexus, like he did with the seal, and blow the light into his body. My mind is absolutely silent, but I feel the energy pulsing through my body and into his. I sense his abdomen rise ever so slightly under my lips. I sit back on my heels and rest my hand against his chest, and feel his heart beating a little stronger...but not much.

He lies motionless, and I'm grasping at straws. I know he is still adrift between here and the next world. I must go get him, like he did with Steven, and bring him back into this world. But how? I don't know how to do this. Please help me.

I close my eyes and ask the universe to take me to the in-between world. I wait. And I wait, hoping for some magical opening to occur. Nothing happens. I feel I am adrift as well, only I'm stuck in this world.

I decide to go with my gut. "I'm right here," I tell him. "Just feel me." I close my eyes and breathe, trying to feel I am breathing with him, in him, for him.

Slowly, slowly, I begin to see Kaimana's outline in the distance.

"Come," he softly coaxes with outstretched arms.

"No, my love. I can't come there. You must come to me...come back now. This life isn't finished for either of us yet."

His image is clearer now, but he's still reaching out for me to follow him. "This is the real life, here, not the other," he calls to me. "We can accomplish much more here. It is not what you think. Come."

I feel desperate. I open my eyes and place my hand on Kaimana's heart, and tap gently against his chest. "You have to trust me," I tell him. "You've been hypnotized by death. But now you must come back...back to your body. You must wake up."

Nothing.

I tap a little harder. "Wake up! I am in the heiau waiting for you. There are many others waiting. Akahi is waiting, your wonderful home, the ocean, your patients and all those who love you on the island...your orchids...everything that you love is waiting."

And then a larger truth comes out of me. "Kaimana," I command, making a fist and thumping on his heart, "please don't make me lose you again!"

Suddenly the light breaks through the crack in the wall, streaming so brightly it's difficult to keep my eyes open. Kaimana begins to shake violently. His chest heaves as his breathing deepens, but then it catches and he begins to sputter. I turn him over on his side and he coughs up water and blood and sand. I am overjoyed to hear his lungs working again.

I pour some water into the lid of the canteen and hold it to his lips, supporting his head. "Drink, Kaimana," I tell him. Drink in my love. He takes two sips, but cannot handle much before he chokes. He's obviously too weak to sit up so I curl my body around his.

"So cold," he says shivering.

I kiss his shoulders and rub his torso until the shaking and chills let up. We lie still...and then he reaches for my hand and places it on his heart. I try not to sob. His breathing becomes quiet, and I'm afraid he will go unconscious again. But then he begins to snore, so I let him rest.

This body coming back to life, this soul leaning into me, my hand resting against his healing heart...in the history of my life, this is the best moment. I know now we will make it, but even if we died right here I would be happy. I prop myself up on my elbow and gently run my fingers through his hair, combing it away from his face. I warm his ears with the palms of my hands and rest my cheek against his cheek. He coughs again and opens his eyes. There's so much love coming toward me.

"You brought me back, didn't you?" he says, so quietly I can barely hear the words.

"Oh, darling, it was nothing," I answer, trying to sound cavalier.

Kaimana grins and turns his head to softly kiss my hand. I am overtaken with tenderness, and lower my salty lips gently onto his.

55

OUT OF CHAOS
COMES THE KNOWN

After a few hours' sleep I'm able to get Kaimana on his feet, and we slowly make our way out of the cave. He can only manage five or six steps at a time. Several times he nearly collapses into the waves. Finally we make it out of the cave, but I am so frickin' nervous. I know I must get him to a hospital as soon as possible.

He dozes on and off in the car, and when I make the big turns or dodge fallen rocks his body leans heavily into mine. It's so frustrating having to drive slowly over debris and wobbly bridges, but I try to transform my agitation—I focus on my breath and clear my mind, making it a meditation practice. Honestly, it's not really working.

Just outside Seal Cove I see David, Jess, and Marco standing by the big military jeep. Relieved beyond belief, I pull over to the side of the road.

"Are you okay?" David yells, walking toward my car.

"We need help!" I answer, breathless. "He needs medical care right away!"

I get out of the car and Jess opens the passenger side. Together we gently pull Kaimana out. David rushes over to help us.

I take hold of David's hand. I'm so grateful, and realize my cold hands are shaking in his stable grip. "Thank you," I tell him earnestly.

"It will be okay, Katie."

We lay Kaimana down on the back seat of the military jeep. I climb in next to Marco and ask him to drive as quickly as possible to the nearest hospital.

"Due respect, Ma'am, the hospital is overflowing with patients and is short on personnel and supplies. I recommend we take him to the Army medical base. If I deliver him there, they won't turn him away."

I give him a look of gratitude and he takes off, spraying gravel behind us. I am so engrossed in Kaimana that I forget to say goodbye to David and Jess. I look back and see them watching us through the dust, David's arm around our daughter. I don't know when I will see them like this together again, but I can feel the love they have for each other and for me.

56

BACK INTO BALANCE

Kaimana has been in the hospital a week, and he's finally regaining his strength. He attributes his recovery to my healing in the heiau. I would love to believe that's what did it. Whatever the reason, at long last we are able to make the long drive back to his house...to my new home.

Maui is healing nicely, too. The roads have been cleared for the most part, and they're dry again. Of course, Kaimana wants to visit Akahi, and he's anxious to go to Lani Lanakila. But I place him under strict doctor's orders to rest, and surround him with the beautiful flowers and good nourishing food that friends and patients have brought as gifts. This man is so loved.

"Where is my savior goddess?" he yells from the bedroom. His voice is full of energy and passion.

"She's right here, my beloved." I arrive with a plate of pineapple so juicy that the golden liquid spills over the sides of the plate. I feed it piece by piece slowly and lovingly into his gorgeous mouth.

"I can't wait until we can make love again," I tell him, rubbing his feet with almond oil scented with jasmine.

"Has there been a moment yet when we are not making love?"

I stop rubbing his arches for a moment, because I just want to let the truth of those words drift down into my heart and germinate. Just because this man is not physically inside you doesn't mean we are not making love. Yes, my body sighs.

In the warm afternoon we sit side by side in the little flower house and repot what is alive enough to grow again. We've thrown open the shutters to let the sunlight pour in, and we talk about our life together and what we will create. I tell him my ideas for a clinic, and talk of how I'll approach the people of San Francisco for funding. The two of us will go back and present the situation at the tent city with photographs and our stories. I am giddy at the idea of introducing my friends to this magical person.

"How are you feeling about David?" he asks quietly, cleaning off the wilted leaves of a hibiscus flower.

"Do you mean how do I feel about getting a divorce?"

He nods.

"I feel that it is absolutely right. My relationship with David is a relic of who I was a very long time ago. I'm not that woman anymore. And, Kaimana, you helped me see that. I couldn't possibly stay with David now."

Kaimana nods and gives my shoulder a gentle squeeze. "As long as you feel certain that it's right for you. I feel very secure in our love, Kate. Do not ever feel pressure from me, please. I trust our timing."

"I know you do. And I have never felt stronger than when I made the decision to trust my intuition and return to you. I do want to be fair to David—although I can smell a young blonde around him as we speak."

"Do you care?"

"Not as long as he's happy. Speaking of happy—I haven't heard from Jess for a few days. When she stopped by the medical base she said she might hang around and take a little vacation before she goes back to San Francisco. I'm hoping she hooked up with a cute guy somewhere on the island."

"Jess is a beautiful woman, like you. And I think the love we have between us helps her create a vision for what she can manifest."

"What a lovely thought. I so want her to trust herself enough to get into a relationship that lasts...like ours. She thinks you're pretty hot! She asked me if there's a HotShamans.com website she can check out."

"Of course there is. Tell her to google 'Lusty Lemurian Lovers.' I am quite certain there is an eight-hundred number she can call to make the connection."

57

HOMECOMING

We've been home a week now enjoying each other, and watching as the Pacific comes back into turquoise balance, taking walks in the light rains, enjoying patients as they arrive with armloads of goodies. In our quiet moments we kiss and caress, but don't go any further. This has been an eye-opening experience, this non-intercourse life. I have smooched and licked my way through toes, lobes, and lashes, and spent sacred time sending love into the phoenix's broken wing with my warm lips. I know now there are a million ways to make love. All you need is incentive—of which I have plenty.

Kanoa is healing nicely, too...physically and emotionally. Kaimana instructed me to put a few drops of one of his homemade tinctures in Kanoa's water bowl, which he didn't touch for hours. Then all at once he slurped it clean. That's when his trust came back big time. Later he actually jumped up on the bed and rolled on his back with a big toothy grin. It was during the full heat of the afternoon, but to our surprise he snuggled up between us and snored in oblivion. We don't know what he lived through these past weeks, so we figure he deserves to take on a new persona...why shouldn't he act like a dog if he wants to?

A Hawaiian family arrives with special spam patties and pork-fried rice that their children have made especially for Kaimana. We thank them to honor their offering, but then wonder what to do with the crusty little gems. I haven't eaten meat in months, and even if I had, spam, a staple here, would be at the bottom of my list. Not knowing what to do, we leave the platter out and take a walk on the beach. We return to find Kanoa scarfing down the last piece. Pig munching pig. Oy vey zmir!

58

LOVE BEFORE ME,
LOVE BEHIND ME,
LOVE ON ALL SIDES OF ME

The plan is that we'll spend the day at Lani Lanakila, then I'll drive back and Kaimana will spend the night with Akahi. He has much to tell him.

It's hot out here in the tent city, in the high nineties. And it's crowded. There are still many islanders here who have been left homeless by the earth changes. We push through the throngs and see Akahi in the distance, walking around the outside of the clinic tent with a large pot of water, filling a ladle and offering it to outstretched hands. With so many people gathering at the tent city, the old healer has answered the call to help. He sees us and smiles peacefully. I like that smile. It lightens my feet!

"Time for work!" Kaimana kisses my hand and walks off to join Akahi. They bow deeply to one another, and stand for a long moment looking warmly into one another's eyes...not a word is spoken. Kaimana bows once more, then makes his way into the tent.

I stand to the side, taking in the wanderers and goings-on. Suddenly the world seems to stop, and I see my darling daughter.

"Mom! Mom! Over here!" Jess rushes toward me and gives me an exuberant hug. She's completely in her element.

"C'mon," I tell her, taking her hand. "There's someone I want you to meet."

I lead her toward the tent, and Akahi walks toward me with a big smile. Again I open my arms to hug him, and again he steps back and bows. I bow back. I can't help grinning to myself. I introduce Jess, and she bows...at least my kid is a fast learner.

Akahi puts down his bucket of water and smiles that peaceful smile again. "Kate, I hope that you and your daughter will join me for tea one day very soon." There is a look in his eyes that seems to say, "Good job, Kate. Well done."

Jess and I finally make it past the entourage waiting at the door. Kaimana pokes his head out to call the next person. He sees us approaching and holds the door open for us.

"You are just in time," he says with a terrific smile, kissing me on the cheek. And then, under his breath, "Beautiful one."

Then he turns to Jess and takes both of her hands in his. "Welcome, Jess."

She promptly gives him a big hug. "You look great! I mean—now that your injuries have healed...that is." She blushes, then glances at me, and a breathless "Wow!" bursts out of her mouth. She laughs in embarrassment, then composes herself. "Well, medicine man, show me where to begin!"

Within moments Jess is reading pulses and taking temperatures. I watch them both working in unison, the two people I love most in the world, getting to know one another, helping people mend their broken spirits...Kaimana in his way, Jess in hers. As I turn to leave, my daughter gives me a look, nodding her head in validation for my choice of partners. She walks over, squeezes my arm, and whispers in my ear, "Nice goin', Katie!"

Back outside I ask a soldier to accompany me to the building that holds the babies and sick children. It's a long, arduous walk, with so many needy folks hanging out with nowhere to go, and being fearful is an old habit. But then I stop, remembering that in the last two weeks things have shifted in this community—and also in me. I tell the serviceman that I'm okay, and walk on, feeling safe and comfortable.

When I get to the Mama's Arms building, I can hardly believe my eyes. I've heard the bad news, that several of the outer islands were severely affected by the earth changes. Many of the residents of those islands have made their way here, so now there are three times as many children as before.

But there's good news, too. Parents who have just arrived with their own kids are helping out, and there are many more adults here to hold the babies, nurse them, diaper them, play with them. And, oh my God, somehow fans have been delivered inside the compound, so that oppressive heaviness in the air isn't nearly as bad as before. Also, all of the windows crumbled in the quake, so—the Universe provides—now there's a breeze blowing through where there had previously been none. The cupboards are full of supplies brought in by relief workers, so they're well stocked with canned milk, baby food, and cereal. There's even a new old refrigerator. It's amazing the good that has come from such turmoil.

A warm hand slips into mine. I turn and face Ilima, the darling pregnant girl I met at Kaimana's house. Her warm gesture and the radiance in her eyes wrap my heart in a blanket of love.

"Aloha, Mrs. Doctor...Kate. So happy you here." She looks pretty tired, but she's no longer the broken, frightened child I saw before. Her eyes are strong and her smile is absolutely luminescent.

I put my other hand on her very pregnant belly. "Soon!"

She nods, grinning widely, and puts her hand over mine. "You help me?"

"Yes, ma'am."

"Good!" she says.

She makes a little bow and I bow back, then she turns to walk back toward the older kids, and we both carry on doing our good work.

THE BANYAN TREE AT DUSK

I want to lose myself in this sea of humanity, where I am more a healer than I have ever been in a white man's hospital. Without benefit of high-tech medical equipment or even an expensive watch around my wrist, I move with a different rhythm and spontaneity. Everything depends on intuition and my connection to nature and the elements. The stresses of that other world seem to have been washed out to sea.

Jess comes to tell me that Kaimana will meet me under the Banyan tree by the laundry area at dusk. This is where the intuitive connection to nature comes in. Does dusk mean a particular time? How should the sky look? What color is the light? Where is the tide? With no watch to synchronize, I'm left to rely on another kind of knowing. These are things native people know and depend on every day to make their lives flow. With their reverence for the land...for the abundance of nature that they rely on for sustenance, the ocean that bathes them and washes their clothes, the palm leaves that fan them, the sun that enriches the red soil...there's an attunement that I'm just learning to experience. Now I find that I hunger for it, and the peace that comes with it. Even the new rows of toilet holes are being dug and attended to in a relaxed and organized manner. And it seems no one is too important to lift a shovel.

I'm so busy looking down little throats and listening to frightened heartbeats that the afternoon light is fading out before I know it. I walk around and thank all of the volunteers for their hard work, and make sure there are enough "nannies" to see the little ones through the evening. Everyone, no matter who they are, makes eye contact with me, and most offer a warm smile...even to this lily white haole. We are dwelling in some kind of miracle that perhaps could only have been created through something as explosive as a crack in the earth's shell. I feel no separation in this room...we are all of the same heart, and we all feel it. Lani Lanakila has somehow become a peaceful sanctuary of hope and help.

The air is still steaming as I head out into the tropical evening. God, I want to lie back in a cool tub filled with some of those pink plumeria blossoms and their scent of limes and honey. I want to wash my hair with coconut and jasmine. At the edge of the clearing a cluster of multi-colored pareos hang as shower curtains, behind which one can bathe using hands and a bucket of water. I recognize several of the imposing Pacific island men who were less than welcoming to me the first time I came here. Now they bow and smile kindly as they stand protecting the women's stalls. Okay, then! As tempting as those well-guarded showers are, the line of women waiting to use them is too long for me to wait my turn and still get to the banyan tree at dusk. I open my shirt and smell my underarms...definitely ripe. I am emanating L'eau de Longshoreman. But you know what? I find it rather sexy and alive, not like my usual antiperspirant fragrance, which by comparison smells so...well, dead. Pretty, but dead.

The banyan tree spreads its arms over what seems like a quarter acre of land. Slowly the hundreds of birds who dwell there are returning to their respective branches for the night. The humans are gathering here tonight, too. Scores of people sit on the ground beneath the tree, listening to lovely Hawaiian guitar music. I've heard rumors that there will be hula later.

"Where are you, my love?" I call silently.

"Over here, over here...." I hear him in my heart.

My soul is magnetized to his energy and I walk into his open arms. We stand amid the others, lost in the touch and smell and flavors of our bodies.

"I missed you today," he says. "But I had the grand pleasure of working alongside your remarkable daughter." He pulls away and looks deep into my eyes. "Kate, I like her very much."

I pull him close and say, "I know." Nothing could make me happier.

Someone brushes past us, and Kaimana takes my hand. "Come, I know where we can go."

He leads the way and we walk in silence. Step by step I lose my weariness from the day and regain my stamina. We don't speak, but say all there is to say through our eyes and hands and breath. We walk for a half mile or so, and I feel more peaceful with every step. Kaimana expertly navigates the steep, rutted footpath around rocky overhangs and down to the beachhead. Soon we are standing before a beautiful little bay where the ocean is strangely serene. We step into the warm water, and it's clear enough that I can see my toes clinging to the sand beneath the waves. We wade in up to our knees and sit down in the surf.

It is as if our mouths have never parted, and our newest kiss is as vast and full as our first. This time, though, there are no made-up boundaries to dismantle, only the pure exuberance of a patient love now being fulfilled. We kiss and laugh and say sweet things to one another...but there are too many kisses for there to be much talk. And then we lie down and let the ocean wash over us. Kaimana's long hair winds around my neck, and I kiss his shoulders and arms as he eases his body onto mine. The moment he enters me I cry out...I have desired him so deeply, and my heart still burns from the days when I tortured myself with the thought that I would never find him again. I bite into his shoulder and the heels of my feet dig into the broken shells and sand. The release seems endless for both of us.

We have made love one trillion times in other realms and endless fantasies, but now we are entwined under the platinum light of the spring moon. It seems we are all moving together...the incoming surf, his outgoing sighs, the fragrance of lotus-filled wind, the salty flavor of flesh on my tongue.... I have found my place in the universe on a little bay, beneath a phoenix rising toward the Pleiadian stars. I am one with all of it, this journey that was born from a shaman's kiss.

ABOUT THE AUTHOR

CAROL SIMONE, also known as "Simone," is a spiritual catalyst in private practice since 1986, coaching and teaching in the fields of meditation and self-empowerment, metaphysics, hypnotherapy, shamanism, and creative expression. She writes and performs ceremonies and invocations for private celebrations and public events, and has been a frequent celebrant for the city of San Francisco. She hosted the radio programs *Inside the Healing Circle* and *San Francisco Nights*, and is the author of *The Goddess of 5th Avenue* and *Why Women Wear Hats* and the editor of *Networks: An Anthology of San Francisco Bay Area Women Poets*. She is also the creator of *Being Quan Yin*, an empowerment meditation CD.

Simone resides in northern California with her husband and Rumi, their beloved bearded collie. All of her work is devoted to Quan Yin, the bodhisattva of compassion.

For more information about Simone's work, including workshops, private sessions, and ongoing apprentice-ships, please visit her website at www.CarolSimone.com.

ACKNOWLEDGEMENTS

THANK YOU, MAUI, for all you have given me for so many years. An imprint of your turquoise beauty and elegant grace lives deeply in my soul. And thank you, too, for reawakening in me my lifetimes in the ancient civilization of Lemuria. I will continue to write about your peaceful, feminine, and healing energies for the rest of my days.

I wish to thank the venerable Thich Nhat Hanh, Gangaji, and Dr. Wayne Dyer for the courageous energy they transmit that helped invoke this shamanic tale. Also deep bows to Viet Nguyen, Dr. Gerald Cohen, Dr. Jennifer Lendl, and Dr. Connie Hernandez for their open-hearted expertise and wisdom.

Thank you also to departed teachers: Jason Oliver, for your incredible understanding of ho'opono'pono and the importance of clearing karmic family patterns. And Walden Welch, astrologer extraordinaire, your loving kindness and brilliant readings gave me the ultimate permission to journey into my mystical self. Even now I feel you reaching out with guidance from another realm.

I am forever grateful to my editor, Jan Allegretti, who aligned herself to every one of my characters with heartfelt wisdom and expertise and helped render them in such a lovely way. What a gift to totally surrender my work to another person. It has been life-changing trusting you.

K. N., thank you for being who you are and for helping me bring authenticity to this book. Your generosity and kindness mean so much to me.

Boundless gratitude to my husband, Locke McCorkle, for his steadfast support and love throughout this project. You are my hero. And also to Helene Rothschild, whose intuitive mentoring and compassion helped me find the inspiration to make my vision come true. You are the best.

Turquoise Light Productions

Turquoise Light Productions is a gathering place for artists who express themselves in a variety of media. Our mission is to manifest their inspiration to empower the planet through love and compassion.

Made in the USA
San Bernardino, CA
02 August 2014